PENGUIN CLASSICS

THE CONFERENCE
OF THE BIRDS

FARID UD-DIN ATTAR, the Persian mystic-poet, was born during the twelfth century, probably in the 1140s, at Neishapur (where Omar Khayyam had also been born) in north-eastern Iran, and died in his home town, probably during the Mongol invasion of the 1220s. By profession he was a maker and seller of medicines and perfumes. His most important works apart from *The Conference of the Birds* are *The Book of the Divine*, *The Book of Affliction*, *The Book of Secrets* and *Memorials of the Saints*, a hagiographic prose work on the lives of prominent religious figures, chiefly Sufis.

DICK DAVIS was born in 1945 and educated at King's College, Cambridge, where he read English, and at the University of Manchester (PhD in Persian Literature). He is Professor of Persian and Chair of the Department of Near Eastern Languages and Cultures at Ohio State University, USA. Apart from *The Conference of the Birds*, he has translated Ferdowsi's *Shahnameh* and Gorgani's *Vis and Ramin* for Penguin Classics, and also edited Edward FitzGerald's *Ruba'iyat of Omar Khayyam* for Penguin. He is a Fellow of the Royal Society of Literature.

AFKHAM DARBANDI was born in 1948 in Tehran, where she grew up. She trained as a nurse and then as a translator. Apart from *The Conference of the Birds*, she has translated the modern Persian novel *The Marsh* by Jafaar Sadeghi-Modaress. She and Dick Davis were married in 1974, and have two daughters, Mariam and Mehri.

FARID UD-DIN ATTAR

The Conference of the Birds

Translated with an Introduction by
AFKHAM DARBANDI *and* DICK DAVIS

PENGUIN BOOKS

PENGUIN CLASSICS

Published by the Penguin Group
Penguin Books Ltd, 80 Strand, London WC2R 0RL, England
Penguin Group (USA) Inc., 375 Hudson Street, New York, New York 10014, USA
Penguin Group (Canada), 90 Eglinton Avenue East, Suite 700, Toronto, Ontario, Canada M4P 2Y3
(a division of Pearson Penguin Canada Inc.)
Penguin Ireland, 25 St Stephen's Green, Dublin 2, Ireland (a division of Penguin Books Ltd)
Penguin Group (Australia), 250 Camberwell Road, Camberwell, Victoria 3124, Australia
(a division of Pearson Australia Group Pty Ltd)
Penguin Books India Pvt Ltd, 11 Community Centre, Panchsheel Park, New Delhi – 110017, India
Penguin Group (NZ), 67 Apollo Drive, Rosedale, Auckland 0632, New Zealand
(a division of Pearson New Zealand Ltd)
Penguin Books (South Africa) (Pty) Ltd, 24 Sturdee Avenue, Rosebank, Johannesburg 2196, South Africa

Penguin Books Ltd, Registered Offices: 80 Strand, London WC2R 0RL, England

www.penguin.com

This translation first published in Penguin Classics 1984
This revised edition first published in Penguin Classics 2011

1

Translation of main text copyright © Afkham Darbandi and Dick Davis, 1984
Introduction and translation of Prologue and Epilogue © Dick Davis, 2011
All rights reserved

The moral right of the translators has been asserted

Set in 10.25/12.25 pt Postscript Adobe Sabon
Typeset by Palimpsest Book Production Limited, Falkirk, Stirlingshire
Printed in Great Britain by Clays Ltd, St Ives plc

ISBN: 978-0-140-44434-6

www.greenpenguin.co.uk

Penguin Books is committed to a sustainable
future for our business, our readers and our
planet. This book is made from paper certified
by the Forest Stewardship Council.

This translation is dedicated to the memory of
Mariam Darbandi, 1956–83

Contents

Introduction

In his poetry, and especially perhaps in his best-known work, *The Conference of the Birds*, Attar shows himself to be one of the most attractive and memorable of all the many medieval Persian poets whose verse has come down to us; his poetry combines the intimate with the splendid, the worldly with the spiritual, and the specific with the universally human. His achievement is all the more remarkable because his subject matter, the nature of religious and metaphysical truth, is one that, in Attar's time and subsequently, has often lent itself to grim-faced homily rather than to beguiling anecdote, to prescriptive regulation rather than to humour and raciness, and to an elevated monotony of tone rather than to the flips and twists of manner appropriate to a master storyteller intent on keeping his audience on the edge of their seats.

Not that Attar is in any sense a trivial poet without a serious message to pass on; he is in deadly earnest, and he leaves us in no doubt of his perception of the gravity of what he wishes to convey. But he delivers this message by means of anecdotes that can be, in turn, serious or funny, sweet or bitter, pithy or expansive, comforting or disconcerting. He is one of the earliest Persian religious poets to do this successfully and extensively, and his manner had a huge effect on poets who came after him and dealt with similar subject matter. The most obvious beneficiary of this technique of constantly shifting banter and admonition, surprise endings and bewildering beginnings, of pathos and bathos, and the heavenly and earthly appearing cheek by jowl, was Rumi, whose poetry is permeated with the spirit of Attar, and from whose work Rumi also borrowed various specific tropes and anecdotes, as, in a number of verses, he himself acknowledges.[1]

As is the case with many medieval Persian poets, especially the better-known ones, a number of entertaining and inspirational anecdotes gradually gathered around Attar's name, but in reality the details of his biography remain almost entirely opaque to us; except in its broadest outlines we know virtually nothing about his life. The little that we do know can be stated very quickly: he was born around the middle of the twelfth century (1146 and 1158 have been suggested as possible dates), and he died in the 1220s, probably when the invading Mongols overran the province (Khorasan) and city (Nieshapur) in which he lived, and slaughtered a great number of the inhabitants. Various manuscripts of *The Conference of the Birds* claim 1175, 1178 or 1187 as the date of its completion; if either of the two earlier dates is accurate, 1158 seems far too late for Attar's birth, as it would mean that he composed the poem in his teens, and this, given the sophistication of its technique and the wealth of learning it displays, seems highly unlikely. If we take the earlier of the two suggested birth dates (1146) and the last of the claimed dates of composition (1187), this would mean the poem was written when he was about forty, and this seems a reasonable supposition.

Attar (which is a pen-name; virtually all medieval Persian poets wrote under chosen rather than given names) appears to have lived for most of his life in Nieshapur, in north-eastern Iran, and his chosen name suggests that he was a perfume seller and pharmacist (and perhaps a physician, as the trades were sometimes combined); there are corroborative details of his perfumer/pharmacy profession in his poems. The name Attar is the same word from which we derive 'attar', meaning a distilled scent, in phrases like 'attar of roses': when, at the opening of the Epilogue to *The Conference of the Birds*, Attar says that he has filled the world with 'these mysteries' musky scent', he is making a punning reference to his pen-name. More than sixty works have been attributed to him at different times, but the number that can be ascribed to him with any certainty is relatively few: his works in verse include *The Conference of the Birds*, *The*

Book of the Divine, *The Book of Secrets*, *The Book of Affliction*, a collection of lyrical poems and another of quatrains. As well as these volumes of verse, Attar also wrote an important prose work, *Memorials of the Saints*, a collection of hagiographic accounts of prominent religious figures, mainly but not exclusively Sufis. In a number of his poems he includes anecdotes about many of the figures whose biographies he gives in *Memorials of the Saints*.

As to his personal beliefs, the Prologue to *The Conference of the Birds* makes it abundantly clear that he was a Sunni Muslim, that is a Muslim who accepts the authority and legitimacy of the four caliphs (Abu Bakr, Omar, Osman and Ali) who succeeded the Prophet Mohammad as head of the Muslim community, rather than a Shi'a Muslim, that is one who accepts the legitimacy only of the fourth of the Sunni caliphs, Ali, and who believes that the preceding three were usurpers of a position that should have been Ali's on the death of Mohammad. In this, Attar is among the great majority of medieval Persian poets, virtually all of whom were Sunnis (the important exceptions are Naser Khosrow,[2] who was an Esmaili Shi'a, and perhaps Ferdowsi,[3] who might have been either an Esmaili Shi'a or a Twelver Shi'a).[4] Iran did not become a predominantly Shi'a country until the sixteenth century, by which time the great efflorescence of Persian medieval poetry was drawing to a close.

Among the attractive but apocryphal stories told about Attar is that he dandled the young Rumi on his knee and predicted his future greatness, when Rumi's family was travelling west through Khorasan, probably in order to stay ahead of the Mongols. Another is that he was converted to Sufism when a wandering dervish (religious mendicant) entered his shop and asked if he (Attar) could die as he (the dervish) could: 'Certainly,' replied Attar. Whereupon the dervish put his begging bowl on the ground, laid his head upon it, uttered the word 'God' and promptly died. When apocryphal tales are told about the lives of great men, there is usually a reason for their fabrication; they attempt to fill what is perceived as a gap that shouldn't ideally be there. The first of these anecdotes seems to have been invented for a relatively trivial and cosy reason: to provide a satisfying personal link between an older poet and his young successor, on whose work he was to have a great influence, and also to suggest a kind of laying-on-of-hands transmission of insight and mastery. But the second anecdote points to a more interesting puzzle. In ascribing Attar's introduction to Sufism to this dramatic encounter with a dervish ready to give up everything, including his life, for his faith, it reads like an attempt to fill a lacuna in the record: what exactly was Attar's relationship to Sufism, and how did he become a Sufi? Indeed, *did* he become a Sufi? The honest answer to these questions is that we don't know.

Nevertheless Attar's poem is clearly about Sufism, the doctrine propounded by the mystics of Islam, and it is necessary to understand the basics of this doctrine if the poem is to be fully appreciated. Sufism was an esoteric system, partly because it was continuously accused of being heretical, partly because it was held to be incomprehensible to those who had not received the necessary spiritual training. It was handed down within orders of adepts, who were forbidden to reveal the most important tenets of belief (though some occasionally did), from sheikh to pupil (throughout *The Conference of the Birds* the word 'sheikh' denotes a spiritual leader, not a secular chief). Different Sufis living at different times have clearly believed different things, and most Sufi authors tend to retreat into paradox at crucial moments, either because they feel their beliefs are genuinely inexpressible in any other form, or because they fear orthodox reprisal.

The doctrine is elusive, but certain tenets emerge as common to most accounts. These, briefly, are: only God truly exists – all other things are an emanation of Him, or are His 'shadow'; religion is useful mainly as a way to reaching a truth beyond the teachings of particular religions – however, some faiths are more useful than others, and Islam is the most useful; man's distinctions between good and evil have no meaning for God, who knows only Unity; the soul is trapped within the cage of the body but can, by looking inward, recognize its essential affinity with God; the awakened soul, guided by God's grace, can progress along a Way which leads to annihilation in God.

Almost the whole of Attar's oeuvre is taken up with these and similar notions, and it seems natural to suppose that he was himself a Sufi. But there is no record of which Sufi order he belonged to, of who initiated him to Sufism, or of who his sheikh was. Sufis were insistent that people could not just spontaneously 'become' Sufis; they had to receive instruction, and very lengthy instruction at that – biographies of prominent Sufis are generally meticulously specific about by whom, and in which Sufi order, the person in question was instructed. There was, however, the possibility of a rare exceptional case; some major Sufi figures were said to have been instructed in dreams, usually by dead Sufis (Attar has a number of anecdotes about men being instructed by means of dreams). Rumi claimed that Attar was instructed in just this fashion by the Sufi martyr Hallaj, who had been executed in Baghdad in 922, for, among other things, publicly exclaiming 'I am the Truth' (or 'I am God', the phrase can be interpreted either way); Attar's works show that he had a particular interest in Hallaj, and this may be what suggested the idea to Rumi. Leaving aside the instruction-by-dreams notion, scholars have suggested various possibilities as to who Attar's sheikh might have been, but their suggestions are all highly speculative; other scholars have suggested that Attar wasn't really a Sufi at all, more a kind of sympathetic fellow-traveller.

Some of Attar's own writings appear to support this latter idea. The biographies in his prose work *The Memorials of the Saints* can seem more like enthusiastic admiration from a book-ish, scholarly acolyte than acknowledgement from a fellow practitioner. Similarly, in the Epilogue to *The Conference of the Birds* Attar quite frequently seems to disclaim any pretensions to being a Sufi; at one point he says that he is 'not a traveller' (line 4577), and that he doesn't consider himself as one of the birds who have gone along the Way (which symbolizes the Sufi path to God). The brief anecdotes in this section, a number of which are about figures who are not 'really' Sufis, can perhaps be read as being, obliquely, mainly about himself (this seems likely as most of the rest of the Epilogue is also about himself). At this point readers might be tempted to invoke the humility topos; that is, to assume that Attar is being excessively modest about his Sufi credentials. However, as we shall see, humility was not what was predominantly on Attar's mind while he was writing the poem's Epilogue, and medieval Persian poems' conclusions were not, traditionally, a site for humble gestures.

There remains the problem that, if he was not a member of a Sufi order, how did he come by the ideas embodied in his poem, which are not in any obvious way those of orthodox Sunni Islam? Perhaps they are simply what was in the air in his cultural milieu (which must in that case have been, religiously, a very liberal one), but animated by his own intuition and poetic genius. Or perhaps he did in fact belong to an order after all, even though there is no record of this, and he himself seems to imply that he didn't. We don't know.

Certainly there were hints and models for him in previous works to which he may have had access, either directly or by report. Ibn Sina,[5] Ghazali[6] and Khaqani[7] had all written works in which birds functioned as symbols of the searching soul, and in the Indian *Panchatantra*, reworked in Persian as *Kalileh and Demneh*, a section describing squabbling birds could also have provided Attar with a model as to how to present his birds standing in for humans. In *Kalileh and Demneh* animals talk and act as humans; the fables that make up the book usually have a moral point to them, and their narratives are allegories of human characteristics and failings. This is precisely the method of Attar's *Conference of the Birds*, and the two works also show a similar kind of folksy humour.

The Conference of the Birds is a Sufi poem, and its subject matter is the mysticism of Islam. Mysticism tells us emphatically that the meaning of things does not lie on their surface, but must be searched for; it is the search that gives purpose and direction to the Sufi's life, and, in the case of reading Sufi literature, to the reader's act of reading. Allegory is therefore the perfect form for a mystical poem, because the form exemplifies what the content is telling us. In allegory, the meaning does not lie on the surface but must be dug for; the surface is merely a symbol of the meaning, and can in fact be a veil to it. Overt, complicated allegories like *The Conference of the Birds* are rarely written now, and most of us have lost the habit of reading them and decoding as we go. However, they were a very common form for narratives in the Middle Ages (flourishing equally well in the worlds of medieval Islam and medieval Christianity), and we can say that allegorical complications tended to drive plots in many medieval narratives in the same way that psychological complications drive the plots of most modern narratives. We cannot simply *read* such works; we have to read and symbolically interpret as we proceed.

The hoopoe in Attar's poem is presented as the birds' guide and leader; he is therefore the equivalent of a sheikh leading a group of religious adepts, or would-be adepts, along their path. His relation to the other birds mirrors Attar's relation to his audience: he expounds the doctrine they wish to hear and admonishes them to act on it. At the beginning of the narrative the various birds are identified by their species, with each representing a human type: the nightingale is the lover, the finch is the coward, and so on. Most of the poem is then organized around the hoopoe's answers to the birds' objections to a journey to find their king, the fabulous Simorgh; this journey represents the Sufi path to God. Once the journey begins there are more questions, and more story-answers.

Many of the stories the hoopoe tells the birds to encourage them along the Way seem obscure at first reading. The obscurity is certainly, in part at least, intentional; the reader is being asked to look at some problem in an unfamiliar way, and logic is often deliberately flouted so that we are, as it were, teased or goaded – rather than logically led – into understanding. In interpreting the stories, it's a good idea to bear two things in mind. First, each story is part of a section that begins with the hoopoe giving a piece of explanatory advice to a particular bird; the stories within that section are illustrative of that advice, and so if a tale seems resistant to interpretation, the first thing to do is to turn the page back and reread the hoopoe's initial words. Second, throughout the poem we see its larger structure and import encapsulated in the discrete tales that make up the bulk of the narrative: what is writ large in the whole poem is inscribed in miniature in the tales. Since the poem as a whole is about the soul's relationship with God, it's therefore a good idea to take

a story that seems recalcitrant to interpretation as an allegory of
the soul's relationship with God. If there are two main actors in
any given story, it's a good bet – it doesn't always work but it does
most of the time – that one of them represents the human soul
and the other God. Here is a story that occurs in a section in which
the hoopoe is speaking about people who are deceived by appear-
ances, who want something superficially attractive but actually
worthless, and who in this way lose what really *is* valuable:

> A royal hunt swept out across the plain.
> The monarch called for someone in his train
> To bring a greyhound, and the handler brought
> A dark, sleek dog, intelligent, well-taught;
> A jewelled gold collar sparkled at its throat,
> Its back was covered by a satin coat –
> Gold anklets clasped its paws; its leash was made
> Of silk threads twisted in a glistening braid.
> The king thought him a dog who'd understand,
> And took the silk leash in his royal hand;
> The dog ran just behind his lord, then found
> A piece of bone abandoned on the ground –
> He stooped to sniff, and when the king saw why
> A glance of fury flashed out from his eye.
> 'When you're with me,' he said, 'your sovereign king,
> How dare you look at any other thing?'
> He snapped the leash and to his handler cried:
> 'Let this ill-mannered brute roam far and wide.
> He's mine no more – better for him if he
> Had swallowed pins than found such liberty!'
> The handler stared and tried to remonstrate:
> 'The dog, my lord, deserves an outcast's fate;
> But we should keep the satin and the gold.'
> The king said: 'No, do just as you are told;
> Drive him, exactly as he is, away –
> And when he comes back to himself some day,
> He'll see the riches that he bears and know
> That he was mine, a king's, but long ago.'

lines 2266–81

A difficulty for contemporary readers, especially perhaps young contemporary readers, in interpreting such a tale is that they tend to look in a narrative for a character they like and with whom they can empathize, and they then see the tale from that character's point of view. In this tale the only character we are likely to empathize with or feel any sympathy for is the unfortunate dog. So a contemporary western reader's first reaction tends to begin at the 'How could he be so mean to his dog?' level, which is not a useful way to read an allegory. If we instead remember the suggestion that one character is likely to represent God and the other the human soul, it soon becomes clear that God must be represented by the king (even though he seems a rather unpleasant character), and the dog must represent the human soul. Why does God (the king) become angry with the human soul (the dog)? Because the dog prefers something worthless (a bone) to following the king as he should, and this is easily translatable to the ways in which a soul spends time concerned with things other than God, which according to the Sufis should be its true and indeed sole concern. And what about leaving the dog his gold collar when he's sent out of the king's presence? That too is not too hard to interpret once we have grasped the basic symbolic structure of the story: God has given the errant soul something special to remind it of its true owner – the splendid collar must represent grace, a divine spark, a memory of God's reality, something of that sort.

A word of warning. In this story God is represented by a king, and that seems a natural enough comparison, but often in Sufi tales it is the socially *inferior* person who represents God or the divine. This is part of the Sufi love of paradox, a way of jolting the reader out of his normal expectations of the world (we've seen a tiny example of this jolting just now: 'You feel sorry for the dog? You're not supposed to feel sorry for him; that's irrelevant'). In the story that immediately precedes the one about the dog, a merchant has a beautiful slave whom he loves but whom, in a moment of foolishness, he sells for gold; he then regrets what he has done and tries everything he can to get her back, but without success. Here the merchant is like the dog; he is distracted from the valuable entity he already possesses by something worthless. In this story the social superior, the merchant, is the deluded human soul, and the divine is represented by the beauty of the abandoned slave. Another point to notice: in the story about the dog, the dog's gold collar represents something good (the memory of God), but in the story about the merchant gold represents something bad (the worthless ware of the physical world). Objects and individuals don't maintain their allegorical significance from one story to another, so the meanings of the symbols in each story have to be worked out anew.

Certain of the beliefs central to Sufism seem to engage Attar's imagination more than others. Two themes in particular are diffused throughout almost the entire poem – the necessity for destroying the Self, and the importance of passionate love. Both are mentioned in every conceivable context and not only at the 'appropriate' moments in the narrative. The two are connected: the Self is seen as an entity dependent on pride and reputation; there can be no progress until the pilgrim is indifferent to both, and the surest way of making him indifferent is the experience of overwhelming love. Now the love Attar chooses to celebrate (and the stories that deal with love are easily the most detailed and the longest of the poem) is of a particular kind; it is always love that flies in the face of either social or sexual or religious convention. It may be love between a social superior and inferior (such as between a princess and a slave); it is very commonly homosexual love; or, as in the longest story of the poem, about Sheikh San'an, it may be love between people of different religions. In each case the love celebrated is seen by the world as, in some sense, scandalous. Love as a social, sexual or religious scandal is an instance of ignoring the world's demands, of renouncing their authority, in order to fulfil a more overwhelming need, and this is the Sufi duty – to turn away from the duties the world insists on in order to seek the true beloved, God.

Readers acquainted with medieval European literature will find Attar's method familiar: parallels to works such as *The Owl and the Nightingale* and Chaucer's *Parliament of Fowls* immediately suggest themselves. Indeed, it is remarkable how close Attar's poem frequently is in tone and technique to later medieval European classics. Like Chaucer's *Canterbury Tales*, it is a group of stories bound together by the convention of a pilgrimage, and as in Chaucer's work the convention allows the author to present a panorama of contemporary society; both poems accommodate widely differing tones and subjects, from the scatological to the exalted to the pathetic; both authors delight in quick character sketches and brief vignettes of quotidian life. With Dante's *Divine Comedy* Attar's poem shares its basic technique, multi-layered allegory, and a structure that leads us from the secular to the divine, from a crowded random world described with a great poet's relish for language and observation, to the ineffable realm of the Absolute. And in all three authors we can discern a basic catholicity of sympathy at odds with the stereotypes of inflexible exclusiveness often associated with both medieval Roman Catholicism and medieval Islam.

When this translation was first published in 1984, Afkham Darbandi and I were most concerned with providing an attractive verse version of Attar's narrative to an Anglophone audience. The story of *The Conference of the Birds* seemed to us to be one that audiences from many cultures could appreciate and enjoy, and the feedback that we have received about the translation, over the years, has amply borne out our hopes. In 1984, we omitted the poem's Prologue and Epilogue from our translation because they are extraneous to the story itself, and because they are much more local in their concerns than the story is; that is, we felt they might appeal to a non-Persian-speaking (and largely non-Muslim) audience less emphatically than the narrative itself would. We felt encouraged in this decision because the prologues and epilogues of Persian narrative poems are distinctly marked off from the main text, so that it is not necessary to read them in order to understand the narrative (and many casual readers of such poems in Persian in fact skip them). However, for this reissue of the translation we have decided to provide the reader with the complete text, since the Prologue and Epilogue contain much that is of interest. The reader still of course, if he or she wishes, has the option of going straight to the story itself.

The Prologue consists largely of praise of the founding figures
of Islam (and it presupposes a fair amount of knowledge of the
traditions of early Islam on the part of the reader, which is why
there are many more notes to this section than to the rest of the
poem). This praise is followed by a vigorous polemic against
'faction', by which Attar means Shi'ism, and to give the polemic
added weight he puts part of it into the mouth of Ali, who
defends those caliphs the Shi'a reject in Ali's name. In common
with most Sufis, Attar is insistent that many religious traditions
can lead to ultimate transcendental truth, and so this sudden
animus against one particular religious tradition can come as
a surprise, particularly to a reader previously unaware of the
arguments involved. Attar's argument is for inclusiveness, and
it is exclusiveness against which he inveighs. He explicitly says
elsewhere, in a number of his poems, that Christians and Jews
and pagans can reach divine truth just as Muslims can (Sufis
were virtually unique in this belief in the medieval period;
certainly there is no Christian writer of the time who would
have dared claim such a thing). But when it comes to the Shi'a,
Attar sees his problem as the old conundrum of how much
tolerance one should extend to the intolerant. His argument
against the Shi'a is that they exclude from consideration the
first three caliphs recognized by Sunni Islam. In his terms, he
excludes the excluders; everyone else is welcome. Of course this
is not at all how the Shi'a would see the question, and we are
left with the paradoxical situation of a poem that explicitly
advocates religious acceptance and inclusion inveighing against
a particular religious orientation. It's perhaps worth pointing
out, though, that Attar's poem has always been immensely popu-
lar in Shi'a Iran, and continues to be so (and this is perhaps a
confirmation of the fact that many readers skip the prologues
to long narrative poems).

The Epilogue is mainly interesting because it is here that Attar
talks extensively about himself, his achievement, his sense of
himself as a great poet, and also his feeling of spiritual inadequacy.
His praise of himself as a poet, coming as it does at the end of a
poem that insistently recommends overcoming the self and its
pride as a prerequisite of salvation, can come as something of a

surprise, even perhaps a let-down. To English-speaking readers it's a bit too like Lord Longford saying, 'In 1969, I published a small book on Humility. It was a pioneering work which has not, to my knowledge, been superseded.' But the reasons for Attar's apparent volte-face lie in the development of Persian poetic genres. One of the major forms for short poems in the early medieval period was the praise poem, which ended in elaborate eulogy of a patron, who was often named in the last lines. Out of this form grew the more intimate and lyrical ghazal, which concluded not with the name of the patron but with the name of the poet. Praise had surrounded the name at the end of the praise poem, and this convention was transferred to the name at the end of the ghazal, so that the poet often praises himself in his poems' concluding lines; this practice became so conventional that it was given a specific name (*fakr*). Attar has transferred this convention, as other narrative poets did too, to the end of his narrative.

But Attar's praise of himself as a poet certainly rings true; the convention has allowed him to say something that we believe he means. At one point he calls himself the 'seal' of the poets (line 4510); this is high self-praise indeed, since this is the word used of the Prophet Mohammad, who is 'the seal'[8] of the prophets – that is, the last, and greatest, who confirms the revelations of those gone before him. He also gives us other fascinating and more personal glimpses of himself as a poet: he boasts that he has never written a poem for a patron (this alone marks him out as remarkable among medieval poets), and he comments too on his sense of isolation. It's true that he denigrates poetry (as Rumi was to do after him; this use of verse to say that writing verse is a nuisance and a waste of time became something of a convention for Sufi poets), but he's also insistent that he's very good at it. The mixture of self-praise and self-denigration, even though it is shot through with poetic convention, comes across as wonderfully real in psychological terms. And Attar's fraught but finally proud sense of himself as a poet is balanced by his profound sense of spiritual inadequacy when he measures himself against the Sufi masters who, as his *Memorials of the Saints* testifies, preoccupied him. It's rare that a medieval poet gives us such an intricate self-portrait, one that swings from immense self-confidence to vehement self-deprecation and back again, and its very contradictions make it seem the more humanly plausible.

As well as this self-portrait, the Epilogue contains an attack on Philosophy, and again, as with the Prologue's attack on Shi'ism, we might be slightly taken aback. The argument between Sufism and Philosophy had been famously played out in the life of Ghazali, who had died in 1111, a few decades before Attar's birth. Ghazali, whose fame was immense in his lifetime and subsequently, had lived and died in Khorasan, where Attar also lived and died, and it is likely that Attar grew up within a local intellectual aura that still venerated Ghazali's teachings. One of Ghazali's major works was a refutation of the complex Neo-Platonic philosophy which had been elaborated by earlier Islamic philosophers, and was ultimately based on Greek sources; later in life Ghazali turned emphatically towards Sufism. He was popularly seen as a philosopher who had used the tools of Philosophy to destroy Philosophy, which was associated with Greek civilization, and in its place he had advocated a Sufi version of faith. We see the same rejection and emphasis in Attar's works, and it seems reasonable to consider him as a kind of lay disciple of Ghazali.

The Epilogue, and so the poem as a whole, ends with Attar thinking about his own death. It is entirely typical of his technique as a Sufi poet that, after brooding on his future funeral for a number of lines, he should choose to end *The Conference of the Birds* with an anecdote that amounts to a flip cautionary rebuke to God, one that implicitly asks Him not to act like a lowly, rather dim-witted bath-attendant, and which talks about something that for most Muslims is very far from the divine indeed: bodily dirt. The whole poem is immensely serious in its underlying concerns, and Attar concludes with a prayer that we cannot doubt is heartfelt. But the verse also, in these closing lines, metaphorically thumbs its nose at seriousness; the most solemn, exalted moment for a person of faith – that of death – is illustrated by a slightly coarse story about a tactless bath-attendant. Nothing could express the Sufi take on life more appositely.

Dick Davis, 2011

NOTES

1. *Rumi . . . in a number of verses, he himself acknowledges*: Rumi (1207–73), more commonly known in Persian as Mowlavi, is generally regarded as the greatest of Persian mystical poets. The authenticity of the verses referred to has been questioned, but even if they are not by Rumi, they became incorporated into his text relatively early on, which indicates that the perception of his indebtedness to Attar was one that was familiar to Rumi's near contemporaries.

2. *Naser Khosrow*: (1004–88) a Persian poet who was converted to Esmaili Shi'ism (see note 4 below) during his travels outside Iran; much of his poetry deals with specifically Ismaili themes, though often in an arcane and disguised way.

3. *Ferdowsi*: (940–*c*. 1020) the major epic poet of Iran. His poetry does not have specifically Shi'a content, but a brief passage in the exordium to his great epic poem *The Shahnameh* has led some scholars to believe that he may have had Shi'a allegiances.

4. *Esmaili Shi'a or a Twelver Shi'a*: both Esmaili and Twelver Shi'a accept that the imamate (leadership of the Islamic community) is vested in the descendants of Ali. The Esmailis believe that the last such leader was Esmail, the eldest son of the sixth leader; the Twelvers believe that the younger brother of Esmail and his descendants were also imams of the community, known collectively as the Twelve Imams.

5. *Ibn Sina*: (980–1037) a Persian philosopher and polymath, known in the west as Avicenna; most of his works were written in Arabic, though one important philosophical work by him is in Persian.

6. *Ghazali*: (1058–1111) a major Islamic theologian and philosopher.

7. *Khaqani*: (1122–90) a Persian poet; his most famous work is a poem on the ruins of Ctesiphon, the ancient pre-Islamic capital of Iran.

8. *'the seal'*: Qur'an 33:40.

A Note on the Translation

Like all medieval Persian narrative poems, Attar's *Conference of the Birds* is in couplets. In the metre used by Attar for this particular poem each couplet has twenty-two syllables, with the rhymes occurring at the eleventh and twenty-second syllable. Since the form has obvious similarities to the English pentameter couplet, commonly called the heroic couplet, which has twenty syllables with the rhymes occurring at the tenth and twentieth syllable and which has been used for narrative poems in English since the medieval period, this form seemed the obvious choice for our translation. In general we have translated one couplet in Persian by one couplet in English, although there is not always an exact correspondence, and we have occasionally incorporated triplets into the text. The chief model for the verse, not slavishly followed but continually borne in mind, has been the narrative translations of Dryden, which aim for the tricky combination of both semantic accuracy and fidelity to nuances of tone and linguistic register. To take Dryden's verse translations as a model might seem wilfully anachronistic, but we followed Dryden's method, in so far as we could, because this produced what we took to be the most convincing results; that is, we felt that the combination of meanings, varying tonal registers, and emotional impact of Attar's original Persian is more successfully conveyed in this manner than by other approaches.

For the narrative of the story as a whole, that is for the English text originally published in 1984, we used the version of the *Manteq al-Tayr (Conference of the Birds)* edited by Dr Sadeq Gouharin (Tehran, 1978). Since this time, a number of critical editions of the poem have appeared, and for the translation of the Prologue and Epilogue we have used the text edited by Dr Mohammad-Reza Shafi'i Kadkani (Tehran, 2004). Manuscripts of any given medieval Persian poem tend to contain many discrepancies, and the manuscripts of Attar's *Conference of the Birds* are no exception. This means that the texts of such poems, as they are printed in different editions, often vary from one another in the number of lines they include as authentic. The small discrepancies between the two editions we have used are the reason for the apparent slight jump in line numbering between the end of the narrative and the beginning of the Epilogue.

THE CONFERENCE
OF THE BIRDS

PROLOGUE

All praise to Him, who as Creator gives
A soul to dust, so that it moves and lives;
Whose breath gives life to creatures, who decrees
His throne's foundation on the watery seas;
Who gave the heavens pre-eminence and laid
The earth here as the humblest place He made
(One He gives movement to perpetually,
And to the other immobility).
The heavens are like a tent He raised, although
No pole supports it from the earth below.
He made the seven planets in six days,
He made the nine spheres[1] with a two-word phrase,
And on the moving firmament at night
He set the stars as seals of golden light.
He gave life different forms, each like a snare
That traps the bird that is the spirit there.
The seas wept in submission and revered Him,
The mountains bowed before His might and feared
    Him;
He made the sea shore thirst, and He alone
Drew musk from blood, and rubies from a stone;
He gave the soul its pure consistent core,
And did all this from dust and nothing more.

By His religion's laws He tamed and checked
The workings of the stubborn intellect,
And with the soul He made the flesh alive
While faith ensured the living soul would thrive.

He set high mountains as His chieftains, proud
And strong and tall, beneath which countries bowed;
He made flowers bloom in fire,[2] He cleared a track
Through waters when He held the ocean back;[3]
He caused a gnat to buzz in someone's brain
Four hundred years, and sent His foe insane;[4]
He made a spider weave a web to save
The lord of all the world, within a cave;[5]
He made an ant, a hair-tip's size, present
Itself to Solomon in argument;[6]
He robed Abbasid caliphs[7] in their glory
And told them Ta and Sin's mysterious story;[8]
He saw the needle (Jesus' robes concealed it),[9]
And stitched the secret there, and so revealed it;
He tipped the tulip flowers with blood, and made
The water lily's flower a smoky shade;
He soaked dust grains in blood, and in the ground
Bright agates and red rubies could be found;
And day and night the sun and moon adore Him,
And bow their heads down to the earth before Him –
How could they not bow down, since all creation
Derives its being from profound prostration?
His generosity ensures day's light,
His drawing back the darkness of the night.

He made its golden torque the parrot's pride,
He made the hoopoe as our journey's guide;
The bird of heaven flies to Him, and throws
Itself against His door with suppliant blows.
He gives the heavens alternate day and night,
Withdrawing darkness and bestowing light;
He breathed on dust and man was made, He made
The universe from foam and smoky shade.
At times He'll let a dog approach His throne,
At times a cat's the way His Way is shown;
When He selects a lowly dog, He can
Transform this dog into a lion-like man,

And for the heavens He has placed upon
Their spheres as steersman the revolving sun.
He makes a staff like Solomon's, or teaches
An ant the means of making human speeches;
He makes a staff take on a snake-like form,[10]
Or from an oven He can start a storm.[11]
He makes a camel come out from a stone,[12]
Or makes a golden calf cry out and groan.[13]

He pours down silver in the winter's cold,
And then, when autumn comes, He scatters gold;
As though one drew blood with a dart, His power
Makes little rose buds burst with blood, and flower;
He gives the jasmine flower its fourfold hood,
He gives the tulip flower its cap of blood;
He crowns the wild narcissus with bright gold,
Where dew forms pearls, a marvel to behold.
Through Him our Reason lives, our hearts are given,
Through Him the earth is fixed, through Him moves
     heaven;
He makes the mountains firm, and makes the sea
Liquid with shame before His sovereignty.
The earth is dust before His might, no more,
The skies are but the knocker on His door;
There are eight spheres of heaven, hell has seven;
Hell is a spark to Him; His threshold's heaven.
Within His unity, creation's drowned –
Drowned? No! Annihilated, never found!
From fish to moon,[14] all particles attest
To Him, and make His essence manifest,
Although the earth and heavens, one by one,
Sufficiently attest to all He's done:
He brings forth fire and earth, blood, wind-blown air,
And shows His secrets to us everywhere.

For forty days He fashioned us from dust,
Then placed the soul within us, as a trust;

The soul gave life to lifeless dust, and He
Then gave us Reason so that we should see;
When Reason saw, He gave Intelligence
To bring us Knowledge, Understanding, Sense –
When man was granted Knowledge, he confessed
To wonder, weakness, as though dispossessed,
And bowed before His throne, as in the end
All bow there, be they enemy or friend.
His wisdom guides all, rules all and restrains all,
And what's more wonderful is it sustains all.
He nailed the mountains to the earth, then He
Washed clean the earth's face with the mighty sea.
Earth rests upon a cow, a wondrous pair,
The cow upon a fish,[15] the fish on air;
The air on what? On what is substanceless,
The Nothingness that is all Nothingness.
Think of the art and skill of this great King
Who upon nothing's rested everything,
Since all that is must rest, by His decree,
On nothing, it *is* nothing, certainly.
He's manifest within the least, the Whole,
That's but a fragment of His perfect soul;
His throne's upon the sea, earth floats on air,
But He is all, and He is everywhere!

The world is names and signs, in truth it's He
Whose being is its sole reality.
This world, the world to come, and all besides,
Are Him; know this, that nothing else abides.
There is one essence, but diffused, deflected,
There is one word, but variously inflected;
A man must know the King, and recognize Him,
Although a hundred different clothes disguise Him;
It's not an error, in this way to see Him,
Since He is all, and everything must be Him –
The error's when a man presumes to state
That what he sees and God are separate.

Alas, men have no strength! Although the sun
Is shining, blindness hampers everyone!
See this, and lose your Self, your Reason, see
That He is all there is and all is He.
How strange it is that men seek pardon, say
That they repent, then try to run away!
O You, who in Your hiding are revealed,
You're all the world, it's man who is concealed;
Flesh hides the soul, and there, within it, You,
The soul's soul, hide, quite hidden from our view.
Before all, and beyond all, You who see
That everything's from Your reality,
Your roof and gate are filled with sentries – how
Is any man to find or reach You now?
Our soul and Reason can't discern Your presence,
And no one knows Your attributes or essence,
Although You are the treasure that's inside
Each soul, where soul and body are allied.

No soul can grasp You, and the prophets cast
Their lives away to reach to You at last;
If Reason sought You out, it would be far
From ever knowing what You truly are.
You are eternal Being, and all hands
Submit, obediently, to Your commands;
You're in the soul, outside the soul, and You
Are not what I declare, but are that too.
In Your court wisdom reels; by pathless ways,
In seeking You, our errant wisdom strays;
Through You I see the world, and yet I see
No sign of You in its immensity;
All men attest to You, and yet You've shown
No sign – to You alone the secret's known!
The heavens have found no trace of You, the skies
Can't glimpse Your track, for all their staring eyes;
The earth can find no scrap of You, no shred,
In all the dust it heaps upon its head.

For love of You the sun goes mad, each night
It smears its face with mud, and hides its light;
The moon too melts for You – we see it yield
To You in awe, and throw away its shield;
The sea's in turmoil in its longing for You,
Dragging its stained skirt and dry lips before You;
The mountains have such heights they have to climb
To reach You, while they're mired in mud and slime,
And fire, on fire to reach You, strains and glares
And throws out stubborn flames, and angry flares;
The wind's gone wild without You, choleric
And mad, an empty-handed lunatic,
And water in its longing, filled with fears,
Displays its ardour in dissolving tears,
While earth has piled itself against Your door,
Its head in ashes now for evermore.

But how much should I say, when I've no way
To say Your attributes in what I say?
If you, my heart, will seek, and try to find,
Watch well what is before and what behind,
And see the seekers at His court's door who
Have crowded on this Way to Him, like you;
Each atom reaches here through its own gate,
Each takes a different road to gain this state,
And what do you know of the Way before
You now, the path you'll follow to His door?
Seek Him in what you see, and He's not there,
Seek Him in secrets and He's everywhere,
Search for Him in the world, He hides away,
Search in what's dark and He's as clear as day,
Seek Him in both, since He is both and either,
And you will find that He is there in neither.
But since you haven't lost a thing, don't seek it,
And since your formulation's wrong, don't speak it!
The things you seek and know are you, and so
It's you, a hundred ways, you're forced to know.

Know Him by Him, not by yourself; His Way's
His own, from Him, it's not what wisdom says;
He cannot be described by any man –
No wretch, no sage, can do this; no one can!
Weakness and Knowledge are milk-sisters who
Fail equally to say whatever's true;
Men's words about Him are but dreams, and they
Cannot define Him by the words they say;
They say He's good or bad; but all they've said
Is really words about themselves instead.
He is beyond all knowing, since His grace
Cannot be seen or traced to any place;
No sign of Him's the only sign He gives,
And man must give to Him the life he lives
Since man, no matter how he turns and twists,
Knows nothing of Him, save that He exists.
The atoms in both worlds are your illusion,
And all you know of Him is mere confusion;
Where He is, man is not, man couldn't thrive there,
So how could any person's soul arrive there?
He is a hundred thousand times beyond man's soul,
And all I've said falls far short of the Whole –
Reason despairs, consumed by its lament,
Souls bite the finger of astonishment,
Reason can't reach this treasure's home, and where
The soul resides this treasure isn't there.

What is the soul, but crazed with longing for Him?
What is the heart, but soaked with blood before Him?
You seek the Truth, and you should cease to seek
To frame it in the metaphors you speak;
The soul and Reason are confounded by Him,
Reason's amazed, the soul's dumbfounded by Him,
And all His envoys, all His prophets, caught
No more than glimpses of the Whole they sought,
And bowed down in the dust in reverence
And willingly confessed their ignorance.

How can I boast I know reality?
He knows, and He alone, and only He,
Because in both worlds He alone exists –
Who's there besides Him? These are dreams and mists!
Waves rise from Him, He is an endless sea,
And you know nothing – learn your ABC!
Whoever does not find that sea will find
That he is nothing, lost and left behind.
How can what's talked about exist? And how
Can any 'I', proud 'I', declare that now?
Don't say that 'He', no word can specify Him,
Don't breathe a word, since none identify Him;
No word or phrase contains Him or confines Him,
No man has insight into what defines Him.
You, cease to be! This is Perfection's way;
And lose your Self, there is no more to say –
Lose your poor Self in Him; this is the goal,
The rest is mere distraction for your soul.
Choose Oneness, shun duality and find
One heart, one place to pray, one focused mind.
You're Adam's child, but ignorant; strive rather
To have the sense and wisdom of your father,
To whom the various beings God created
From Nothingness bowed down as subjugated;
When making Adam's nature He concealed it
Behind a hundred different veils to shield it,
And said: 'O Adam, they bow down before you,
Be generous to them as they adore you.'
And he who did not bow[16] was cursed, and driven
Deprived of Knowledge from the court of heaven;
His features were all blackened, as he cried:
'Don't leave me, Lord, alone and vilified!'
And God replied: 'Accursed and loathsome thing,
Adam's My regent here, your lord and king;
Be as his talisman today, tomorrow
Burn rue against the Evil Eye and sorrow.'

What is more wonderful than when the soul
Enters the flesh, and part becomes the Whole –
The soul so high, the earthly flesh so low,
Now one, with soul above, and earth below?
When high and low united in one span
Earth's most mysterious miracle was man,
But no one grasps this mystery, this state,
That's not for any beggar to debate;
We cannot understand, we cannot know,
And in our hearts we'll always feel this woe.
Silence is best. Why talk about it, why,
Since courage here's as feeble as a sigh?
Yes, many know the surface of this sea
But no one's plunged into its mystery;
There's treasure in those depths, and for its sake
The world, this talisman, will crack and break;
The treasure will be yours, since when the flesh
Is gone the soul will rise up from its mesh;
Your soul will be the talisman then, bidden
To be the body bearing what is hidden.
Go forward, don't ask where, and don't complain,
Don't ask for remedies to ease your pain.
How many sink within this ocean, drowned
Within its depths, of whom no trace is found!
A world's a mote within this endless sea,
A mote's a world in its immensity
(The world's a bubble in this sea – take note
Of this – as is the tiniest little mote;
One mote or world the less, what difference
Could this make in an ocean so immense?);
I've given Reason, soul, faith, heart to see
This mote in its ideal entirety.
Don't ask about His throne; don't talk at all,
Stifle your questions now, however small –
Your Reason's puzzled even by a hair,
Sew both your lips together, and beware!
No one can comprehend this mote, so cease
To ask so many questions; go in peace.

lines 139–158

What is this universe, this baseless place,
This topsy-turvy and unstable space?
And when you'd think of Him, you try, and fail
To pass beyond the veils within that veil.
But how can our confused perplexity
Begin to understand His sovereignty?
How can the turning heavens penetrate
His secrets in their still unstable state?
How can they see beyond that veil when they
Are set upon their whirling, wandering way?
When for so many years they've turned around
So that the ground's the sky, the sky's the ground?
And if they've failed to see beyond this veil
How is it possible that you'll prevail?
The world is lessons, longing, discontent,
Bewilderment within bewilderment;
The Way grows longer every hour, and we
Each hour sink deeper in perplexity;
D'you know what travellers see? They see that they
Must go for ever further on the Way –
If there were ends to what is infinite,
Or numbers stopped, they might encompass it.

I've seen a wondrous workshop where men shed
The selves that they were born with, as if dead.
Since to the Self the Self cannot be shown,
A mote's self by a mote remains unknown.
All's turned around and upside-down, all
Bite their hands, and turn their faces to the wall.
My Self annoys me, I want only You,
And Yours is all the good and bad I do;
I'm nothing without You, Your glance will make me
Complete and perfect: look, and don't forsake me;
Glance at my blood-drenched, suffering heart, and
          choose me,
Rescue me from the many, don't refuse me.
If for the briefest moment You reject me,
No one will seek my dust out, or respect me.

lines 159–176

But who am I that You should choose to prize me?
It is enough for me that You despise me –
How can I claim that I'm Your poor Hindu[17]
When I'm Your street-dog's slave, if he's near You?
My soul's Your slave, though, black with longing for
    You,
A black slave, branded, desperate to adore You.
Yes, I'm Your Hindu slave, if any man is,
My heart's as black now as an African is;
Don't sell your branded slave, but have me wear
Your earring,[18] as I'm Yours now, everywhere;
No one's excluded from Your grace; for me
Your ring and brand suffice eternally.
May happiness not visit any who
Aren't happy in their hearts to long for You;
You are my balm, but hurt me now, since I
Without that touch of pain will surely die –
All disbelief and faith are atoms to
The pain that Attar knows in serving You.

O Lord, You hear me cry: 'O Lord'; You're there
Throughout my darkest night, in my despair.
This night's so long, send me day's happiness,
Send me Your gracious light, in my distress;
Be my support in darkness, stand beside me,
Since there is no one else to help or guide me;
Give me faith's glorious light, annihilate
My Self's dark night, that holds me in this state.
I am an atom lost here in the shade,
I lack the substance of which Being's made;
I am a beggar of the sovereign sun –
Of all its rays may I be touched by one,
So that this dizzy mote that's me may dance
And clap my hands within His radiance
And rising through this aperture take flight
Into the real and living world of light.
Until my soul is ready to depart
I'm still that person that I was at heart,

But when my soul departs, at my last breath,
I've only You as I encounter death.
When I forsake this earth, how I shall grieve
And suffer, if You're absent as I leave!
But souls You're with can journey on, since You
Can do whatever You intend to do.

Those who have travelled on this Way before
Were motivated by religion's lore,
But found their souls bewildered, stupefied
With weakness and desire, dissatisfied.
Look at what Adam bore, the lifetime's woe
Our ancestor was forced to undergo,
And Noah, who survived the flood, whose life
Was harried by a thousand years of strife;
And look at Abraham whose home became
A cruel contraption filled with fire and flame,
And Esmail, who trembled to discover
He was to be the sacrificial lover;
And look at Jacob, wild with grief, and blind
From weeping for the son he could not find,
And Joseph, who found greatness, but who first
Endured the well, and was enslaved and cursed;
And look at suffering Job, who was the prey
Of worms and wolves that gnawed his flesh away,
And Jonah, who was lost, and whose sad tale
Brought him inside the belly of the whale;
And look at Moses' fate, marked from the womb
(Pharaoh his nurse, his cradle as his tomb),
And David, who made coats of mail, who melted
With inward heat and grief the steel he smelted;
And look at Solomon, whose wealth was scattered
Upon the winds, whose kingdom demons shattered,
And ardent Zacharia then, who said
No word as men sawed open his poor head;
And look at John, his life snuffed out, his fate
To have his head displayed upon a plate,

And Jesus at the cross's foot, whom Jews
So often sought to harry and abuse;
Look at the best of prophets, see what he
Endured from unbelievers' tyranny –
And this choice seemed an easy thing to you?
To lose your soul's the least you'll have to do!

But why should I say more? Why should I talk?
I've plucked the roses, every single stalk,
And suddenly I find I'm dizzy, weak,
Bewildered now, and with no power to speak;
In seeking wisdom's Way, I'm lost, forlorn,
I'm like a little child that's just been born,
And how can I, so small and destitute,
Reach from the womb now to the Absolute?
Unknowable, invisible, You reign
Beyond all attributes of loss and gain –
Unaided by good Moses' piety,
Unharmed by evil Pharaoh's infamy.
O God, immeasurable, boundless, who
Is limitless and infinite like You?
Surely no worldly thing is infinite,
What could exist without an end to it?
O world, mankind is mute; our senses fail
With wonder while You're hidden by this veil;
Remove the veil, don't let my soul's life burn
With longing any longer, let me learn!
I'm dizzy, lost in seas of discontent,
Save me from my confused predicament:
I'm reeling in a whirlpool, kept outside
The inwardness this veil exists to hide –
Save Your slave now from this estranging sea;
You plunged me in it, You must rescue me!
My Self is drowning me; come, seize my hand,
Since if You don't, I'll never gain dry land.
My folly's smeared my soul with dirt; I swear
That being filthy's something I can't bear –

Cleanse my poor soul of filth, or spill my blood,
Kill me, and make me one with dirt and mud.
Men fear You but I fear my Self; this devil
Replaces all the good You give with evil!
I'm dead, I crawl upon the earth; oh, give
My soul life, my Creator, let me live!
Heathens, believers, all are blood-soaked here,
They're dizzy, or they stray and disappear –
The dizzy ones are those elected by You,
The wanderers are those rejected by You.
O King, I drown in blood, and like the skies
I whirl round in perpetual surprise.
You've said: 'I am beside you, night and day;
Seek constantly, don't ever turn away.'
If we're together then as sun and shade,
And You're the sun, and we're the shade You've made,
Why is it, Lord, You can't bestow upon
Your shadows here the radiance of the sun?
My heart is filled with grief, my soul with pain,
My longing's like a cloud, my tears like rain,
But I must seek You out – to stop and say
My grief to You would mean I'll lose my way.
Guide me since I am lost, bestow on me
Good Fortune since I come in poverty;
Those souls who dwell with You are fortunate,
They're lost in You, it is themselves they hate.
I don't despair, but worry drives me on –
Of every hundred thousand, He'll choose one.

The bandit and the bread

A bandit dragged a wretch home to his lair
And tied him up, and meant to kill him there;
He drew his knife to sever the man's head
Just as his wife gave him a bit of bread.
He was about to kill the wretch, then saw the bit
Of bread, and asked how he had come by it:

'Who handed you that scrap of bread I see?'
The wretch replied: 'Your wife gave it to me.'
And hearing him the bandit said: 'Then I
Can't be the lawful means by which you die,
Since, when a man breaks bread with us, to draw
A knife against him is to break our law;
A man who shares our bread's our friend – how can
I even think of killing such a man?'

I've travelled on your Way since I was able,
My Lord, and all my bread is from Your table;
When bread is shared and broken with us we
Feel grateful for such generosity,
And You're, a hundred thousand times, the source
Of bread for me, an infinite recourse.
O Lord, I'm like a man who's drowned in blood,
Whose boat is stuck in barren sands and mud;
Take my hand, help me now; how long must I
Flounder here helpless like a struggling fly?
You pardon us, and yet I burn, I'm sure,
A hundred ways – what more must I endure?
My blood's ashamed, and boils in its confusion,
My sins are legion, cover their profusion;
I've sinned a hundred ways from negligence
And found each time Your kind benevolence.
My King, You saw the wretch I was; I vow
The sins You saw are gone; look at me now –
I sinned from ignorance and carelessness;
Forgive my sins, and pity my distress;
My eyes seem dry now to the outward view
But inwardly I weep and wail for You.
The good and bad I've done, O Lord, must be
Imputed to the carnal part of me;
Forgive my many weaknesses, erase
My loss of dignity, and my disgrace.

Praise of the Prophet

Lord of the world and faith, Mohammad, throne
And moon of all that's known and is unknown,
Bright sun of law and sea of certainty,
Light of the world and sign of clemency –
Pure souls are dust to his soul, and adore him,
The world itself is merely dust before him.
Lord of both worlds, sovereign of all, the sun
Of human souls, the faith of everyone,
Lord of ascension, throne of earthly might,
Shadow of God, sun of essential light,
Both worlds are as his hunting spoils, the throne
Of heaven prostrates itself to him alone;
In this world and the next world he precedes us,
To all that's hidden, all that's plain, he leads us.
Greatest and best of prophets, leader of
The purest souls, of saints consumed by love;
The rightly guided and the guide to all,
To all that's hidden, all that's visible,
Greater than any words that I can say,
Of all things best, and first in every way;
The Arbiter of Judgement Day, as he
Has called himself, earth's Source of Clemency.

His being named both worlds, and peace was given
By means of his name to the throne of heaven.
Like dew drops rising from a sea of grace
Creation followed him and found its place,
His light became the goal of all creation;
All Being is from him, all deprivation;
And when God saw this perfect light, He lit
A hundred further seas of light from it;
He made him for Himself, and then created
For him the world that he illuminated –
Creation has no goal but him, and he
Remains unrivalled in his purity.

The first thing to emerge from darkest night
Was, without doubt, his pure refulgent light;
From this there came the world, heaven's throne, the
     pen
And tablet that record the fates of men;
A trace of this light made the world, a trace
Created Adam and the human race.
This light appeared, and fell down in prostration
Before its God, the Lord of all creation;
For centuries it worshipped prostrate there,
For lifetimes it stood still in fervent prayer,
For years it raised itself erect to say
Its faith's confession humbly, and to pray –
The prayers this sea of secrets prayed were made
The image of the prayers the faithful prayed.[19]
Like sunlight then, and moonlight, this bright light
Spread everywhere, for aeons, in God's sight
Until it made a pathway, suddenly,
Into the depths of Truth's unbounded sea.
And when it saw the sea of secrets' face
The light flared up and seethed, imbued with grace,
And seven times it sought itself, and seven
Celestial spheres then formed the vault of heaven,
And every glance God gave, the light returned
Desire now as a star that flared and burned,
Until the light grew peaceful and became
The throne of heaven both in form and name;
This was his essence, given as reflection,
As angels were his qualities' perfection.

His breathing made the world's bright lights appear,
His thoughtful heart made hidden secrets clear;
The secret of the soul, though, had to be
Reserved to God's breathed-in divine decree,
Since when His breath and mystery joined they formed
The many souls with which creation swarmed.
Because the Prophet's light was sent for all,
All follow it when it is visible,

And he was sent to all, of every clime,
To all mankind until the end of time,
And even Satan, when he heard him speak,
Said Islam was the Way that he would seek.
One night God also let him to try to win
Demonic djinns[20] back from their life of sin,
And on another night he summoned all
God's angels and His prophets to his call.
He summoned animals to hear his preaching,
And goats and lizards answered to his teaching;
He preached to idols everywhere, and hurled
Them from their pedestals throughout the world.
That pure soul summoned atoms; grains of sand
Became like prayer-beads, praying in his hand –
Among the prophets, who was of his worth?
And which of them was sent to all the earth?
His light's the cause of all that lives, his essence
Precedes all essences by its pure presence.
His duty was to summon both worlds, all
Their atoms, visible, invisible –
All peoples came to be his congregation,
His grace is harvested by every nation,
And it will be enough to hear him say:
'These are my people here' on Judgement Day,
Since, for this guiding light's sake, God will send
Salvation to his people without end.

Where he's the guide, the beneficiary's
The man who acts upon his faith's decrees,
And we should weep for any action where
His guidance and his insight are not there.
He is all creatures' refuge, and his will's
The goal that every pilgrimage fulfils;
He is the world's sage, wise in every way,
And others are but servants who obey;
But who has even dreamed he knows or sees
The nature of this Prophet's qualities?

He saw all, and he was all, unsurpassed,
And saw the future as he saw the past.
God gave him as the prophets' seal to us,
Miraculous, and good, and generous;
And filled him with His grace, so that he'd show
The Truth to all mankind, both high and low.
And in his life here, even heathen crime
Remained unpunished, till a future time.
To him alone were all God's secrets given
When one night he ascended into heaven,
The lord of all, whose shadeless shadow blessed
The outspread world beneath, from east to west –
God gave to him the best of books, and he
Received all Truth, in its entirety.
The mothers of the faithful were his wives,
Apostles gave, to his ascent, their lives;
He leads the prophets, and the wise men who
Acknowledge him become like prophets too.
To honour him completely and proclaim him
God had the Torah and the Gospels name him,
And by his worth a stone was made to be
The holy ka'aba,[21] robed in majesty.
Men prayed before his dust, and what was void
And ugly for the faithful was destroyed;
He broke all idols and idolatries,
His is the best of all communities.
In drought years, spittle from his mouth ensured
That in dry wells pure water was restored;
His finger split the moon, the sun went back
At his command upon its ancient track,
Between his shoulder blades a sun-like seal
Proclaimed his prophet-hood as true and real.
The best of times, the best of towns, were when
And where men's leader was the best of men –
The ka'aba then became God's house, and those
Who followed him found shelter from their foes.
By his grace Gabriel put on the cloak
Of humankind before him there and spoke;

lines 318–336

The earth became more stalwart then, a place
Of worship, reverent purity and grace,
And secrets, more than any books have shown,
By one who could not read, were seen and known –
That God's word was his word sufficed, the best
Of times was his, exceeding all the rest,
And all words but his word will fade away
Entirely, on God's final Judgement Day.

Until his final breath, his ardent prayer
Was to pursue his longing everywhere,
And plunging in the sea of secrets he
Desired to worship God more fervently –
His heart was that deep sea, and what commotion
Will seethe and churn within the deepest ocean!
He said to Bilal: 'Call for prayer, release
My troubled soul from bondage, give it peace!'
And coming to himself, bewildered, he
Would say to his loved wife then: 'Speak to me!'
And how a soul survives such coming, going,
My mind can't formulate, and there's no knowing!
Reason can't reach his peace, or Knowledge find
A way to know the states within his mind –
When God and Abraham conversed, for fear
Of burning Gabriel could not come near.
And when the Simorgh[22] was made manifest
Astonished Moses was a finch at best.
Approaching His blessed precincts, Moses heard
'Remove your shoes' as God's commanding word,
And then, his shoes removed, he glowed and shone
With light as in God's vale he journeyed on.
Faith's flame, in his ascension, heard the sound
Of Bilal's sandalled feet upon the ground,
Although, despite his kingship, this was where
Moses went shoeless, and his feet were bare;
Look at the favour God bestowed upon
Even the servant of His chosen one –

Mohammad's servant, with his feet still shod,
Walked in the precincts of the court of God.
When Moses saw Mohammad's servant's place
Of intimacy there, and noble grace,
He said: 'O God, I pray that You let me
Enrol myself in his community!'
While Moses sought this rank he never gained it,
Though Jesus also sought it and attained it,
And when he leaves this refuge surely he
Will bring mankind to this community;
From the fourth heaven he'll descend to place
Upon the dusty earth his prostrate face,
And he will be as our Creator names him,
The Prophet's faithful herald, who proclaims him.
If someone says: 'But how can anyone
Come back again to this world once he's gone?'
The answer to each problem that arises,
And to whatever doubts the heart surmises,
Is that Mohammad only, of all men,
Saw both worlds plainly and returned again –
And what as Knowledge other prophets learned
Mohammad with his very sight discerned.
God placed a glorious crown upon his head,
The mountains bowed before him then in dread;
He is the king, the sultan, it is he
Who rules all subjects here eternally.
The world is perfumed with his musky hair,
Thirst for him dries the oceans with despair –
Who does not thirst to see him, when each stone,
Each block of timber, thirsts for him alone,
And when the palm-tree groaned for him when he
Preached from a pulpit, not beneath the tree?[23]
The heavens were filled with his illumination,
But the poor palm bemoaned their separation.

For shame, sweat flows from me like blood; how can
I find the words to speak of such a man?
He is all eloquence, I'm dumb; how could
My faltering words describe him as they should?
How can a wretch like me depict his nature?
No one can do this but the world's Creator.
The world is dust to you, for all its worth,
Infinite souls, to your soul, are but earth;
Prophets describe you with bewilderment,
Wise men are fuddled and incompetent.
It's with your smiling that the sun appears,
The clouds obey you when they weep your tears;
Both worlds are dust before you, though you kept
A threadbare carpet as the place you slept;
Raise your head from that carpet, see how far,
O generous one, beyond its worth you are!
All laws dissolve in your law, and all essence
Is lost within the splendour of your presence;
Your laws will last for ever, and your name
And God's enjoy equivalent acclaim.
All prophets, all God's messengers, obey
The laws you gave, and walk along your Way –
Since none can go before you, it is true
That all, without a doubt, must follow you;
You are the first in this world and the last,
At one time both its future and its past.
No one can even reach the dust around you,
No one can share the glories that surround you,
Since God has given both worlds' sovereignty
To you, Mohammad, for eternity.
O messenger of God, I grasp at air,
For shame heap dust upon my head and hair.
Whom have I in both worlds but you, the friend
Of friendless men, till life and breath shall end?
Look for a moment at my deep distress,
Help me escape now from my helplessness;
I've wrecked my life with sin, but abjectly
I beg that you will intercede for me;

And though 'Be wary' troubles me, the force
Of God's 'Do not despair' is my recourse:
Both day and night I mourn a hundred times,
Longing for you to expiate my crimes,
Since but a word from you turns violence
And sinful wrongs into obedience.
You intercede for dirt, and may the blaze
Of intercession's candle light our days,
And we like moths shall suddenly take flight
And beat our fluttering wings about your light,
Since those who see your flame, like moths, will fly
Wholeheartedly into that fire to die.
Your sight suffices souls, and the foundation
Of both worlds' being is your approbation;
Your kindness heals my heart's pains, and the grace
That shines within my soul's your sun-like face;
My soul stands as a servant at your door,
My tongue's a drawn sword ready to make war,
And all the jewels my speaking tongue disperses
Along your pathway are my heartfelt verses –
My soul's a sea that scatters jewels, a sea
That takes its being from your sign in me,
And since my soul has found your sign there's been
The sign within my soul that's never seen.
O rarest jewel, my need is this, that you
Glance in your grace on all I am and do,
And with that signless grace make me your own –
Signlessly, always, keep me yours alone.
Purge me of doubts, vain thoughts, idolatry,
Cleanse me by your essential purity,
And by the name we share[24] ensure my name
And face will not be black with sin and shame.
I am your child, black waters now surround me,
Along your Way this flood has almost drowned me,
And yet my hope is that you'll seize my hand
And set me on your Way, upon dry land.

The baby who tumbled in the river

A baby tumbled from a river bank;
The mother watched in terror as it sank,
Threshing its arms and legs; in her despair
She saw it swept toward a mill wheel there,
And dashed to open wide the sluice's gate
And save her child before it was too late.
The rushing water flowed aside, and bore
The baby out of danger to the shore;
The mother snatched her baby up, and pressed
Him to her heart, and fed him from her breast.

Your mercy's like a mother's, generous
And kind, but what mill-races wait for us!
And when we tumble in their turbulence
We're swept along by passion's vehemence,
And like that baby then, we thresh and turn
In terror as the swirling waters churn.
Glance at us then, the children of your Way,
Be merciful, before we're swept away;
Have pity on our hearts' bewildered state
And open wide for us the sluice's gate;
Feed us from Mercy's kindly breast, and see
We aren't denied the milk of Charity.
You came, beyond portrayal and description,
Beyond all explanation and depiction,
And we, who cannot reach your saddle, stay
As dust beneath the dust along your Way.
Your friends are but your dust, and all the rest
Of humankind is your dust's dust at best;
Those who don't bow before your friends can be
Considered as your followers' enemy.
The first is Abu Bakr, Ali the last,
Four pillars of the ka'aba, firm and fast;

One as your confidant and your vizier,[25]
One as a sun of justice, bright and clear,[26]
One as a sea of patient modesty,[27]
One as a lord of generosity.[28]

Praise of Abu Bakr the sincere

First of caliphs and friends, and second brave
Companion of the Prophet in the cave,[29]
Lord of the faith, pivot of Truth, in all
Made eminent and unsurpassable!
Whatever God poured from the court of heaven
Into the Prophet's mind, was also given
To Abu Bakr, so that his heart then spilled,
In turn, the Truth with which it had been filled.
He breathed in both worlds with a gulp of air
And sealed his lips with stones and held them there,
And then he bowed his head throughout the night,
And groaned and prayed until the morning light –
His musky sighs reached China, where they lent
To Tartar deer's blood their pervasive scent,
And from this came the sun of faith's command:
'Seek Knowledge, unto China's distant land.'
He put stones in his mouth; his wisdom knew
That he would then pronounce no word but 'Hu!'[30]
The stones constrained his tongue in such a way
That 'Hu', God's name, was all that he could say.
A stone is weighty; when can men without
Such weightiness be useful or devout?
When Omar glimpsed his value he confessed:
'Would that I were a hair upon that chest!'
Since You appointed him as second, we
Accept him as the Prophet's deputy.

Praise of Omar

The lord of law, faith's sun and burning light,
Great judge of Truth, God's shadow in men's sight,
The seal of justice, Truth and equity,
The door to insight and sagacity,
He for whom God sent Ta Ha to begin
His chapter,[31] and to cleanse him of all sin;
The 'Ha' of Ta Ha in his heart became
A cry for 'Hu', and glory to his name!
And Omar, by the Prophet's great decree,
Will cross the bridge first to eternity
And grasp the knocker on the gates of heaven –
All glory to the rank he will be given!
Since God first put His hand in his, He'll take him
At last where He abides, and not forsake him.
His law fulfilled the faith, his power released
The Nile, and by his might earth's trembling ceased;
He was the torch of paradise whose light
Wholly effaced men's shadows from their sight;
So how was it the devil fled in fear
Whenever Omar's shadow would appear?
And when his tongue spoke truly he was blessed
Within his heart, where God was manifest.
At times his soul would burn with love, and then
His tongue would burn with truths he taught to men,
And when the Prophet saw his burning, he
Named him the torch of heaven's eternity.

Praise of Osman

Tradition's lord, light absolute, created
To be the master twice illuminated,[32]
Faith's chieftain, Osman, Affan's offspring, drowned
In seas of gnosis, sacred and profound!

The elevation of faith's banner came
From Osman's, faith's commander's, fame;
The heart of twofold light within Osman
Was where the glory of both worlds began.
'A second Joseph',[33] 'Mine of virtue's light',
The Prophet called him, and 'A sea of might'.
He risked his life for friends and relatives;
In saving them it is his soul he gives,
Since it was favouring his own that led
His foes to cut his body from his head.[34]
He was the world's guide and its ornament,
And Islam spread beneath his government;
His time saw Islam everywhere respected,
And God's Qur'an collated and collected.
The Lord of Lords said of Osman: 'He even
Shames with his splendour angels lodged in heaven';
Likewise the Prophet said: 'God will not weigh
The life that Osman led, on Judgement Day.'
The Prophet vouched for Osman's faith when he
Was absent from the oath of loyalty,[35]
Although those present there agreed that they
Could not, like him, have safely stayed away.

Praise of Ali

The lord of Truth, faith's pole, the good man's guide,
The gate to where all sciences abide,
The cupbearer by whom heaven's water's poured,
The Prophet's cousin, lion of the Lord,
The chosen one in whom the Prophet saw
His daughter's husband,[36] and his son-in-law,
He came to guide and to explain; his task
Was to resolve all questions men might ask.
He clears all claims that mortals might dispute,
Without a doubt his word is absolute,
And since he knows God's secrets, how could sense
Cast doubt upon his insight's prescience?

lines 455–471

'Of all men he's most just', 'In every way
His essence is from God', the proverbs say.
Christ's breath revived the dead, Ali's restored
A hand that had been severed by a sword,[37]
And on the Prophet's shoulders, it was he
Who smashed the ka'aba's idols utterly.
He knew of secrets hidden from men's sight,
And so his hand, like Moses', shone with light –
If this had not been so, how could he clasp
The mighty zulfiqar[38] within his grasp?
At times he'd rage at what he'd done, and then
He'd whisper in a well's depths, far from men;
Finding no one in whom he could confide,
He'd go into himself, and there he'd hide.

Ali speaks against faction[39]

'Oh, sunk in faction's coils, and caught within
Your state of endless bigotry and sin,
You boast of soul and sense, and yet you seethe
With prejudice in every breath you breathe!
The caliphate's not personal; could there be
In Abu Bakr and Omar bigotry?
If they'd been biased they'd have surely tried
To have their sons succeed them when they died,
And in so doing taken rights from those
Who played a part in whom the faithful chose;
And not to fight against this would have meant
Establishing a fateful precedent.
No one opposed their caliphate, and so
Choose or reject them with a "Yes!" or "No!"
If you reject the Prophet's friends, then you
Reject the message of the Prophet too,
Whose words were: "All of my Companions shine
As stars! The best of times to live is mine!
The best of men are my close friends, those near
To me in love, and those I hold most dear."

But if these "best" seem evil to you, how
Can men declare that you see clearly now?
How can you claim the Prophet's friends would choose
A worthless creature whom they should refuse,
And put him in Mohammad's noble place?
How could they bear such folly and disgrace!
And if belief in them is wrong, you make
Collating the Qur'an's words a mistake.
But no, the Prophet's close Companions were
Just in their actions, and they did not err.
Reject but one of them, and you reject
Thirty-three thousand[40] whom you should accept.
Those who with every breath do all they should,
"Hobbling the camel"[41] since this too is good,
Who act so scrupulously – how can you
Think they would take what is another's due?
If Abu Bakr had wanted this, would he
Have said: "Depose me now, get rid of me"?
Likewise, if Omar breathed one selfish breath
Would he have whipped his guilty son to death?[42]
No, Abu Bakr was just, free from all greed,
Devoted to God's court in thought and deed;
He gave his wealth, his soul, his daughter to
God's cause; such men aren't wicked – shame on you!
Free of all superficialities
His mind communed with inward mysteries,
And when he sat upon the pulpit he
Acted with reverence and humility.
He saw all things so clearly! Who can say
That such a man's unjust in any way?
And Omar, who uprooted thorns, or made
New bricks to build with, justice was his trade:[43]
He'd search the town for wormwood, everywhere
He strode he looked for it with constant care –
Always controlling his desires, he fed
Himself each day with seven bites of bread,
And never used the public funds to get
The daily salt and vinegar he ate.

His mattress was the sand when he was tired,
His whip was all the pillow he required;
He'd take a water skin to ease the plight
Of some poor widow when she slept at night,
Then roused his heart, and through the darkness kept
A careful watch while all around him slept.
He said to Hozifeh once: "Can you see
Hypocrisy in Omar now, in me?
Where is the man who has the honest grace
To tell me all my faults, and face to face?"
If Omar had usurped the caliphate
Why were his clothes in such a wretched state?
Ten patches pieced together, roughly sewn,
Were all the clothes that he could call his own.
If this is how he led the faith, it's clear
There was no greed or favouritism here;
A man who totes bricks, mixes mud, won't make
A show of hardship just for nothing's sake –
If he had run the caliphate to please
Himself he would have lived in princely ease.
And in his time so many heathen lands
Were emptied of their evil at his hands;[44]
So, if you're prejudiced against him, I
Say you're unjust, and you deserve to die.
No poison killed him,[45] but your rage will be
A poison that will kill you finally.
Don't judge the caliphate, you graceless fool,
By your ideas of what it is to rule;
If this were *your* fate you would soon discover
A hundred griefs before the task was over.
If someone seized the caliphate he'd find
A hundred sorrows would assail his mind,
Since it's not easy, while we live, to be
Responsible for a community.'

Omar and the caliphate

Omar addressed Oveis in rage: 'I'll sell
The caliphate and bid its power farewell;
If someone wants to buy it now for gold,
For just one dinar, here it is; it's sold!'
Oveis heard Omar's words and said: 'So leave it,
Just go; whoever wants it can retrieve it;
Someone is sure to pick it up again,
Some passer-by who'd really like to reign.'
But the Companions, when they heard that he
Meant to relinquish power, wailed piteously;
They said as one: 'You are our guide, don't make
Your people leaderless, for pity's sake!
Since in his wisdom Abu Bakr chose you
To lead us, and to do what you must do,
His soul will suffer if you turn aside
And leave the way his orders specified.'
And hearing this Omar felt even more
Constrained by duty than he had before.

The death of Ali

When Fate decreed a wretch's mortal blow
Should strike Ali at last, and lay him low,[46]
They brought Ali a potion, and he said:
'Where is the man who left me here for dead?
Give him the potion first, then me, since he
Must travel too, and he'll accompany me.'
They brought the potion, but the man resisted.
'This is revenge, it's poison!' he insisted.
And Ali said: 'By God who is in heaven,
If he had drunk the potion I was given,
I would not enter paradise, I swear,
Unless I had that man beside me there.'

This ugly soul had killed him, but he tried
To lead the man to heaven when he died;
He loved his enemy so much, could he
Consider Abu Bakr with enmity?
He pitied his own murderer, how could
Omar seem anything to him but good?
The boundless world will not produce a friend
For Abu Bakr like Ali till time's end;
How long must you say: 'Ali was oppressed,
Denied his rightful power and dispossessed'?
My boy, Ali's the lion of God, the crown
Of Truth, and no one brings a lion down!

Mohammad at the well

Mohammad halted at a well head's side;
'Bring water for my thirsty troops,' he cried.
The man he'd sent dashed back and said to him:
'It's blood that fills this well, up to the brim!'
Mohammad said: 'You think this is the well's
Own doing? No, it's here that Ali tells
His secrets to the depths; in sympathy
The water's turned into the blood you see.'

Could one whose soul has suffered such distress
Feel even an ant's weight of bitterness?
Your soul's become a faction-ridden riot,
But Ali's soul was not like this: be quiet!
Don't think that you're like him, since he was
    drowned
Within the seas of Truth that he had found,
And was so lost within his work that he
Had no time for your foolish fantasy.
If Ali felt the hatred that you boast
He would have fought against the Prophet's host;
He was much more a man than you, far more –
Why then did he, not once, begin a war?

He could have justly sought the caliphate
If Abu Bakr did not deserve this state.
When Aysha moved against him,[47] it was right,
At that point, to resist her men and fight,
To answer force with force, and not to yield
When faced with armies on the battlefield
(Those who could fight the Prophet's daughter – who
Was Ali's wife – opposed her father too).
My boy, the letters that form Ali's name
Are all the knowledge of him you can claim!
He was prepared – a hundred times – to give
His life; you cling to life, and long to live.

When any of the Prophet's friends were killed
Ali bemoaned the blood that had been spilled,
And cried: 'Oh, why can't it be me who dies?
My wretched life's now worthless in my eyes!'
The Master said: 'But you must stay alive,
Ali, preserved for us; you must survive.'

Bilal

Bilal was whipped; a hundred times the rod
Struck him, to force him to deny his God;
'The One!' he cried, 'the One!' as red blood poured
From all the wounds with which his flesh was scored.

If a thorn pierced your foot, you'd quite forget
The friends and foes that you had made and met,
And should a man a thorn can discompose
Rule a community, do you suppose?
They[48] could do this, not you, so for how long
Will you persist in being blind and wrong?
Your tongue's the saviour of idolatry,
It wounds the saintly with its idiocy;
Your chatter stains your record, yet you'd win
Salvation if you held this chatter in.

lines 556–571

Ali and Abu Bakr

Ali and Abu Bakr were both immersed
Within the sea of Truth that they traversed,
And when the Prophet hid within a cave
Ali slept in the Prophet's bed to save
The life of his great guide and leader by
Offering himself, in lieu of him, to die;
And Abu Bakr had shown himself as brave
By driving off the snakes within the cave.
Both were prepared to give their lives, to make
This sacrifice, if need be, for his sake,
And yet you cry up this or that brave man
And show yourself as blindly partisan.
You're his, you say, or his, yet where in you
Is all the suffering these two men went through?
Be ready, as these two men were, to die,
Or stop this captious, carping hue and cry!
'Ali' you say, or 'Abu Bakr', but show
No knowledge of the God you ought to know.
But leave all this as signed and sealed, and fight
To be a man like Rabe'eh, day and night;
That woman was a hundred men, from head
To foot she was replete with holy dread,
And, free of foolish chatter, she was drowned
For ever in the sacred light she found.

Rabe'eh

Someone once questioned her: 'What would you say
About the Prophet's friends, good Rabe'eh?'
She said: 'I haven't done with God yet, how
Can I discuss the Prophet's friendships now?
If I weren't wholly lost in God, I might
Be able to consider men aright.

Am I not she who, while I prayed, a thorn
Had pierced my eye, and the eye's flesh was torn,
So that blood dripped upon my prayer-mat there,
And I prayed on regardless, unaware?
One who has such divine concerns, how can
She care about this woman or that man?
Since I don't know myself, how could I claim
To talk of other men with praise or blame?'

You're neither God nor Prophet, you can't say
You do or don't accept men on this Way;
You're dust along this road; so be that, dust –
Stop all this 'yes' and 'no', it isn't just!
You're dust, so talk about the dust, but see
All men you meet as made of purity.

The Prophet's prayer

The Prophet prayed: 'I ask that You allow
Me to direct my people's business now,
So that no one should ever know or guess
This people's grievous sins and wickedness.'
And God replied: 'Great lord, if you could see
The vast extent of their iniquity,
You could not bear the shame of it, you'd hide
Yourself away, you'd be so mortified!
Your heart rejected Aysha, whom you loved,
Because of slanders that remained unproved,[49]
You heard the gossip of dishonest men
And sent her to her father's house again,
You turned from one you held most dear; and in
This people there are many filled with sin.
You could not bear it; no, let God direct them,
Put them in His hands now, He will protect them.
If you desire the world should never learn
Of all your people's sins, then I in turn,

My dearest jewel, desire that you should never
Learn of your people's sinfulness for ever,
So step aside, and day and night let Me
Be in command of your community.'
The Prophet did not lead, so what makes you
Think leading men is something you can do?

Stop judging, give up prejudice, don't say
So much so often; set out on the Way.
What *they* did once, do that! And never cease
To follow your own path; now go in peace!
Like Abu Bakr be honest, or decide
That justice, like Omar's, will be your guide,
Or like Osman be meek and courteous,
Or like Ali be wise and generous,
Or just be silent; put your head down, go –
That's my advice, it's all you need to know.
But are you honest, are you wise? No, you're
A Self, with every breath grown more impure;
Destroy that infidel the Self, and be –
Once it is killed – a man of faith, set free.
And take no part in faction (as though you
Possessed a prophet's knowledge of what's true).
In law one witness won't suffice, don't prate
About Companions and the caliphate!
I take no part in all such argument;
God keep me from a factional intent,
And purify my soul, so that my writing
Is free from partisanship and backbiting.

THE CONFERENCE
OF THE BIRDS

Dear hoopoe, welcome! You will be our guide;
It was on you King Solomon relied
To carry secret messages between
His court and distant Sheba's lovely queen.
He knew your language and you knew his heart –
As his close confidant you learned the art
Of holding demons captive underground,
And for these valiant exploits you were crowned.
And you are welcome, finch! Rise up and play
Those liquid notes that steal men's hearts away;
Like Moses you have seen the flames burn high
On Sinai's slopes and there you long to fly,
Like him avoid cruel Pharaoh's hand, and seek
Your promised home on Sinai's mountain peak.
There you will understand unspoken words
Too subtle for the ears of mortal birds.
And welcome, parrot, perched in paradise!
Your splendid plumage bears a strange device,
A necklace of bright fire about the throat;
Though heaven's bliss is promised by your coat,
This circle stands for hell; if you can flee
Like Abraham from Nimrod's enmity,
Despise these flames – uninjured you will tread
Through fire if first you cut off Nimrod's head,
And when the fear of him has died put on
Your gorgeous coat; your collar's strength has gone!
Welcome, dear partridge – how you strut with pride
Along the slopes of wisdom's mountain-side;

Let laughter ring out where your feet have trod,
Then strike with all your strength the door of God;
Destroy the mountain of the Self, and here
From ruined rocks a camel will appear;
Beside its new-born noble hooves, a stream
Of honey mingled with white milk will gleam –
Drive on this beast and at your journey's end
Saleh will greet you as a long-lost friend.
Rare falcon, welcome! How long will you be
So fiercely jealous of your liberty?
Your lure is love, and when the jess is tied,
Submit, and be for ever satisfied.
Give up the intellect for love and see
In one brief moment all eternity;
Break nature's frame, be resolute and brave,
Then rest at peace in Unity's black cave.
Rejoice in that close, undisturbed dark air –
The Prophet will be your companion there.[1]
And welcome, francolin! Since once you heard
And answered God's first all-commanding word,
Since love has spoken in your soul, reject
The Self, that whirlpool where our lives are wrecked;
As Jesus rode his donkey, ride on it;
Your stubborn Self must bear you and submit –
Then burn this Self and purify your soul;
Let Jesus' spotless spirit be your goal.
Destroy this burden, and before your eyes
The Holy Ghost in glory will arise.
Welcome, dear nightingale – from your sweet throat
Pour out the pain of lovers note by note.
Like David in love's garden gently sigh;
There sing the songs that make men long to die,
Oh, sing as David did, and with your song
Guide home man's suffering and deluded throng.
The Self is like a mail coat – melt this steel
To pliant wax with David's holy zeal,
And when its metal melts, like David you
Will melt with love and bid the Self adieu.

And welcome, peacock – once of paradise,
Who let the venomous, smooth snake entice
Your instincts to its master's evil way,
And suffered exile for that fateful day;
He blackened your untutored heart and made
A tangled darkness of the orchard's shade –
Until you crush this snake, how can you be
A pilgrim worthy of our mystery?
Destroy its ugly charm and Adam then
Will welcome you to paradise again.
Cock pheasant, welcome! With your piercing sight,
Look up and see the heart's source drowned in light;
You are imprisoned in your filthy well,
A dark and noisome, unremitting hell –
Rise from this well as Joseph did and gain
The throne of Egypt's fabulous domain,
Where you and Joseph will together reign.
Dear pigeon, welcome – with what joy you yearn
To fly away, how sadly you return!
Your heart is wrung with grief, you share the gaol
That Jonah knew, the belly of a whale –
The Self has swallowed you for its delight;
How long will you endure its mindless spite?
Cut off its head, seek out the moon and fly
Beyond the utmost limits of the sky;
Escape this monster and become the friend
Of Jonah in that ocean without end.
Welcome, sweet turtle-dove, and softly coo
Until the heavens scatter jewels on you –
But what ingratitude you show! Around
Your neck a ring of loyalty is bound,
But while you live you blithely acquiesce
From head to claw in smug ungratefulness;
Abandon such self-love and you will see
The Way that leads us to reality.
There knowledge is your guide, and Khezr will bring
Clear water drawn from life's eternal spring.

And welcome, hawk! Your flight is high and proud,
But you return with head politely bowed –
In blood and in affliction you must drown,
And I suggest you keep your head bent down!
What are you here? Mere carrion, rotten flesh,
Withheld from Truth by this world's clumsy mesh;
Outsoar both this world and the next, and there,
Released from both, take off the hood you wear –
When you have turned from both worlds you will land
On Zulgharnin's outstretched and welcome hand.
And little goldfinch, welcome! May your fire
Be an external sign of fierce desire.
Whatever happens, burn in those bright flames,
And shut your eyes and soul to earthly claims.
Then, as you burn, whatever pain you feel,
Remember God will recompense your zeal;
When you perceive His hidden secrets, give
Your life to God's affairs and truly live –
At last, made perfect in reality,
You will be gone, and only God will be.

The birds assemble and the hoopoe tells
them of the Simorgh[2]

The world's birds gathered for their conference
And said: 'Our constitution makes no sense.
All nations in the world require a king;
How is it we alone have no such thing?
Only a kingdom can be justly run;
We need a king and must inquire for one.'

They argued how to set about their quest.
The hoopoe fluttered forward; on his breast
There shone the symbol of the Spirit's Way
And on his head Truth's crown, a feathered spray.

Discerning, righteous and intelligent,
He spoke: 'My purposes are heaven-sent;
I keep God's secrets, mundane and divine,
In proof of which behold the holy sign
Bismillah³ etched for ever on my beak.
No one can share the grief with which I seek
Our longed-for Lord, and quickened by my haste
My wits find water in the trackless waste.
I come as Solomon's close friend and claim
The matchless wisdom of that mighty name
(He never asked for those who quit his court,
But when I left him once alone he sought
With anxious vigilance for my return –
Measure my worth by this great king's concern!).
I bore his letters – back again I flew –
Whatever secrets he divined I knew;
A prophet loved me; God has trusted me;
What other bird has won such dignity?
For years I travelled over many lands,
Past oceans, mountains, valleys, desert sands,
And when the Deluge rose I flew around
The world itself and never glimpsed dry ground;
With Solomon I set out to explore
The limits of the earth from shore to shore.
I know our King – but how can I alone
Endure the journey to His distant throne?
Join me, and when at last we end our quest
Our King will greet you as His honoured guest.
How long will you persist in blasphemy?
Escape your self-hood's vicious tyranny –
Whoever can evade the Self transcends
This world and as a lover he ascends.
Set free your soul; impatient of delay,
Step out along our sovereign's royal Way:
We have a king; beyond Kaf's mountain peak⁴
The Simorgh lives, the Sovereign whom you seek,
And He is always near to us, though we
Live far from His transcendent majesty.

lines 689–716

A hundred thousand veils of dark and light
Withdraw His presence from our mortal sight,
And in both worlds no being shares the throne
That marks the Simorgh's power and His alone –
He reigns in undisturbed omnipotence,
Bathed in the light of His magnificence –
No mind, no intellect can penetrate
The mystery of His unending state:
How many countless hundred thousands pray
For patience and true knowledge of the Way
That leads to Him whom reason cannot claim,
Nor mortal purity describe or name;
There soul and mind bewildered miss the mark
And, faced by Him, like dazzled eyes, are dark –
No sage could understand His perfect grace,
Nor seer discern the beauty of His face.
His creatures strive to find a path to Him,
Deluded by each new, deceitful whim,
But fancy cannot work as she would wish;
You cannot weigh the moon like so much fish!
How many search for Him whose heads are sent
Like polo-balls in some great tournament
From side to giddy side – how many cries,
How many countless groans assail the skies!
Do not imagine that the Way is short;
Vast seas and deserts lie before His court.
Consider carefully before you start;
The journey asks of you a lion's heart.
The road is long, the sea is deep – one flies
First buffeted by joy and then by sighs;
If you desire this quest, give up your soul
And make our Sovereign's court your only goal.
First wash your hands of life if you would say:
"I am a pilgrim of our Sovereign's Way";
Renounce your soul for love; He you pursue
Will sacrifice His inmost soul for you.

It was in China, late one moonless night,
The Simorgh first appeared to mortal sight –
He let a feather float down through the air,
And rumours of its fame spread everywhere;
Throughout the world men separately conceived
An image of its shape, and all believed
Their private fantasies uniquely true!
(In China still this feather is on view,
Whence comes the saying you have heard, no doubt,
"Seek knowledge, unto China seek it out.")
If this same feather had not floated down,
The world would not be filled with His renown –
It is a sign of Him, and in each heart
There lies this feather's hidden counterpart.
But since no words suffice, what use are mine
To represent or to describe this sign?
Whoever wishes to explore the Way,
Let him set out – what more is there to say?'

The hoopoe finished, and at once the birds
Effusively responded to his words.
All praised the splendour of their distant King;
All rose impatient to be on the wing;
Each would renounce the Self and be the friend
Of his companions till the journey's end.
But when they pondered on the journey's length,
They hesitated; their ambitious strength
Dissolved: each bird, according to his kind,
Felt flattered but reluctantly declined.

The nightingale's excuse

The nightingale made his excuses first.
His pleading notes described the lover's thirst,
And through the crowd hushed silence spread as he
Descanted on love's scope and mystery.
'The secrets of all love are known to me,'

He crooned. 'Throughout the darkest night my song
Resounds, and to my retinue belong
The sweet notes of the melancholy lute,
The plaintive wailing of the lovesick flute;
When love speaks in the soul my voice replies
In accents plangent as the ocean's sighs.
The man who hears this song spurns reason's rule;
Grey wisdom is content to be love's fool.
My love is for the rose; I bow to her;
From her dear presence I could never stir.
If she should disappear the nightingale
Would lose his reason and his song would fail,
And though my grief is one that no bird knows,
One being understands my heart – the rose.
I am so drowned in love that I can find
No thought of my existence in my mind.
Her worship is sufficient life for me;
The quest for her is my reality
(And nightingales are not robust or strong;
The path to find the Simorgh is too long).
My love is here; the journey you propose
Cannot beguile me from my life – the rose.
It is for me she flowers; what greater bliss
Could life provide me – anywhere – than this?
Her buds are mine; she blossoms in my sight –
How could I leave her for a single night?'

The hoopoe answers him

The hoopoe answered him: 'Dear nightingale,
This superficial love which makes you quail
Is only for the outward show of things.
Renounce delusion and prepare your wings
For our great quest; sharp thorns defend the rose
And beauty such as hers too quickly goes.
True love will see such empty transience
For what it is – a fleeting turbulence

That fills your sleepless nights with grief and blame –
Forget the rose's blush and blush for shame!
Each spring she laughs, not *for* you, as you say,
But *at* you – and has faded in a day.

The story of a dervish and a princess

There was a king whose comely daughter's grace
Was such that any man who glimpsed her face
Declared himself in love. Like starless dusk
Her dark hair hung, soft-scented like fine musk;
The charm of her slow, humid eyes awoke
The depths of sleeping love, and when she spoke,
No sugar was as sweet as her lips' sweet;
No rubies with their colour could compete.
A dervish saw her, by the will of Fate.
From his arrested hand the crust he ate
Dropped unregarded, and the princess smiled.
This glance lived in his heart – the man grew wild
With ardent love, with restless misery;
For seven years he wept continually
And was content to live alone and wait,
Abject, among stray dogs, outside her gate.
At last, affronted by this fool and tired
Of his despair, her serving-men conspired
To murder him. The princess heard their plan,
Which she divulged to him. "O wretched man,"
She said, "how could you hope for love between
A dervish and the daughter of a queen?
You cannot live outside my palace door;
Be off with you and haunt these streets no more.
If you are here tomorrow you will die!"
The dervish answered her: "That day when I
First saw your beauty I despaired of life;
Why should I fear the hired assassin's knife?
A hundred thousand men adore your face;
No power on earth could make me leave this place.

But since your servants want to murder me,
Explain the meaning of this mystery:
Why did you smile at me that day?" "Poor fool,
I smiled from pity, almost ridicule –
Your ignorance provoked that smile." She spoke,
And vanished like a wisp of strengthless smoke.'

The parrot's excuse

The pretty parrot was the next to speak,
Clothed all in green, with sugar in her beak,
And round her neck a circle of pure gold.
Even the falcon cannot boast so bold
A loveliness – earth's variegated green
Is but the image of her feathers' sheen,
And when she talks the fascinating sound
Seems sweet as costly sugar finely ground;
She trilled: 'I have been caged by heartless men,
But my desire is to be free again;
If I could reassert my liberty
I'd find the stream of immortality
Guarded by Khezr – his cloak is green like mine,
And this shared colour is an open sign
I am his equal or equivalent.
Only the stream Khezr watches could content
My thirsting soul – I have no wish to seek
This Simorgh's throne of which you love to speak.'

The hoopoe answers her

The hoopoe said: 'You are a cringing slave –
This is not noble, generous or brave,
To think your being has no other end
Than finding water and a loyal friend.

Think well – what is it that you hope to gain?
Your coat is beautiful, but where's your brain?
Act as a lover and renounce your soul;
With love's defiance seek the lover's goal.

A story about Khezr

Khezr sought companionship with one whose mind
Was set on God alone. The man declined
And said to Khezr: "We two could not be friends,
For our existences have different ends.
The waters of immortal life are yours,
And you must always live; life is your cause
As death is mine – you wish to live, while I
Impatiently prepare myself to die;
I leave you as quick birds avoid a snare,
To soar up in the free, untrammelled air."'

The peacock's excuse and the hoopoe's answer

Next came the peacock, splendidly arrayed
In many-coloured pomp; this he displayed
As if he were some proud, self-conscious bride
Turning with haughty looks from side to side.
'The Painter of the world created me,'
He shrieked, 'but this celestial wealth you see
Should not excite your hearts to jealousy.
I was a dweller once in paradise;
There the insinuating snake's advice
Deceived me – I became his friend, disgrace
Was swift and I was banished from that place.
My dearest hope is that some blessèd day
A guide will come to indicate the way
Back to my paradise. The King you praise
Is too unknown a goal; my inward gaze

Is fixed for ever on that lovely land –
There is the goal which I can understand.
How could I seek the Simorgh out when I
Remember paradise?' And in reply
The hoopoe said: 'These thoughts have made you
    stray
Further and further from the proper Way;
You think your monarch's palace of more worth
Than He who fashioned it and all the earth.
The home we seek is in eternity;
The Truth we seek is like a shoreless sea,
Of which your paradise is but a drop.
This ocean can be yours; why should you stop,
Beguiled by dreams of evanescent dew?
The secrets of the sun are yours, but you
Content yourself with motes trapped in its beams.
Turn to what truly lives, reject what seems –
Which matters more, the body or the soul?
Be whole: desire and journey to the Whole.

A story about Adam

A novice asked his master to explain
Why Adam was forbidden to remain
In his first undivided happiness.
The master said: "When he, whose name we bless,
Awoke in paradise a voice declared:
'The man whose mind and vision are ensnared
By heaven's grace must forfeit that same grace,
For only then can he direct his face
To his true Lord.'" The lover's life and soul
Are firmly focused on a single goal;
The saints in paradise teach that the start
Of drawing near is to renounce the heart.'

The duck's excuse

The coy duck waddled from her stream and quacked:
'Now none of you can argue with the fact
That both in this world and the next I am
The purest bird that ever flew or swam;
I spread my prayer-mat out, and all the time
I clean myself of every bit of grime
As God commands. There's no doubt in my mind
That purity like mine is hard to find;
Among the birds I'm like an anchorite –
My soul and feathers are a spotless white.
I live in water and I cannot go
To places where no streams or rivers flow;
They wash away a world of discontent –
Why should I leave this perfect element?
Fresh water is my home, my sanctuary;
What use would arid deserts be to me?
I can't leave water – think what water gives;
It is the source of everything that lives.
Water's the only home I've ever known;
Why should I care about this Simorgh's throne?'

The hoopoe answers her

The hoopoe answered her: 'Your life is passed
In vague, aquatic dreams which cannot last –
A sudden wave and they are swept away.
You value water's purity, you say,
But is your life as pure as you declare?
A fool described the nature both worlds share:
"The unseen world and that which we can see
Are like a water-drop which instantly
Is and is not. A water-drop was formed
When time began, and on its surface swarmed

The world's appearances. If they were made
Of all-resisting iron they would fade;
Hard iron is mere water, after all –
Dispersing like a dream, impalpable."'

The partridge's excuse

The pompous partridge was the next to speak,
Fresh from his store of pearls. His crimson beak
And ruddy plumage made a splendid show –
A headstrong bird whose small eyes seemed to glow
With angry blood. He clucked: 'My one desire
Is jewels; I pick through quarries for their fire.
They kindle in my heart an answering blaze
Which satisfies me – though my wretched days
Are one long turmoil of anxiety.
Consider how I live, and let me be;
You cannot fight with one who sleeps and feeds
On precious stones, who is convinced he needs
No other goal in life. My heart is tied
By bonds of love to this fair mountain-side.
To yearn for something other than a jewel
Is to desire what dies – to be a fool;
Nothing is precious like a precious stone.
Besides, the journey to the Simorgh's throne
Is hard. I cannot tear myself away;
My feet refuse as if caught fast in clay.
My life is here; I have no wish to fly;
I must discover precious stones or die.'

The hoopoe answers him

The hoopoe said: 'You have the colours of
Those jewels you so inordinately love,
And yet you seem – like your excuses – lame.
Your beak and claws are red as blood or flame,

Yet those hard gems from which you cannot part
Have only helped you to a hardened heart;
Without their colours they are nothing more
Than stones – and to the wise not worth a straw.

King Solomon and his ring

No jewel surpasses that which Solomon
Wore on his finger. It was just a stone,
A mere half-*dang*[5] in weight, but as a seal
Set in his ring it brought the world to heel.
When he perceived the nature of his rule –
Dependent on the credit of a jewel –
He vowed that no one after him should reign
With such authority.' (Do not again,
Dear God, I pray, create such puissant kings;
My eyes have seen the blight their glory brings.
But criticizing courts is not my task;
A basket-weaver's work is all I ask,
And I return to Solomon's great seal.)
'Although the power it brought the king was real,
Possession of this gem meant that delay
Dogged his advance along the spirit's Way –
The other prophets entered paradise
Five hundred years before the king. This price
A jewel extracted from great Solomon,
How would it hinder such a dizzy one
As you, dear partridge? Rise above this greed;
The Simorgh is the only jewel you need.'

The homa's excuse

The homa next addressed the company.
Because his shadow heralds majesty,[6]
This wandering portent of the royal state
Is known as Homayun, 'The Fortunate'.

He sang: 'O birds of land and ocean, I
Am not as other birds, but soar and fly
On lofty aspiration's lordly wings.
I have subdued the dog desire; great kings
Like Feridun and Jamshid owe their place
To my dark shadow's influence. Disgrace
And lowly natures are not my concern.
I throw desire its bone; the dog will turn
And let the soul go free. Who can look down
On one whose shadow brings the royal crown?
The world should bask in my magnificence –
Let Khosroe's glory stand in my defence.
What should this haughty Simorgh mean to me?'

The hoopoe answers him

The hoopoe said: 'Poor slave to vanity,
Your self-importance is ridiculous;
Why should a shadow merit so much fuss?
You are not now the sign of Khosroe's throne,
More like a stray dog squabbling for a bone.
Though it is true that you confer on men
This majesty, kings must sink down again
And bear the punishments of Judgement Day.

King Mahmud after death

There was a man, advanced along the Way,
Who one night spoke to Mahmud in a dream.
He said: "Great king, how does existence seem
To one beyond the grave?" Mahmud replied:
"I have no majesty since I have died;
Your greetings pierce my soul. That majesty
Was only ignorance and vanity;
True majesty belongs to God alone –
How could a heap of dust deserve the throne?

Since I have recognized my impotence,
I blush for my imperial pretence.
Call me 'unfortunate', not 'king'. I should
Have been a wanderer who begged for food,
A crossing-sweeper, any lowly thing
That drags its way through life, but not a king.
Now leave me; I have nothing more to say;
Hell's devils wait for me; I cannot stay.
I wish to God the earth beneath my feet
Had swallowed me before I heard the beat
Of that accursèd homa's wings; they cast
Their shade, and may they shrivel in hell's blast!"'

The hawk's excuse

The hawk came forward with his head held high;
His boasts of grand connections filled the sky.
His talk was stuffed with armies, glory, kings.
He bragged: 'The ecstasy my sovereign brings
Has turned my gaze from vulgar company.
My eyes are hooded and I cannot see,
But I perch proudly on my sovereign's wrist.
I know court etiquette and can persist
In self-control like holy penitents;
When I approach the king, my deference
Correctly keeps to the established rule.
What is this Simorgh? I should be a fool
If I so much as dreamed of him. A seed
From my great sovereign's hand is all I need;
The eminence I have suffices me.
I cannot travel; I would rather be
Perched on the royal wrist than struggling through
Some arid *wadi* with no end in view.
I am delighted by my life at court,
Waiting on kings or hunting for their sport.'

The hoopoe answers him

The hoopoe said: 'Dear hawk, you set great store
By superficial graces, and ignore
The all-important fact of purity.
A king with rivals in his dignity
Is no true king; the Simorgh rules alone
And entertains no rivals to His throne.
A king is not one of those common fools
Who snatches at a crown and thinks he rules.
The true king reigns in mild humility,
Unrivalled in his firm fidelity.
An earthly king acts righteously at times,
But also stains the earth with hateful crimes,
And then whoever hovers nearest him
Will suffer most from his destructive whim.
A courtier risks destruction every hour –
Distance yourself from kings and worldly power.
A king is like a raging fire, men say;
The wisest conduct is to keep away.

A king and his slave

There was a monarch once who loved a slave.
The youth's pale beauty haunted him; he gave
This favourite the rarest ornaments,
Watched over him with jealous reverence –
But when the king expressed a wish to shoot,
His loved one shook with fear from head to foot.
An apple balanced on his head would be
The target for the royal archery,
And as the mark was split he blenched with fear.
One day a foolish courtier standing near
Asked why his lovely face was drained and wan,
For was he not their monarch's chosen one?

The slave replied: "If I were hit instead
Of that round apple balanced on my head,
I would be then quite worthless to the king –
Injured or dead, lower than anything
The court can show; but when the arrow hits
The trembling target and the apple splits,
That is his skill. The king is highly skilled
If he succeeds – if not, the slave is killed."'

The heron's excuse

The heron whimpered next: 'My misery
Prefers the empty shoreline of the sea.
There no one hears my desolate, thin cry –
I wait in sorrow there, there mourn and sigh.
My love is for the ocean, but since I –
A bird – must be excluded from the deep,
I haunt the solitary shore and weep.
My beak is dry – not one drop can I drink –
But if the level of the sea should sink
By one drop, jealous rage would seize my heart.
This love suffices me; how can I start
A journey like the one that you suggest?
I cannot join you in this arduous quest.
The Simorgh's glory could not comfort me;
My love is fixed entirely on the sea.'

The hoopoe answers him

The hoopoe answered him: 'You do not know
The nature of this sea you love: below
Its surface linger sharks; tempests appear,
Then sudden calms – its course is never clear,
But turbid, varying, in constant stress;
Its water's taste is salty bitterness.

How many noble ships has it destroyed,
Their crews sucked under in the whirlpool's void:
The diver plunges and in fear of death
Must struggle to conserve his scanty breath;
The failure is cast up, a broken straw.
Who trusts the sea? Lawlessness is her law;
You will be drowned if you cannot decide
To turn away from her inconstant tide.
She seethes with love herself – that turbulence
Of tumbling waves, that yearning violence,
Are for her Lord, and since she cannot rest,
What peace could you discover in her breast?
She lives for Him – yet you are satisfied
To hear His invitation and to hide.

A hermit questions the ocean

A hermit asked the ocean: "Why are you
Clothed in these mourning robes of darkest blue?[7]
You seem to boil, and yet I see no fire!"
The ocean said: "My feverish desire
Is for the absent Friend. I am too base
For Him; my dark robes indicate disgrace
And lonely pain. Love makes my billows rage;
Love is the fire which nothing can assuage.
My salt lips thirst for Kausar's[8] cleansing stream."
For those pure waters tens of thousands dream
And are prepared to perish; night and day
They search and fall exhausted by the Way.'

The owl's excuse

The owl approached with his distracted air,
Hooting: 'Abandoned ruins are my lair,
Because, wherever mortals congregate,
Strife flourishes and unforgiving hate;

A tranquil mind is only to be found
Away from men, in wild, deserted ground.
These ruins are my melancholy pleasure,
Not least because they harbour buried treasure.
Love for such treasure has directed me
To desolate, waste sites; in secrecy
I hide my hopes that one fine day my foot
Will stumble over unprotected loot.
Love for the Simorgh is a childish story;
My love is solely for gold's buried glory.'

The hoopoe answers him

The hoopoe answered him: 'Besotted fool,
Suppose you get this gold for which you drool;
What could you do but guard it night and day
While life itself – unnoticed – slips away?
The love of gold and jewels is blasphemy;
Our faith is wrecked by such idolatry.
To love gold is to be an infidel,
An idol-worshipper who merits hell.
On Judgement Day the miser's secret greed
Stares from his face for everyone to read.

The miser who became a mouse

A miser died, leaving a cache of gold;
And in a dream what should the son behold
But his dead father, shaped now like a mouse
That dashed distractedly about the house,
His mouse-eyes filled with tears. The sleeping son
Spoke in his dream: "Why, father, must you run
About our home like this?" The poor mouse said:
"Who guards my store of gold now I am dead?
Has any thief found out its hiding-place?"
The son asked next about his mouse-like face

And heard his father say: "Learn from my state;
Whoever worships gold, this is his fate –
To haunt the hidden cache for evermore,
An anxious mouse that darts across the floor."'

The finch's excuse

The timid finch approached. Her feeble frame
Trembled from head to foot, a nervous flame;
She chirped: 'I am less sturdy than a hair
And lack the courage that my betters share;
My feathers are too weak to carry me
The distance to the Simorgh's sanctuary.
How could a sickly creature stand alone
Before the glory of the Simorgh's throne?
The world is full of those who seek His grace,
But I do not deserve to see His face
And cannot join in this delusive race –
Exhaustion would cut short my foolish days,
Or I should turn to ashes in His gaze.
Joseph was hidden in a well and I
Shall seek my loved one in the wells nearby.'

The hoopoe answers her

The hoopoe said: 'You teasing little bird,
This humble ostentation is absurd!
If all of us are destined for the fire,
Then you too must ascend the burning pyre.
Get ready for the road, you can't fool me –
Sew up your beak, I loathe hypocrisy!
Though Jacob mourned for Joseph's absent face,
Do you imagine you could take his place?

Jacob's dream when Joseph was lost

When Jacob lost his son his eyes grew blind;
Tears flooded for the child he could not find.
His lips repeatedly formed Joseph's name –
To his despair the angel Gabriel came
And said: "Renounce this word; if you persist,
Your own name will be cancelled from the list
Of prophets close to God." Since this command
Came from his God, dear Joseph's name was banned
Henceforth from Jacob's lips; deep in his soul
He hid the passions he could not control.
But as he slept one night the long-lost child
Appeared before him in a dream, and smiled;
He started up to call him to his side –
And then remembered, struck his breast and sighed.
When from his vivid dream the old man woke,
The angel Gabriel came to him, and spoke:
"Though you did not pronounce your lost son's name,
You sighed – the exhalation meant the same
As if you had renounced your vow; a sigh
Reveals the heart as clearly as a cry.'"

The other birds protest and the hoopoe tells them of their relationship with the Simorgh

The other birds in turn received their chance
To show off their loquacious ignorance.
All made excuses – floods of foolish words
Flowed from these babbling, rumour-loving birds.
Forgive me, reader, if I do not say
All these excuses to avoid the Way;
But in an incoherent rush they came,
And all were inappropriate and lame.

How could they gain the Simorgh? Such a goal
Belongs to those who discipline the soul.
The hoopoe counselled them: 'The world holds few
As worthy of the Simorgh's throne as you,
But you must empty this first glass; the wine
That follows it is love's devoted sign.
If petty problems keep you back – or none –
How will you seek the treasures of the sun?
In drops you lose yourselves, yet you must dive
Through untold fathoms and remain alive.
This is no journey for the indolent –
Our quest is Truth itself, not just its scent!'

When they had understood the hoopoe's words,
A clamour of complaint rose from the birds:
'Although we recognize you as our guide,
You must accept – it cannot be denied –
We are a wretched, flimsy crew at best,
And lack the bare essentials for this quest.
Our feathers and our wings, our bodies' strength
Are quite unequal to the journey's length;
For one of us to reach the Simorgh's throne
Would be miraculous, a thing unknown.
At least say what relationship obtains
Between His might and ours; who can take pains
To search for mysteries when he is blind?
If there were some connection we could find,
We would be more prepared to take our chance.
He seems like Solomon, and we like ants;
How can mere ants climb from their darkened pit
Up to the Simorgh's realm? And is it fit
That beggars try the glory of a king?
How ever could they manage such a thing?'

The hoopoe answered them: 'How can love thrive
In hearts impoverished and half alive?
"Beggars," you say – such niggling poverty
Will not encourage truth or charity.

A man whose eyes love opens risks his soul –
His dancing breaks beyond the mind's control.
When long ago the Simorgh first appeared –
His face like sunlight when the clouds have cleared –
He cast unnumbered shadows on the earth,
On each one fixed His eyes, and each gave birth.
Thus we were born; the birds of every land
Are still his shadows – think, and understand.
If you had known this secret you would see
The link between yourselves and majesty.
Do not reveal this truth, and God forfend
That you mistake for God Himself God's friend.
If you become that substance I propound,
You are not God, though in God you are drowned;
Those lost in Him are not the Deity –
This problem can be argued endlessly.
You are His shadow, and cannot be moved
By thoughts of life or death once this is proved.
If He had kept His majesty concealed,
No earthly shadow would have been revealed,
And where that shadow was directly cast
The race of birds sprang up before it passed.
Your heart is not a mirror bright and clear
If there the Simorgh's form does not appear;
No one can bear His beauty face to face,
And for this reason, of His perfect grace,
He makes a mirror in our hearts – look there
To see Him, search your hearts with anxious care.

A king who placed mirrors in his palace

There lived a king; his comeliness was such
The world could not acclaim his charm too much.
The world's wealth seemed a portion of his grace;
It was a miracle to view his face.
If he had rivals, then I know of none;
The earth resounded with this paragon.

lines 1078–1099

When riding through his streets he did not fail
To hide his features with a scarlet veil.
Whoever scanned the veil would lose his head;
Whoever spoke his name was left for dead,
The tongue ripped from his mouth; whoever thrilled
With passion for this king was quickly killed.
A thousand for his love expired each day,
And those who saw his face, in blank dismay
Would rave and grieve and mourn their lives away –
To die for love of that bewitching sight
Was worth a hundred lives without his light.
None could survive his absence patiently,
None could endure this king's proximity –
How strange it was that men could neither brook
The presence nor the absence of his look!
Since few could bear his sight, they were content
To hear the king in sober argument,
But while they listened they endured such pain
As made them long to see their king again.
The king commanded mirrors to be placed
About the palace walls, and when he faced
Their polished surfaces his image shone
With mitigated splendour to the throng.

If you would glimpse the beauty we revere
Look in your heart – its image will appear.
Make of your heart a looking-glass and see
Reflected there the Friend's nobility;
Your Sovereign's glory will illuminate
The palace where He reigns in proper state.
Search for this King within your heart; His soul
Reveals itself in atoms of the Whole.
The multitude of forms that masquerade
Throughout the world spring from the Simorgh's shade.
If you catch sight of His magnificence
It is His shadow that beguiles your glance;
The Simorgh's shadow and Himself are one;
Seek them together, twinned in unison.

lines 1100–1121

But you are lost in vague uncertainty . . .
Pass beyond shadows to reality.
How can you reach the Simorgh's splendid court?
First find its gateway, and the sun, long-sought,
Erupts through clouds; when victory is won,
Your sight knows nothing but the blinding sun.

A story about Alexander the Great

When Alexander, that unconquered lord,
Who subjugated empires with his sword,
Required a lengthy message to be sent
He dressed up as the messenger and went.
"The king gives such an order," he would say,
And none of those who hurried to obey
Once guessed this messenger's identity –
They had no knowledge of such majesty,
And even if he said: "I am your lord,"
The claim was thought preposterous and ignored.
Deluded natures cannot recognize
The royal way that stands before their eyes.

Ayaz' sickness

Ayaz, afflicted with the Evil Eye,
Fell ill. For safety he was forced to lie
Sequestered from the court, in loneliness.
The king (who loved him) heard of his distress
And called a servant. "Tell Ayaz," he said,
"What tears of sympathy I daily shed.
Tell him that I endure his suffering,
And hardly comprehend I am the king;
My soul is with him (though my flesh is here)
And guards his bed solicitous with fear;
Ayaz, what could this Evil Eye not do,
If it destroys such loveliness as you!"

lines 1122–1141

The king was silent; then again he spoke:
"Go quickly as a fire, return like smoke;
Stop nowhere, but outrun the brilliant flash
That lights the world before the thunder's crash.
Go now; if you so much as pause for breath
My anger will pursue you after death."
The servant scuttled off, consumed with dread,
And like the wind arrived at Ayaz' bed –
There sat his sovereign, by the patient's head!
Aghast, the servant trembled for his life
And pictured in his mind the blood-smeared knife.
"My king," he said, "I swear, I swear indeed,
That I have hurried here with utmost speed –
Although I see you here I cannot see
How in the world you have preceded me;
Believe my innocence, and if I lie
I am a heathen and deserve to die."
His sovereign answered him: "You could not know
The hidden ways by which we lovers go;
I cannot bear my life without his face,
And every minute I am in this place.
The passing world outside is unaware
Of mysteries Ayaz and Mahmud share;
In public I ask after him, although
Behind the veil of secrecy I know
Whatever news my messengers could give;
I hide my secret and in secret live."'

The birds question the hoopoe and he advises them

An ancient secret yielded to the birds
When they had understood the hoopoe's words –
Their kinship with the Simorgh was now plain
And all were eager to set off again.

The homily returned them to the Way
And with one voice the birds were heard to say:
'Tell us, dear hoopoe, how we should proceed –
Our weakness quails before this glorious deed.'

'A lover,' said the hoopoe, now their guide,
'Is one in whom all thoughts of Self have died;
Those who renounce the Self deserve that name;
Righteous or sinful, they are all the same!
Your heart is thwarted by the Self's control;
Destroy its hold on you and reach your goal.
Give up this hindrance, give up mortal sight,
For only then can you approach the light.
If you are told: "Renounce our faith," obey!
The Self and faith must both be tossed away;
Blasphemers call such action blasphemy –
Tell them that love exceeds mere piety.
Love has no time for blasphemy or faith,
Nor lovers for the Self, that feeble wraith.
They burn all that they own; unmoved they feel
Against their skin the torturer's sharp steel.
Heart's blood and bitter pain belong to love,
And tales of problems no one can remove;
Cupbearer, fill the bowl with blood, not wine –
And if you lack the heart's rich blood take mine.
Love thrives on inextinguishable pain,
Which tears the soul, then knits the threads again.
A mote of love exceeds all bounds; it gives
The vital essence to whatever lives.
But where love thrives, there pain is always found;
Angels alone escape this weary round –
They love without that savage agony
Which is reserved for vexed humanity.
Islam and blasphemy have both been passed
By those who set out on love's path at last;
Love will direct you to Dame Poverty,
And she will show the way to blasphemy.

When neither blasphemy nor faith remain,
The body and the Self have both been slain;
Then the fierce fortitude the Way will ask
Is yours, and you are worthy of our task.
Begin the journey without fear; be calm;
Forget what is and what is not Islam;
Put childish dread aside – like heroes meet
The hundred problems which you must defeat.

The story of Sheikh San'an

San'an was once the first man of his time.
Whatever praise can be expressed in rhyme
Belonged to him: for fifty years this sheikh
Kept Mecca's holy place, and for his sake
Four hundred pupils entered learning's way.
He mortified his body night and day,
Knew theory, practice, mysteries of great age,
And fifty times had made the Pilgrimage.
He fasted, prayed, observed all sacred laws –
Astonished saints and clerics thronged his doors.
He split religious hairs in argument;
His breath revived the sick and impotent.
He knew the people's hearts in joy and grief
And was their living symbol of Belief.
Though conscious of his credit in their sight,
A strange dream troubled him, night after night;
Mecca was left behind; he lived in Rome,
The temple where he worshipped was his home,
And to an idol he bowed down his head.
"Alas!" he cried, when he awoke in dread,
"Like Joseph I am in a well of need
And have no notion when I shall be freed.
But every man meets problems on the Way,
And I shall conquer if I watch and pray.
If I can shift this rock my path is clear;
If not, then I must wait and suffer here."

Then suddenly he burst out: "It would seem
That Rome could show the meaning of this dream;
There I must go!" And off the old man strode;
Four hundred followed him along the road.
They left the ka'aba[9] for Rome's boundaries,
A gentle landscape of low hills and trees,
Where, infinitely lovelier than the view,
There sat a girl, a Christian girl who knew
The secrets of her faith's theology.
A fairer child no man could hope to see –
In beauty's mansion she was like a sun
That never set – indeed the spoils she won
Were headed by the sun himself, whose face
Was pale with jealousy and sour disgrace.
The man about whose heart her ringlets curled
Became a Christian and renounced the world;
The man who saw her lips and knew defeat
Embraced the earth before her bonny feet;
And as the breeze passed through her musky hair
The men of Rome watched wondering in despair.
Her eyes spoke promises to those in love,
Their fine brows arched coquettishly above –
Those brows sent glancing messages that seemed
To offer everything her lovers dreamed.
The pupils of her eyes grew wide and smiled,
And countless souls were glad to be beguiled;
The face beneath her curls glowed like soft fire;
Her honeyed lips provoked the world's desire;
But those who thought to feast there found her eyes
Held pointed daggers to protect the prize,
And since she kept her counsel no one knew –
Despite the claims of some – what she would do.
Her mouth was tiny as a needle's eye,
Her breath as quickening as Jesus' sigh;
Her chin was dimpled with a silver well
In which a thousand drowning Josephs fell;
A glistering jewel secured her hair in place,
Which like a veil obscured her lovely face.

lines 1203–1224

The Christian turned, the dark veil was removed,
A fire flashed through the old man's joints – he loved!
One hair converted hundreds; how could he
Resist that idol's face shown openly?
He did not know himself; in sudden fire
He knelt abjectly as the flames beat higher;
In that sad instant all he had been fled
And passion's smoke obscured his heart and head.
Love sacked his heart; the girl's bewitching hair
Twined round his faith impiety's smooth snare.
The sheikh exchanged religion's wealth for shame,
A hopeless heart submitted to love's fame.
"I have no faith," he cried. "The heart I gave
Is useless now; I am the Christian's slave."
When his disciples saw him weeping there
And understood the truth of the affair,
They stared, confounded by his frantic grief,
And strove to call him back to his belief.
Their remonstrations fell on deafened ears;
Advice has no effect when no one hears.
In turn the sheikh's disciples had their say;
Love has no cure, and he could not obey.
(When did a lover listen to advice?
When did a nostrum cool love's flames to ice?)
Till evening came he could not move but gazed
With stupefaction in his face, amazed.

When gloomy twilight spread its darkening shrouds –
Like blasphemy concealed by guilty clouds –
His ardent heart gave out the only light,
And love increased a hundredfold that night.
He put aside the Self and selfish lust;
In grief he smeared his locks with filth and dust
And kept his haunted vigil, watched and wept,
Lay trembling in love's grip and never slept.
"O Lord, when will this darkness end?" he cried.
"Or is it that the heavenly sun has died?

Those nights I passed in faith's austerities
Cannot compare with this night's agonies;
But like a candle now my flame burns high
To weep all night and in the daylight die.
Ambush and blood have been my lot this night;
Who knows what torments day will bring to light?
This fevered darkness and my wretched state
Were made when I was made, and are my fate;
The night continues and the hours delay –
Perhaps the world has reached its Judgement Day;
Perhaps the sun's extinguished with my sighs,
Or hides in shame from my belovèd's eyes.
This long, dark night is like her flowing hair –
The thought in absence comforts my despair,
But love consumes me through this endless night;
I yield to love, unequal to the fight.
Where is there time enough to tell my grief?
Where is the patience to regain belief?
Where is the luck to waken me, or move
Love's idol to reciprocate my love?
Where is the reason that could rescue me,
Or by some trick prove my auxiliary?
Where is the hand to pour dust on my head,
Or lift me from the dust where I lie dead?
Where is the foot that seeks the longed-for place?
Where is the eye to show me her fair face?
Where is the loved one to relieve my pain?
Where is the guide to help me turn again?
Where is the strength to utter my complaint?
Where is the mind to counsel calm restraint?
The loved one, reason, patience – all are gone
And I remain to suffer love alone."

At this the fond disciples gathered round,
Bewildered by his groans' pathetic sound.
"My sheikh," urged one, "forget this evil sight;
Rise, cleanse yourself according to our rite."

lines 1246–1269

"In blood I cleanse myself," the sheikh replied;
"In blood, a hundred times, my life is dyed."
Another asked: "Where is your rosary?"
He said: "I fling the beads away from me;
The Christian's belt[10] is my sole sanctuary!"
One urged him to repent; he said: "I do,
Of all I was, all that belonged thereto."
One counselled prayer; he said: "Where is her face
That I may pray toward that blessèd place?"
Another cried: "Enough of this; you must
Seek solitude and in repentant dust
Bow down to God." "I will," replied the sheikh,
"Bow down in dust, but for my idol's sake."
And one reproached him: "Have you no regret
For Islam and those rites you would forget?"
He said: "No man repents past folly more;
Why is it I was not in love before?"
Another said: "A demon's poisoned dart –
Unknown to you – has pierced your trusting heart."
The sheikh said: "If a demon straight from hell
Deceives me, I rejoice and wish her well."
One said: "Our noble sheikh has lost his way;
Passion has led his wandering wits astray."
"True, I have lost the fame I once held dear,"
Replied their sheikh, "and fraud as well, and fear."
One said: "You break our hearts with this disgrace."
He laughed: "The Christian's heart will take their
      place."
One said: "Stay with old friends awhile, and come –
We'll seek the ka'aba's shade and journey home."
The sheikh replied: "A Christian monastery
And not the ka'aba's shade suffices me."
One said: "Return to Mecca and repent!"
He answered: "Leave me here, I am content."
One said: "You travel on hell's road." "This sigh
Would shrivel seven hells," was his reply.
One said: "In hope of heaven turn again."
He said: "Her face is heaven; I remain."

lines 1270–1294

One said: "Before our God confess your shame."
He answered: "God Himself has lit this flame."
One said: "Stop vacillating now and fight;
Defend the ways our faith proclaims as right."
He said: "Prepare your ears for blasphemy;
An infidel does not prate piety."
Their words could not recall him to belief,
And slowly they grew silent, sunk in grief.
They watched; each felt the heart within him fail,
Fearful of deeds Fate hid beneath her veil.

At last white day displayed her golden shield;
Black night declined his head, compelled to yield –
The world lay drowned in sparkling light, and dawn
Disclosed the sheikh, still wretched and forlorn,
Disputing with stray dogs the place before
His unattainable belovèd's door.
There in the dust he knelt, till constant prayers
Made him resemble one of her dark hairs;
A patient month he waited day and night
To glimpse the radiance of her beauty's light.
At last fatigue and sorrow made him ill –
Her street became his bed and he lay still.
When she perceived he would – and could – not move,
She understood the fury of his love,
But she pretended ignorance and said:
"What is it, sheikh? Why is our street your bed?
How can a Muslim sleep where Christians tread?"
He answered her: "I have no need to speak;
You know why I am wasted, pale and weak.
Restore the heart you stole, or let me see
Some glimmer in your heart of sympathy;
In all your pride find some affection for
The grey-haired, lovesick stranger at your door.
Accept my love or kill me now – your breath
Revives me or consigns me here to death.
Your face and curls command my life; beware
Of how the breeze displays your vagrant hair;

The sight breeds fever in me, and your deep
Hypnotic eyes induce love's restless sleep.
Love mists my eyes, love burns my heart – alone,
Impatient and unloved, I weep and groan;
See what a sack of sorrow I have sewn!
I give my soul and all the world to burn,
And endless tears are all I hope to earn.
My eyes beheld your face, my heart despaired;
What I have seen and suffered none have shared.
My heart has turned to blood; how long must I
Subsist on misery? You need not try
To humble wretchedness, or kick the foe
Who in the dust submissively bows low.
It is my fortune to lament and wait –
When, if, love answers me depends on Fate.
My soul is ambushed here, and in your street
Relives each night the anguish of defeat;
Your threshold's dust receives my prayers – I give
As cheap as dust the soul by which I live.
How long outside your door must I complain?
Relent a moment and relieve my pain.
You are the sun and I a shadow thrown
By you – how then can I survive alone?
Though pain has worn me to a shadow's edge,
Like sunlight I shall leap your window's ledge;
Let me come in and I shall secretly
Bring seven heavens' happiness with me.
My soul is burned to ash; my passion's fire
Destroys the world with unappeased desire.
Love binds my feet and I cannot depart;
Love holds the hand pressed hard against my heart.
My fainting soul dissolves in deathly sighs –
How long must you stay hidden from my eyes?"

She laughed: "You shameless fool, take my advice –
Prepare yourself for death and paradise!
Forget flirtatious games, your breath is cold;
Stop chasing love, remember you are old.

It is a shroud you need, not me! How could
You hope for wealth when you must beg for food?"
He answered her: "Say what you will, but I
In love's unhappy torments live and die;
To Love, both young and old are one – his dart
Strikes with unequalled strength in every heart."
The girl replied: "There are four things you must
Perform to show that you deserve my trust:
Burn the Qur'an, drink wine, seel up faith's eye,
Bow down to images." And in reply
The sheikh declared: "Wine I will drink with you;
The rest are things that I could never do."
She said: "If you agree to my commands,
To start with, you must wholly wash your hands
Of Islam's faith – the love which does not care
To bend to love's requests is empty air."
He yielded then: "I must and will obey;
I'll do whatever you are pleased to say.
Your slave submits – lead me with ringlets twined
As chains about my neck; I am resigned!"
She smiled: "Come then and drink," and he allowed
Her to escort him to a hall (the crowd
Of scholars followed, weeping and afraid)
Where Christians banqueted, and there a maid
Of matchless beauty passed the cup around.
Love humbled our poor sheikh – without a sound
He gave his heart into the Christian's hands;
His mind had fled, he bowed to her commands,
And from those hands he took the proffered bowl;
He drank, oblivion overwhelmed his soul.
Wine mingled with his love – her laughter seemed
To challenge him to take the bliss he dreamed.
Passion flared up in him; again he drank,
And slave-like at her feet contented sank –
This sheikh who had the whole Qur'an by heart
Felt wine spread through him and his faith depart;
Whatever he had known deserted him,
Wine conquered and his intellect grew dim;

lines 1338–1362

Wine sluiced away his conscience; she alone
Lived in his heart, all other thoughts had flown.
Now love grew violent as an angry sea,
He watched her drink and moved instinctively –
Half fuddled with the wine – to touch her neck.
But she drew back and held his hand in check,
Deriding him: "What do you want, old man?
Old hypocrite of love, who talks but can
Do nothing else? To prove your love, declare
That your religion is my rippling hair.
Love's more than childish games, if you agree –
For love – to imitate my blasphemy
You can embrace me here; if not, you may
Take up your stick and hobble on your way."
The abject sheikh had sunk to such a state
That he could not resist his wretched fate;
Now ignorant of shame and unafraid,
He heard the Christian's wishes and obeyed –
The old wine sidled through the old man's veins
And like a twisting compass turned his brains;
Old wine, young love, a lover far too old,
Her soft arms welcoming – could he be cold?
Beside himself with love and drink he cried:
"Command me now; whatever you decide
I will perform. I spurned idolatry
When sober, but your beauty is to me
An idol for whose sake I'll gladly burn
My faith's Qur'an." "Now you begin to learn,
Now you are mine, dear sheikh," she said. "Sleep well,
Sweet dreams; our ripening fruit begins to swell."

News spread among the Christians that this sheikh
Had chosen their religion for love's sake.
They took him to a nearby monastery,
Where he accepted their theology;
He burned his dervish cloak and set his face
Against the faith and Mecca's holy place –

After so many years of true belief,
A young girl brought this learnèd sheikh to grief.
He said: "This dervish has been well betrayed;
The agent was mere passion for a maid.
I must obey her now – what I have done
Is worse than any crime beneath the sun."
(How many leave the faith through wine! It is
The mother of such evil vagaries.)
"Whatever you required is done," he said.
"What more remains? I have bowed down my head
In love's idolatry, I have drunk wine;
May no one pass through wretchedness like mine!
Love ruins one like me, and black disgrace
Now stares a once-loved dervish in the face.
For fifty years I walked an open road
While in my heart high seas of worship flowed;
Love ambushed me and at its sudden stroke
For Christian garments I gave up my cloak;
The ka'aba has become love's secret sign,
And homeless love interprets the divine.
Consider what, for your sake, I have done –
Then tell me, when shall we two be as one?
Hope for that moment justifies my pain;
Have all my troubles been endured in vain?"
The girl replied: "But you are poor, and I
Cannot be cheaply won – the price is high;
Bring gold, and silver too, you innocent –
Then I might pity your predicament;
But you have neither, therefore go – and take
A beggar's alms from me; be off, old sheikh!
Be on your travels like the sun – alone;
Be manly now and patient, do not groan!"
"A fine interpretation of your vow,"
The sheikh replied; "my love, look at me now –
I have no one but you; your cypress gait,
Your silver form, decide my wretched fate.
Take back your cruel commands; each moment you
Confuse me by demanding something new.

I have endured your absence, promptly done
All you have asked – what profit have I won?
I've passed beyond loss, profit, Islam, crime,
For how much longer must I bide my time?
Is this what we agreed? My friends have gone,
Despising me, and I am here alone.
They follow one way, you another – I
Stand witless here uncertain where to fly;
I know without you heaven would be hell,
Hell heaven with you; more I cannot tell."
At last his protestations moved her heart.
"You are too poor to play the bridegroom's part,"
She said, "but be my swineherd for a year
And then we'll stay together, never fear."
The sheikh did not refuse – a fractious way
Estranges love; he hurried to obey.
This reverend sheikh kept swine – but who does not
Keep something swinish in his nature's plot?
Do not imagine only he could fall;
This hidden danger lurks within us all,
Rearing its bestial head when we begin
To tread salvation's path – if you think sin
Has no place in your nature, you can stay
Content at home; you are excused the Way.
But if you start our journey you will find
That countless swine and idols tease the mind –
Destroy these hindrances to love or you
Must suffer that disgrace the sad sheikh knew.

Despair unmanned his friends; they saw his plight
And turned in helpless horror from the sight –
The dust of grief anointed each bowed head;
But one approached the hapless man and said:
"We leave for Mecca now, O weak-willed sheikh;
Is there some message you would have us take?
Or should we all turn Christians and embrace
This faith men call a blasphemous disgrace?"

We get no pleasure from the thought of you
Left here alone – shall we be Christians too?
Or since we cannot bear your state should we,
Deserting you, incontinently flee,
Forget that you exist and live in prayer
Beside the ka'aba's stone without a care?"
The sheikh replied: "What grief has filled my heart!
Go where you please – but quickly, now, depart;
Only the Christian keeps my soul alive,
And I shall stay with her while I survive.
Though you are wise your wisdom cannot know
The wild frustrations through which lovers go.
If for one moment you could share my pain,
We could be old companions once again.
But now go back, dear friends; if anyone
Asks after me explain what I have done –
Say that my eyes swim blood, that parched I wait
Trapped in the gullet of a monstrous fate.
Say Islam's elder has outsinned the whole
Of heathen blasphemy, that self-control
Slipped from him when he saw the Christian's hair,
That faith was conquered by insane despair.
Should anyone reproach my actions, say
That countless others have pursued this Way,
This endless Way where no one is secure,
Where danger waits and issues are unsure."
He turned from them; a swineherd sought his swine.
His friends wept vehemently – their sheikh's decline
Seemed death to them. Sadly they journeyed home,
Resigning their apostate sheikh to Rome.

They skulked in corners, shameful and afraid.
A close companion of the sheikh had stayed
In Mecca while the group had journeyed west –
A man of wisdom, fit for any test,
Who, seeing now the vacant oratory
Where once his friend had worshipped faithfully,

Asked after their lost sheikh. In tears then they
Described what had occurred along the way;
How he had bound his fortunes to her hair,
And blocked the path of faith with love's despair;
How curls usurped belief and how his cloak
Had been consumed in passion's blackening smoke;
How he'd become a swineherd, how the four
Acts contrary to all Islamic law
Had been performed by him, how this great sheikh
Lived like a pagan for his lover's sake.
Amazement seized the friend – his face grew pale,
He wept and felt the heart within him fail.
"O criminals!" he cried. "O frailer than
Weak women in your faith – when does a man
Need faithful friends but in adversity?
You should be there, not prattling here to me.
Is this devoted love? Shame on you all,
Fair-weather friends who run when great men fall.
He put on Christian garments – so should you;
He took their faith – what else had you to do?
This was no friendship, to forsake your friend,
To promise your support and at the end
Abandon him – this was sheer treachery.
Friend follows friend to hell and blasphemy –
When sorrows come a man's true friends are found;
In times of joy ten thousand gather round.
Our sheikh is savaged by some shark – you race
To separate yourselves from his disgrace.
Love's built on readiness to share love's shame;
Such self-regarding love usurps love's name."
"Repeatedly we told him all you say,"
They cried. "We were companions of the Way,
Sworn to a common happiness or grief;
We should exchange the honours of belief
For odium and scorn; we should accept
The Christian cult our sheikh could not reject.

But he insisted that we leave – our love
Seemed pointless then; he ordered us to move.
At his express command we journeyed here
To tell his story plainly, without fear."

He answered them: "However hard the fight,
You should have fought for what was clearly right.
Truth struggled there with error; when you went
You only worsened his predicament.
You have abandoned him; how could you dare
To enter Mecca's uncorrupted air?"
They heard his speech; not one would raise his head.
And then, "There is no point in shame," he said.
"What's done is done; we must act justly now,
Bury this sin, seek out the sheikh and bow
Before him once again." They left their home
And made their way a second time to Rome;
They prayed a hundred thousand prayers – at times
With hope, at times disheartened by their crimes.
They neither ate nor slept but kept their gaze
Unswerving throughout forty nights and days.
Their wailing lamentations filled the sky,
Moving the green-robed angels ranked on high
To clothe themselves with black, and in the end
The leader of the group, the sheikh's true friend,
His heart consumed by sympathetic grief,
Let loose the well-aimed arrows of belief.
For forty nights he had prayed privately,
Rapt in devotion's holy ecstasy –
At dawn there came a musk-diffusing breeze,
And in his heart he knew all mysteries.
He saw the Prophet, lovely as the moon,
Whose face, Truth's shadow, was the sun at noon,
Whose hair in two black heavy braids was curled –
Each hair, a hundred times, outpriced the world.
As he approached with his unruffled pace,
A smile of haunting beauty lit his face.

The sheikh's friend rose and said: "God's Messenger,
Vouchsafe your help. Our sheikh has wandered far;
You are our guide; guide him to Truth again."
The Prophet answered: "I have loosed the chain
Which bound your sheikh – your prayer is answered, go.
Thick clouds of dust have been allowed to blow
Between his sight and Truth – those clouds have gone;
I did not leave him to endure alone.
I sprinkled on the fortunes of your sheikh
A cleansing dew for intercession's sake –
The dust is laid; sin disappeared before
His new-made vow. A world of sin, be sure,
Shall with contrition's spittle be made pure.
The sea of righteousness drowns in its waves
The sins of those sincere repentance saves."

With grateful happiness the friend cried out;
The heavens echoed his triumphant shout.
He told the good news to the group; again
They set out eagerly across the plain.
Weeping they ran to where the swineherd-sheikh,
Now cured of his unnatural mistake,
Had cast aside his Christian clothes, the bell,
The belt, the cap, freed from the strange faith's spell.
Seeing his friends approach his hiding-place,
He saw how he had forfeited God's grace;
He ripped his clothes in frenzies of distress;
He grovelled in the dust with wretchedness.
Tears flowed like rain; he longed for death; his sighs'
Great heat consumed the curtain of the skies;
Grief dried the blood within him when he saw
How he had lost all knowledge of God's law;
All he had once abandoned now returned
And he escaped the hell in which he'd burned.
He came back to himself, and on his knees
Wept bitterly for past iniquities.
When his disciples saw him weeping there,
Bathed in shame's sweat, they reeled between despair

lines 1504–1528

And joy – bewildered they drew near and sighed;
From gratitude they gladly would have died.
They said: "The mist has fled that hid your sun;
Faith has returned and blasphemy is gone;
Truth has defeated Rome's idolatry;
Grace has surged onward like a mighty sea.
The Prophet interceded for your soul;
The world sends up its thanks from pole to pole.
Why should you mourn? You should thank God
        instead
That out of darkness you've been safely led;
God who can turn the day to darkest night
Can turn black sin to pure repentant light –
He kindles a repentant spark, the flame
Burns all our sins and all sin's burning shame."

I will be brief: the sheikh was purified
According to the faith; his old Self died –
He put the dervish cloak on as before.
The group set out for Mecca's gates once more.

And then the Christian girl whom he had loved
Dreamed in her sleep; a shaft of sunlight moved
Before her eyes, and from the dazzling ray
A voice said: "Rise, follow your lost sheikh's way;
Accept his faith, beneath his feet be dust;
You tricked him once, be pure to him and just,
And, as he took your path without pretence,
Take his path now in truth and innocence.
Follow his lead; you once led him astray –
Be his companion as he points the Way;
You were a robber preying on the road
Where you should seek to share the traveller's load.
Wake now, emerge from superstition's night."
She woke, and in her heart a steady light
Beat like the sun, and an unwonted pain
Throbbed there, a longing she could not restrain;

lines 1529–1546

Desire flared up in her; she felt her soul
Slip gently from the intellect's control.
As yet she did not know what seed was sown –
She had no friend and found herself alone
In an uncharted world; no tongue can tell
What then she saw – her pride and triumph fell
Like rain from her; with an unearthly shout
She tore the garments from her back, ran out
And heaped the dust of mourning on her head.
Her frame was weak, the heart within her bled,
But she began the journey to her sheikh,
And like a cloud that seems about to break
And shed its downpour of torrential rain
(The heart's rich blood) she ran across the plain.
But soon the desert's endless vacancy
Bewildered her; wild with uncertainty,
She wept and pressed her face against the sand.
"O God," she cried, "extend your saving hand
To one who is an outcast of the earth,
To one who tricked a saint of unmatched worth –
Do not abandon me; my evil crime
Was perpetrated in a thoughtless time;
I did not know what I know now – accept
The prayers of one who ignorantly slept."

The sheikh's heart spoke: "The Christian is no more;
The girl you loved knocks at religion's door –
It is our way she follows now; go back
And be the comforter her sorrows lack."
Like wind he ran, and his disciples cried:
"Has your repentant vow so quickly died?
Will you slip back, a shameless reprobate?"
But when the sheikh explained the girl's sad state,
Compassion moved their hearts and they agreed
To search for her and serve her every need.
They found her with hair draggled in the dirt,
Prone on the earth as if a corpse, her skirt

Torn from her limbs, barefoot, her face death-pale.
She saw the sheikh and felt her last strength fail;
She fainted at his feet, and as she slept
The sheikh hung over her dear face and wept.

She woke, and seeing tears like rain in spring
Knew he'd kept faith with her through everything.
She knelt before him, took his hands and said:
"The shame I brought on your respected head
Burns me with shame; how long must I remain
Behind this veil of ignorance? Make plain
The mysteries of Islam to me here,
And I shall tread its highway without fear."
The sheikh spelt out the faith to her; the crowd
Of gratified disciples cried aloud,
Weeping to see the lovely child embrace
The search for Truth. Then, as her comely face
Bent to his words, her heart began to feel
An inexpressible and troubling zeal;
Slowly she felt the pall of grief descend,
Knowing herself still absent from the Friend.
"Dear sheikh," she said, "I cannot bear such pain;
Absence undoes me and my spirits wane.
I go from this unhappy world; farewell
World's sheikh and mine – further I cannot tell,
Exhaustion weakens me; O sheikh, forgive . . ."
And saying this the dear child ceased to live.
The sun was hidden by a mist – her flesh
Yielded the sweet soul from its weakening mesh.
She was a drop returned to Truth's great sea;
She left this world, and so, like wind, must we.

Whoever knows love's path is soon aware
That stories such as this are far from rare.
All things are possible, and you may meet
Despair, forgiveness, certainty, deceit.
The Self ignores the secrets of the Way,
The mysteries no mortal speech can say;

Assurance whispers in the heart's dark core,
Not in the muddied Self – a bitter war
Must rage between these two. Turn now and mourn
That your existence is so deeply torn!'

The birds set off on their journey, pause, then choose a leader

They heard the tale; the birds were all on fire
To quit the hindrance of the Self; desire
To gain the Simorgh had convulsed each heart;
Love made them clamour for the journey's start.
They set out on the Way, a noble deed!
Hardly had they begun when they agreed
To call a halt: 'A leader's what we need,'
They said, 'one who can bind and loose, one who
Will guide our self-conceit to what is true;
We need a judge of rare ability
To lead us over danger's spacious sea;
Whatever he commands along the Way,
We must, without recalcitrance, obey,
Until we leave this plain of sin and pride
And gain Kaf's distant peak. There we shall hide,
A mote lost in the sun; the Simorgh's shade
Will cover those who travelled and obeyed.
But which of us is worthy of this trust?
A lottery is suitable and just.
The winning lot must finally decide
Which bird should be our undisputed guide.'
A hush fell, arguments were laid aside,
The lots were chosen, and the hoopoe won,
A lucky verdict that pleased everyone.
He was their leader; they would sacrifice
Their lives if he demanded such a price;
And as they travelled on the Way his word
Would spell authority to every bird.

The birds are frightened by the emptiness of the Way,
and the hoopoe tells them a story about Sheikh Bayazid

The hoopoe, as their chief, was hailed and crowned –
Huge flocks of birds in homage gathered round;
A hundred thousand birds assembled there,
Making a monstrous shadow in the air.
The throng set out – but, clearing the first dune,
Their leader sent a cry up to the moon
And panic spread among the birds; they feared
The endless desolation which appeared.
They clung together in a huddling crowd,
Drew in their heads and wings and wailed aloud
A melancholy, weak, faint-hearted song –
Their burdens were too great, the way too long!
How featureless the view before their eyes,
An emptiness where they could recognize
No marks of good or ill – a silence where
The soul knew neither hope nor blank despair.
One said, 'The Way is lifeless, empty – why?'
To which the hoopoe gave this strange reply:
'To glorify the King.

                    One moonlit night
Sheikh Bayazid, attracted by the sight
Of such refulgent brilliance, clear as day,
Across the sleeping city took his way
And thence into the desert, where he saw
Unnumbered stars adorning heaven's floor.
He walked a little and became aware
That not a sound disturbed the desert air,
That no one moved in that immensity
Save him. His heart grew numb and gradually
Pure terror touched him. "O great God," he cried,
"Your dazzling palace beckons far and wide –
Where are the courtiers who should throng this court?"
A voice said: "Wanderer, you are distraught;

lines 1611–1626

Be calm. Our glorious King cannot admit
All comers to His court; it is not fit
That every rascal who sleeps out the night
Should be allowed to glimpse its radiant light.
Most are turned back, and few perceive the throne;
Among a hundred thousand there is one."'

The birds ask the hoopoe to resolve their doubts

The trembling birds stared out across the plain;
The road seemed endless as their endless pain.
But in the hoopoe's heart new confidence
Transported him above the firmaments –
The sands could not alarm him nor the high
Harsh sun at noon, the peacock of the sky.
What other bird, throughout the world, could bear
The troubles of the Way and all its care?

The frightened flock drew nearer to their guide.
'You know the perils of the Way,' they cried,
'And how we should behave before the King –
You served great Solomon in everything
And flew across his lands – therefore you know
Exactly where it's safe and right to go;
You've seen the ups and downs of this strange Way.
It is our wish that as our guide you say
How we should act before the King we seek;
And more, as we are ignorant and weak,
That you should solve the problems in our hearts
Before the fearful company departs.
First hear our doubts; the thing we do not doubt
Is that you'll answer them and drive them out –
We know that on this lengthy Way no light
Will come to clear uncertainty's dark night;
But when the heart is free we shall commit
Our hearts and bodies, all we have, to it.'

lines 1627–1648

The hoopoe stood to speak, and all the birds
Approached to be encouraged by his words;
A hundred thousand gathered with one mind,
Serried in ranks according to their kind.
The dove and nightingale voiced their complaint;
Such beauty made the company grow faint –
A cry of ecstasy went up; a state
Where neither Self nor void predominate
Fell on the birds. The hoopoe spoke; he drew
The veil from what is ultimately true.
One asked: 'How is it you surpass us in
This search for Truth; what is our crippling sin?
We search and so do you – but you receive
Truth's purity while we stand by and grieve.'

The hoopoe tells them about the glance of Solomon

The hoopoe answered him: 'Great Solomon
Once looked at me – it is that glance alone
Which gave me what I know; no wealth could bring
The substance I received from wisdom's king.
No one can gain this by the forms of prayer,
For even Satan bowed with pious care;
Though don't imagine that you need not pray;
We curse the fool who tricks you in this way.
Pray always, never for one moment cease,
Pray in despair and when your goods increase,
Consume your life with prayer, till Solomon
Bestows his glance, and ignorance is gone.
When Solomon accepts you, you will know
Far more than my unequal words can show.'

lines 1649–1666

The story of King Mas'ud and the fisherboy

He said: 'King Mas'ud, riding out one day,
Was parted from his army on the way.
Swift as the wind he galloped till he saw
A little boy sat by the ocean's shore.
The child was fishing – as he cast his hook,
The king dismounted with a friendly look
And sat by him; but the unhappy child
Was troubled in his heart and hardly smiled.
"You seem the saddest boy I've ever seen,"
The monarch said. "What can such sorrow mean?"
"Our father's gone; for seven children I
Must cast my line," was his subdued reply.
"Our mother's paralysed and we are poor;
It is for food that I must haunt this shore –
I come to fish here in the dawn's first light
And cannot leave until the fall of night.
The meagre harvest of my toil and pain
Must last us all till I return again."
The king said: "Let's be friends, do you agree?"
The poor child nodded and, immediately,
His new friend cast their line into the sea.
That day the boy drew up a hundred fish.
"This wealth is far beyond my wildest wish,"
He said. "A splendid haul," the king replied.
"Good Fortune has been busy at your side –
Accept your luck, don't try to comprehend
How this has happened; you'd be lost, my friend.
Your wealth is greater than my own; today
A king has fished for you – I cannot stay."
He leapt onto his horse. "But take your share,"
The boy said earnestly. "That's only fair."
"Tomorrow's catch is mine. We won't divide
Today's; you have it all," the king replied.
"Tomorrow when I fish you are the prey,
A trophy I refuse to give away."

lines 1667–1685

The next day, walking in his garden's shade,
The king recalled the friend that he had made.
A captain fetched the boy, and this unknown
Was at the king's command set on his throne.
The courtiers murmured at his poverty –
"He is my friend, this fact suffices me;
He is my equal here in everything,
The partner of my throne," declared the king;
To every taunt the boy had one reply:
"My sadness vanished when the king passed by."

A murderer who went to heaven

A murderer, according to the law,
Was killed. That night the king who'd killed him saw
The same man in a dream; to his surprise
The villain lorded it in paradise –
The king cried: "You! In this celestial place!
Your life's work was an absolute disgrace;
How did you reach this state?" The man replied:
"A friend to God passed by me as I died;
The earth drank up my blood, but stealthily
That pilgrim on Truth's journey glanced at me,
And all the glorious extravagance
That laps me now came from his searing glance."

The man on whom that quickening glance alights
Is raised to heaven's unsuspected heights;
Indeed, until this glance discovers you
Your life's a mystery without a clue;
You cannot carve your way to heaven's throne
If you sit locked in vanity alone.
You need a skilful guide; you cannot start
This ocean-voyage with blindness in your heart.
It may be you will meet the very guide
Who glanced at me; be sure he will provide –
Whatever troubles come – a place to hide.

lines 1686–1703

You cannot guess what dangers you will find,
You need a staff to guide you, like the blind.
Your sight is failing and the road is long;
Trust one who knows the journey and is strong.
Whoever travels in a great lord's shade
Need never hesitate or be afraid;
Whoever undertakes this lord's commands
Finds thorns will change to roses in his hands.

The story of King Mahmud and the woodcutter

King Mahmud went out hunting. In the chase
His courtiers flagged, unequal to the pace.
An old man led a donkey whose high load
Of brushwood slipped and fell into the road.
The old man scratched his head; the king came near
And said: "Do you need help?" "I do, that's clear,"
The old man said; "if you could lend a hand,
You won't lose much. I see that you command
Your share of grace – such men are always good."
The king got down and helped him with the wood,
His flower-like hands embraced the thorns; and then
He rode back to his waiting lords again.
He said to them: "An old man will appear,
Riding a piled-high donkey – lead him here;
Block all the paths and highways to this place;
I want him to confront me face to face."
The winding roads were blocked up in a ring,
Of which the centre was the waiting king.
The old man mumbled as he rode alone:
"Why won't he go . . . this donkey's skin and bone.
Soldiers! . . . Good day, my lords!" and still the way
Led pitilessly on; to his dismay
There rose ahead a royal canopy,
And there was no escape that he could see.
He rode, for there was nothing else to do,
And found awaiting him a face he knew.

"I made a king hump wood for me," he cried;
"God help all sinners now, I'm terrified."
"What troubles you, my man?" inquired the king.
"Don't play with me, you took in everything,"
The old man said; "I'm just a wretched fool
Who day and night must scour the plain for fuel;
I sell the thorns I get and buy dry bread –
Give me some scraps, and blessings on your head."
The king replied: "Old man, I'll buy your wood –
Come, name a price you think is fair and good."
"My lord, such wood cannot be cheaply sold;
It's worth, I reckon, ten full bags of gold."
The courtiers laughed: "It's worth two barley grains.
Shut up and sell, and thank you for your pains."
"Two grains, my friends, that's true – but this rare buyer
Can surely manage something rather higher?
A great one touched these thorns – his hand brought
        forth
A hundred flowers; just think what that is worth!
A dinar buys one root – a little gain
Is only right, I've had my share of pain;
The wood itself is worthless, I agree –
It is that touch which gives it dignity.'"

❧

A cowardly bird protests

One of the birds let out a helpless squeak:
'I can't go on this journey, I'm too weak.
Dear guide, I know I can't fly any more;
I've never tried a feat like this before.
This valley's endless; dangers lie ahead;
The first time that we rest I'll drop down dead.
Volcanoes loom before the goal is won –
Admit this journey's not for everyone.
The blood of multitudes has stained the Way;
A hundred thousand creatures, as you say,

Address themselves to this great enterprise –
How many die, a useless sacrifice!
On such a road the best of men are cowed,
Hoods hide the frightened features of the proud –
What chance have timid souls? What chance have I?
If I set out it's certain I shall die!'

The hoopoe admonishes him

The hoopoe said: 'Your heart's congealed like ice;
When will you free yourself from cowardice?
Since you have such a short time to live here,
What difference does it make? What should you fear?
The world is filth and sin, and homeless men
Must enter it and homeless leave again.
They die, as worms, in squalid pain; if we
Must perish in this quest, that, certainly,
Is better than a life of filth and grief.
If this great search is vain, if my belief
Is groundless, it is right that I should die.
So many errors throng the world – then why
Should we not risk this quest? To suffer blame
For love is better than a life of shame.
No one has reached this goal, so why appeal
To those whose blindness claims it is unreal?
I'd rather die deceived by dreams than give
My heart to home and trade and never live.
We've seen and heard so much – what have we learned?
Not for one moment has the Self been spurned;
Fools gather round and hinder our release:
When will their stale, insistent whining cease?
We have no freedom to achieve our goal
Until from Self and fools we free the soul.
To be admitted past the veil you must
Be dead to all the crowd considers just.
Once past the veil you understand the Way
From which the crowd's glib courtiers blindly stray.

If you have any will, leave women's stories,
And even if this search for hidden glories
Proves blasphemy at last, be sure our quest
Is not mere talk but an exacting test.
The fruit of love's great tree is poverty;
Whoever knows this knows humility.
When love has pitched his tent in someone's breast,
That man despairs of life and knows no rest.
Love's pain will murder him, then blandly ask
A surgeon's fee for managing the task –
The water that he drinks brings pain, his bread
Is turned to blood immediately shed;
Though he is weak, faint, feebler than an ant,
Love forces him to be her combatant;
He cannot take one mouthful unaware
That he is floundering in a sea of care.

Sheikh Nughani at Neishapur

Sheikh Nughani set out for Neishapur.
The way was more than he could well endure
And he fell sick – he spent a hungry week
Huddled in tattered clothes, alone and weak.
But after seven days had passed he cried:
"Dear God, send bread." An unseen voice replied:
"Go, sweep the dirt of Neishapur's main square,
And with the grain of gold that you find there
Buy bread and eat." The sheikh abruptly said:
"If I'd a broom I wouldn't beg for bread,
But I have nothing, as you plainly see;
Give me some bread and stop tormenting me!"
The voice said: "Calm yourself, you need not weep –
If you want bread take up your broom and sweep."
The sheikh crawled out and publicized his grief
Till he was lent a broom and sweeper's sieve.
He swept the filthy square as he'd been told,
And in his last sieve's dust-heap found the gold.

He hurried to the baker's, bought his bread –
Thoughts of the broom and sieve then filled his head.
He stopped short in his tracks; the shining grain
Was spent and he was destitute again.
He wandered aimlessly until he found
A ruined hut, and on the stony ground
He flung himself headlong; to his surprise
The broom and sieve appeared before his eyes.
Joy seized the old man – then he cried: "O Lord,
Why must I toil so hard for my reward?
You tell me to exhaust myself for bread!"
"Bread needs the sauce of work," the Lord's voice said;
"Since bread is not enough, I will increase
The sauce that makes it tasty; work in peace!"

A simpleton walked naked through the crowd,
And seeing such fine clothes he cried aloud:
"God give me joy like theirs." A voice replied:
"I give the sun's kind warmth; be satisfied."
He said: "My Lord, the sun clothes you, not me!"
The voice said: "Wait ten days, then you will see
The garment I provide." Ten days had gone;
A poor man offered to this simpleton
A ragged cloak made up of scraps and shreds.[11]
"You've spent ten days with patches and old threads
Stitching this cloak," the madman said; "I'll bet
You spoiled a treasury of clothes to get
So many bits together – won't you tell
Your servant where you learned to sew so well?"
The answer came: "In His great court one must
Be humble as His royal highway's dust;
So many, kindled by His glory, come –
But few will ever reach the longed-for home."

A story about Rabe'eh

Saint Rabe'eh for seven years had trod
The pilgrimage to Mecca and her God.
Now drawing near the goal she cried: "At last
I've reached the ka'aba's stone; my trials are past" –
Just at that moment the aspiring saint
Succumbed to woman's intimate complaint –
She was impure; she turned aside and said:
"For seven years a pilgrim's life I've led,
And as I reach the throng of pilgrims He
Plants this unlooked-for thorn to hinder me;
Dear God, give access to Your glorious home,
Or send me back the weary way I've come."
No lover lived as true as Rabe'eh,
Yet look, she too was hindered on the Way.
When first you enter wisdom's sea, beware –
A wave of indecision floods you there.
You worship at the ka'aba's shrine and then
You're weeping in some worthless pagan's den;
If from this whirlpool you can raise your head,
Tranquillity will take the place of dread.
But if you sink into its swirl alone
Your head will seem some mill's enormous stone;
The least distraction will divert your mind
From that tranquillity you hoped to find.

A troubled fool

A saintly fool lived in a squalid place.
One day he saw the Prophet face to face,
Who said to him: "In your life's work I see
The signs of heaven-sent tranquillity."
"Tranquillity! When I can't get away
From hungry fleas by night or flies by day!

lines 1803–1818

A tiny gnat got into Nimrod's brain
And by its buzzing sent the man insane;
I seem the Nimrod of this time – flies, fleas,
Mosquitoes, gnats do with me as they please!"'

A bird complains of his sinfulness

Another bird complained: 'Sin stains my soul;
How can the wicked ever reach our goal?
How can a soul unclean as noisome flies
Toward the Simorgh's mountains hope to rise?
When sinners leave the path, what power can bring
Such stragglers to the presence of our King?'

And the hoopoe answers him

The answer came: 'You speak from ignorance;
Do not despair of His benevolence.
Seek mercy from Him; throw away your shield,
And by submission gain the longed-for field.
The gate stands open to contrition's way –
If you have sinned, squeeze through it while you may,
And if you travel with an honest heart,
You too will play the victor's glorious part.

Shame forced a vicious sinner to repent.
Once more his strength returned, once more he went
Down his old paths of wickedness and lust;
Leaving the Way, he wallowed in his dust.
But pain welled in his heart, his life became –
A second time – the source of bitter shame.
Since sin had brought him nothing but despair,
He wanted to repent, but did not dare;
His looks betrayed more agitation than
Ripe corn grains jumping in a heated pan –

His heart was racked by grief and warring fears;
The highway's dust was laid by his sad tears.
But in the dawn he heard a voice: "The Lord
Was merciful when first you pledged your word.
You broke it and again I gave you time,
Asking no payment for this newer crime;
Poor fool – would you repent once more? My gate
Stands open always; patiently I wait."

Gabriel and the unbeliever

One night in paradise good Gabriel heard
The Lord say: "I am here," and at His word
There came another voice which wept and prayed –
"Who knows whose voice this is?" the angel said.
"It comes from one, of this at least I'm sure,
Who has subdued the Self, whose heart is pure."
But no one in the heavens knew the man,
And Gabriel swooped toward the earth to scan
The deserts, seas and mountains – far and wide
He searched, without success, until he cried
For God to lead his steps. "Seek him in Rome,"
God said. "A pagan temple is his home."
There Gabriel went and saw the man in tears –
A worthless idol ruled his hopes and fears.
Astonished, Gabriel turned and said: "Tell me,
Dear Lord, the meaning of this mystery;
You answer with your kindness one who prays
Before a senseless idol all his days!"
And God replied: "He does not know Our Way;
Mere ignorance has led this man astray –
I understand the cause of his disgrace
And will not coldly turn aside My face;
I shall admit him to My sanctuary
Where kindness will convert his blasphemy."'

lines 1835–1855

The hoopoe paused and raised his voice in prayer,
Then said: 'This man for whom God showed such care
Was one like you – and if you cannot bring
Great virtues to the presence of our king,
Do not alarm yourself; the Lord will bless
The saint's devotions and your nothingness.

A Sufi who wanted to buy something for nothing

A voice rang out one morning in Baghdad:
"My honey's sweet, the best that can be had –
The price is cheap; now who will come and buy?"
A Sufi passing in a street nearby
Asked: "Will you sell for nothing?" But he laughed:
"Who gives his goods for nothing? Don't be daft!"
A voice came then: "My Sufi, turn aside –
A few steps higher – and be satisfied.
For nothing We shall give you everything;
If you want more, that 'more' We'll also bring.
Know that Our mercy is a glittering sun;
No particle escapes its brilliance, none –
Did We not send to sin and blasphemy
Our Prophet as a sign of clemency?"

God remonstrates with Moses

God said: "Gharun has ten times seven times,
Dear Moses, begged forgiveness for his crimes –
Still you ignore him, though his soul is free
From all the twisting growths of blasphemy;
I have uprooted them and now prepare
A robe of grace in answer to his prayer.
You have destroyed him; wound has followed wound;
You force his head to bow down to the ground –
If you were his Creator you would give
Some respite to this suffering fugitive."

lines 1856–1872

One who shows mercy to the merciless
Brings mercy close to Godlike blessèdness;
The ocean of God's grace is infinite –
Our sins are like a tear dissolved in it.
How could His mercy change? – it can contain
No trace of temporal corruption's stain.
One who accuses sinners takes the part
Of tyranny, and bears a tyrant's heart.

A sinner enters heaven

A sinner died, and, as his coffin passed,
A man who practised every prayer and fast
Turned ostentatiously aside – how could
He pray for one of whom he knew no good?
He saw the sinner in his dreams that night,
His face transfigured with celestial light.
"How did you enter heaven's gates," he said,
"A sinner stained with filth from foot to head?"
"God saw your merciless, disdainful pride,
And pitied my poor soul," the man replied.

What generous love His wisdom here displays!
His part is mercy, ours is endless praise;
His wisdom's like a crow's wing in the night –
He sends a child out with a taper's light,
And then a wind that quenches this thin flame;
The child will suffer words of scathing blame,
But in that narrow darkness he will find
The thousand ways in which his Lord is kind.
If all were pure of all iniquity,
God could not show His generosity;
The end of wisdom is for God to show –
Perpetually – His love to those below.
One drop of God's great wisdom will be yours,
A sea of mercy with uncharted shores;

lines 1873–1890

My child, the seven heavens, day and night,
For your sake wage their old unwearied fight;
For your sake angels pray – your love and hate
Reflected back are hell's or heaven's gate.
The angels have bowed down to you and drowned
Your soul in Being, past all plummet's sound –
Do not despise yourself, for there is none
Who could with you sustain comparison;
Do not torment yourself – your soul is All,
Your body but a fleeting particle.
This All will clarify, and in its light
Each particle will shine, distinctly bright –
As flesh remains an agent of the soul,
Your soul's an agent of the sacred Whole.
But "part" and "whole" must disappear at last;
The Way is one, and number is surpassed.
A hundred thousand clouds above you press;
Their rain is pure, unending happiness;
And when the desert blooms with flowers, their scent
And beauty minister to your content;
The prayers of all the angels, all they do,
All their obedience, God bestows on you.

The angels' jealousy of man

Abbasseh said: "At God's last Judgement Day,
When panic urges men to run away
And at the same time paralyses them,
When sinners stumble, overwhelmed by shame,
When terror seizes on the human race,
And each man seeks to hide his anguished face,
Then God, whom all the earth and heavens adore,
Will His unstinted benedictions pour
On man, the handful of unworthy dust.
The angels will cry out: 'Lord, is this just,
That man, before us all, take precedence?'
And God will say: 'There is no consequence

Of loss or gain in this for you, but man
Has reached the limit of his earthly span –
Hunger must always be supplied with bread;
A mortal nation clamours to be fed.'"'

An indecisive bird complains

Another bird declared: 'As you can see,
I lack the organs of virility;
Each moment I prefer a different tree –
I'm drunk, devout, the world's, then (briefly) His;
Caught between "No, it isn't", "Yes, it is".
The flesh will send me drinking, then I'll find
The praise of God awakening in my mind;
What should I do between these two extremes,
Imprisoned by conflicting needs and dreams?'

And the hoopoe answers him

The hoopoe said: 'This troubles everyone;
What man is truly single-minded? None!
If all of us could boast a spotless mind,
Why should the prophets mingle with mankind?
If it is love which prompts your fervent prayers,
A hundred kindnesses will calm your cares.
Life is an obstinate young colt – until
He's broken in by your restraining will
He knows no peace; but you are indolent,
Stretched out beside the oven, warm, content.
Tears temper hearts; but living well's a rust
That inch by inch reduces them to dust –
You're just a eunuch pampering his needs;
Your Self's grown gross, a dog that sleeps and feeds.

lines 1909–1921

A *story about Shebli*

Shebli would disappear at times; no one
In all Baghdad could guess where he had gone –
At last they found him where the town enjoys
The sexual services of men and boys,
Sitting among the catamites; his eye
Was moist and humid, and his lips bone-dry.
One asked: "What brings you here, to such a place?
Is this where pilgrims come to look for grace?"
He answered: "In the world's way these you see
Aren't men or women; so it is with me –
For in the way of faith I'm neither man
Nor woman, but ambiguous courtesan –
Unmanliness reproaches me, then blame
For my virility fills me with shame."
The man of understanding puts aside,
To travel on this path, all outward pride
(The courage of his choice will honour those
Who taught this pilgrim everything he knows).
If you seem more substantial than a hair,
You've made an idol of yourself – take care,
Whatever praise or blame may say of you,
You're an idolater in all you do.
As Truth's sworn slave, beware of Azar's ways
Who carved the stone to which he offered praise –
Devotion is the crown of all mankind;
Leave Uzza and such idols far behind.
You seem a Sufi to the common folk
But hide a hundred idols with your cloak –
If you're a eunuch underneath, don't dress
In clothes of high heroic manliness!

Two Sufis go to court

One day two dressed as wandering Sufis came
Before the courts to lodge a legal claim.
The judge took them aside. "This can't be right,
For Sufis to provoke a lawyers' fight,"
He said. "You wear the robes of resignation,
So what have you to do with litigation?
If you're the men to pay a lawyer's fee,
Off with your Sufi clothes immediately!
And if you're Sufis as at first I thought,
It's ignorance that brings you to this court.
I'm just a judge, unversed in your affair,
But I'm ashamed to see the clothes you wear;
You should wear women's veils – that would be less
Dishonest than your present holy dress."

How will you solve love's secret lore if you –
Not man, not woman – glide between the two?
If on its path love forces you to yield,
Then do so gladly, throw away your shield;
Resist and you will die, your soul is dead –
To ward off your defeat bow down your head!

A pauper in love with the king of Egypt

A poor man fell in love with Egypt's king,
Who heard the news and ordered guards to bring
The wretch to him. "You love the king," he said;
"Now choose: give up your home here or your head –
You must make up your mind between these two,
Exile or death. Well, which seems best to you?"
For all his love this pauper wasn't brave;
His choice was exile rather than the grave.
He left; the king's command came loud and clear:
"Cut off his head at once and bring it here."

lines 1938–1955

The porter said: "But he is innocent;
Why should my lord command this punishment?"
"He did not really love," the king replied.
"Though he pretended love for me, he lied:
If he were valiant in love he would
Have chosen death here as the highest good.
If one prefers his head to love, then he
Must pay to love the traitor's penalty –
Had he required my head, at his command
There would have been no lord to rule this land;
I would have worn his livery, a king
Would have become his slave in everything –
But he resisted love, and it is right
That he should lose his head in such a fight.
The man who leaves me, though he rave and cry,
Is an impostor and his love's a lie –
I say this as a warning to that crowd
Whose boasts of love for me ring long and loud."'

A bird complains of the Self

One of the birds then said: 'My enemy's
That veteran of highway robberies,
My Self; how can I travel on the Way
With such a follower? The dog won't pay
The least attention to a word I say –
The dog I knew is gone and in his place
A slavering wolf stalks by me, pace for pace.'

And the hoopoe answers him

The hoopoe said: 'How has this dog betrayed
And brought to dust whatever plans you made!
The Self's squint-eyed and cannot guide you well,
Part dog, part parasite, part infidel.

When you are praised your Self swells up with pride
(Aware that praise is quite unjustified);
There's no hope for the Self – the dog grows fatter
The more it hears men fawn, deceive and flatter.
What is your childhood but a negligence,
A time of carelessness and ignorance?
What is your youth but madness, strife and danger,
Knowledge that in this world you are a stranger?
What is your age but torpid helplessness,
The flesh and spirit sapped by long distress?
Until this dog, the Self, can be subdued,
Our life is folly, endlessly renewed;
If all of life from birth to death is vain,
Blank nothingness will be our only gain –
Such slaves the Self owns! What a catalogue!
How many rush to worship this foul dog!
The Self is hell – a furnace belching fire,
An icy pit as pride succeeds desire,
And though a hundred thousand die of grief,
That this same dog should die is past belief.

A gravedigger

A man who lived by digging graves survived
To ripe old age. A neighbour said: "You've thrived
For years, digging away in one routine –
Tell us the strangest thing you've ever seen."
He said: "All things considered, what's most strange
Is that for seventy years without a change
That dog, my Self, has seen me digging graves,
Yet neither dies, nor alters, nor behaves!"

lines 1971–1986

Abbasseh's description of the Self

One night Abbasseh said: "The world could be
Thronged with wild infidels and blasphemy,
Or it could be a place of pious works,
Filled with the faithful, keen as zealous Turks.
Instead the prophets came – that infidel
The Self must choose between the faith and hell
(One seemed too difficult, one terrified –
How could the indecisive soul decide?).
Beneath the Self's reign we are infidels
And nourish blasphemy in all our cells;
Its life is stubborn, strong, intractable –
To kill it seems well-nigh impossible.
It draws its strength from both alternatives;
No wonder it so obstinately lives.
But if the heart can rule, then day and night
This dog will labour for the heart's delight,
And when the heart rides out he sprints away
Eager to flush his noble master's prey.
Whoever chains this dog will find that he
Commands the lion of eternity;
Whoever binds this dog, his sandals' dust
Surpasses all the councils of the just."

A king questions a Sufi

A ragged pilgrim of the Sufis' Way
By chance met with a king, and heard him say:
"Who's better, me or you?" The old man said:
"Silence, your words are empty as your head!
Although self-praise is not our normal rule
(The man who loves himself is still a fool),
I'll tell you, since I must, that one like me
Exceeds a thousand like your majesty.

Since you find no delight in faith – alas,
Your Self has made of you, my lord, an ass
And sat on you, and set its load on you –
You're just its slave in everything you do;
You wear its halter, follow its commands,
A no-one, left completely in its hands.
My study is to reach Truth's inmost shrine –
And I am not my Self's ass, he is mine;
Now since the beast I ride on rides on you,
That I'm your better is quite plainly true.
You love the Self – it's lit in you a fire
Of nagging lust, insatiable desire,
A blaze that burns your vigour, wastes your heart,
Leaving infirmity in every part –
Consuming all your strength, till deaf and blind
You're old, forgetful, rambling in your mind."

This man, and hundreds like him, constitute
The mighty phalanx of the Absolute;
When such an army charges you will find
You and your puny Self are left behind.
How you delight in this dog's partnership –
But it's the dog, not you, that cracks the whip!
The forces of the king will separate
This dog and you – why not anticipate
Their order and forestall the pain? If though
You weep that here on earth you cannot know
Enough of this audacious infidel –
Don't worry; you'll be comrades down in hell.

Two foxes

Two foxes met, and tasted such delight
They could not let each other out of sight.
But then a king came hunting on the plain
And parted them. "Where shall we meet again?"
She yelped. He barked back as he reached their hole:
"At the furrier's, dear – hung up as a stole!"'

A bird complains of pride

Another said: 'Whenever I decide
To seek His presence, that arch-devil Pride
Obstructs my path. I can't fight back with force;
Against his specious talk I've no recourse.
How can I find salvation from his lies,
Drink down the wine of meaning and be wise?'

The hoopoe answers him

The hoopoe said: 'This devil never leaves
Until the Self has gone; if he deceives
You now, his cunning is your own deceit –
Your wishes are the devil, you the cheat!
If you accomplish one desire, a shoal
Of struggling demons rises in your soul;
The world's a furnace and a prison cell,
The devil's province, an unending hell –
Draw back your hand from it if you would win
An unmolested life secure from sin.

The devil complains

A sluggard once approached a fasting saint
And, baffled by despair, made this complaint:
"The devil is a highwayman, a thief,
Who's ruined me and robbed me of belief."
The saint replied: "Young man, the devil too
Has made his way here to complain – of you.
'My province is the world,' I heard him say;
'Tell this new pilgrim of God's holy Way
To keep his hands off what is mine – if I
Attack him it's because his fingers pry
In my affairs; if he will leave me be,
He's no concern of mine and can go free.'"

Malek Dinar

One dear to God addressed Malek Dinar:
"I've lost myself – but tell me how you are."
He said: "I get my bread from God's own hands,
Then carry out the Evil One's commands."

Your vaunted faith is wordy insolence;
The devil strikes, and you have no defence –
This world's grief clings to you, yet you decide
You're ready for our quest! God damn your pride!
I said: "Give up the world," and now I say
Stand firm to be admitted to the Way;
If you have given Him this earthly show
When will you spread your hands and let it go?
Your sloth has drowned you in a sea of greed;
You don't know why you wait or what you need –
Though earth and heaven weep you seek out sin;
Greed blunts your faith, passion corrupts within.
What is this world, this nest of greed and lust,
But leavings of oppression, windswept dust?

lines 2035–2052

Here tyranny intensified its reign,
Here cruelty struck and left an emptied plain.
God calls this world a nothing, but its snare
Has trapped you, and you struggle in despair –
When will you die to such unhappiness
And take the hand that leads you from distress?
Can one who's lost in nothing rightly claim
The attributes of man, much less the name?
The creature who abandons what he sought
For nothing's sake is nought and less than nought.
What is this world's work? Idle lethargy,
That idleness a long captivity.
What is the world but a consuming pyre,
Where nation follows nation to the fire?
And when its flames turn night to blinding day,
The lion-hearted hero runs away –
To close your eyes and flee is courage here,
Or like some fluttering moth you'll draw too near
And in the blaze be burned; to worship flame
Is drunken pride, the path to death and shame.
The fire surrounds you, and with every breath
The scorching flames reach out and threaten death;
But they are quenched when we achieve our goal,
And look – there waits asylum for your soul.

A rich lord and a dervish

At public prayers a great lord cried: "O God,
Have mercy on me now and spare the rod!"
A crazy dervish heard his prayer and said:
"You dare to call His mercies on your head
When your behaviour seems to say: 'The earth
Can hardly hold a person of my worth' –
You've raised a palace up against the sky,
Embellished it with gold to daze the eye;
Ten boys and ten young girls await your whim,
What claim have you on mercy or on Him?

Look on your life, on all that you possess –
There isn't room for mercy in this mess!
If Fate gave you my daily round of bread,
Then you could call down mercies on your head.
Shame on you, man! Until you turn aside
From power and wealth and all your stinking pride,
There's nothing to be done – turn now, and see
How like a hero you can still break free."

Death-bed repentance

A true believer said: "There is a crowd
Who when they come to die will cry aloud
And turn to God. But they are fools; they should
Have spent their lives in seeking what is good.
When leaves are falling it's too late to sow;
Repentance on a death-bed is too slow –
The time to turn aside has flown; be sure
Whoever waits till then will die impure."'

A miserly bird

Another bird said: 'I love gold alone;
It's life to me, like marrow to a bone –
When I have gold I blossom like a flower;
With restless pride I revel in its power.'

The hoopoe answers him

The hoopoe said: 'Appearances delight
The heart that cannot see Truth's dawning light;
You are as blind by day as in the night –
Your life's a crawling ant's. What essence lies
In surfaces? A void! Direct your eyes

To meaning's core; gold is a stone, and you
Are like a child attracted by its hue.
It is an idol when it holds the soul
Back from its God – hide it in some dark hole!
And if it is a sovereign remedy
It also has a foul utility
(Men make a ring of it that stops a mule
From being covered). O unhappy fool,
Who's helped by all this gold? And what real pleasure
Can you derive from heaps of glittering treasure?
If you can give a dervish just a grain
You'll nag at him, or wish it back again!
It's true that backed by gold you'll never lack
For friends – your friendship's brand burns every
          back!
Each month you count the profits from your trade;
What trade! Your soul's been sold, the bargain's made.
Life's sweetness passes and you spend your time
Scrabbling for farthings – isn't this a crime?
You give this All for nothing, while your heart
Is given wholly to the merchant's art;
But underneath your gibbet I shall wait
Until its steps are jerked away by Fate.
How many times you'll hang! Each sliding noose
Will seem a hundred burning flames – what use
Will your religion, gold, be to you then?
Or when you're drowned, your business acumen?
In that last tumult as you gasp for air
You'll know your doom and shriek in wild despair.
Remember the Qur'an: "You cannot gain
Salvation while the things you love remain."
You must abandon all things that exist;
Even the soul itself must be dismissed –
Renounce its fellowship; it too must go,
Along with all you own and all you know.
If you have made this world a place for sleep,
Your bed's the load that makes the Way so steep –

Burn it! and pass beyond what merely seems;
You can't deceive the Truth with sleepy dreams.
Let fear persuade you, and the fire is lit;
Burn your bed now if you would rise from it.

The novice who had some gold

A novice hid a little store of gold.
His sheikh knew this, although he'd not been told.
There was a journey that they had to make –
The two set out, the young man and his sheikh;
Then night came to the valley where they walked,
And into two the path they followed forked.
The novice trembled for his hidden gold
(Which makes its owners rather less than bold);
"Which way do you advise?" he asked his sheikh.
"There are two paths; which is the best to take?"
The sheikh said: "Throw out what you cannot hide,
Then either way will do – as you decide."
Let gold win someone's heart, and when that's done
Even the devil, out of fear, will run
(When gold is weighed what arguments ensue:
"One grain too many!" "No, one grain too few!");
In ways of faith he's like an ass that's lame,
Cast down, preoccupied and full of shame –
A king when cheating people, but a fool
When faith is mentioned – a bewildered mule.
The man whom shining gold can lead astray
Is captured by the world, he's lost the Way.
Remember Joseph and beware this well;
Tread carefully; it leads to death and hell.

Rabe'eh and the two grains of silver

A sheikh of Basra said to Rabe'eh:
"How much you have endured along love's Way!
And all this strength is from yourself – tell me
The source of your profound ability,
This inward light which you have neither read
Nor learned nor copied." Saint Rabe'eh said:
"Great sheikh, I simply spin coarse cotton thread;
I sell this and am satisfied to get
Two grains of silver – though I never yet
Held both these grains together in my palm,
But one in either hand. I fear the harm
That follows from the clink of coin on coin,
The sleepless nights when sums of money join."

The worldly man's embroiled in bloody cares,
Laying a hundred thousand different snares
Until unlawfully he gets his gold,
And promptly dies! Before his body's cold,
The eager heir has claimed his property,
His legal right to strife and misery.
You sell the Simorgh for this gold; its light
Has made your heart a candle in the night!
We seek the Way of perfect Unity,
Where no one counts his own prosperity;
But you are like an ant that's led astray
Too easily from our strict, narrow Way –
The strait path offers no deceitful smiles;
What living creature can endure its trials?

The hermit who listened to a bird

A man divinely blessed filled all his days
For twice two hundred years with sacred praise.
He lived alone where no man ever trod
And, hidden by Truth's veil, conversed with God
(His one companion was the Lord, and He
Makes other friends a useless luxury).
His garden had a tree – this tree a guest;
For there a lovely bird had built its nest.
Such sweetly trilling songs poured from its throat,
A hundred secrets lurked in every note!
Charmed by this liquid voice the hermit found
Companionship in its beguiling sound.
God called the prophet of that time and said:
"We must reproach this man: 'The life you've led
Has day and night been given up to prayer;
For years you burned with love – and now you dare
To sell Me for the singing of a bird,
The willing dupe of that fine voice you heard!
I've bought and cared for you – your negligence
Has cheaply sold me off as recompense:
I pay the price for you, you auction Me,
Is this your meaning for "fidelity"?
I am the one Companion you should keep,
Not some quick bargain to be marked down
    "cheap".'"

❦

An ostentatious bird

Another bird declared: 'My happiness
Comes from the splendid things which I possess:
My palace walls inlaid with gold excite
Astonishment in all who see the sight.

They are a world of joy to me – how could
I wrench my heart from this surpassing good?
There I am king; all bow to my commands –
Shall I court ruin in the desert sands?
Shall I give up this realm, and live without
My certain glory in a world of doubt?
What rational mind would give up paradise
For wanderings filled with pain and sacrifice?'

The hoopoe answers him

The hoopoe said: 'Ungrateful wretch! Are you
A dog that you should need a kennel too?
This world's a kennel's filthy murk at best;
Your palace is a kennel with the rest.
If it seems paradise, at your last breath
You'll know it is your dungeon after death.
There'd be no harm in palaces like yours,
Did not the thought of death beat at our doors.

A king who built a splendid palace

A king who loved his own magnificence
Once built a palace and spared no expense.
When this celestial building had been raised,
The gorgeous carpets and its splendour dazed
The crowd that pressed around – a servant flung
Trays heaped with money to the scrabbling throng.
The king now summoned all his wisest friends
And said: "What do I lack? Who recommends
Improvements to my court?" "We must agree,"
They said, "no man could now or ever see,
In all the earth, a palace built like this."
An old ascetic spoke. "One thing's amiss,"

He said; "there's one particular you lack.
This noble structure has a nasty crack
(Though if it weren't for that it would suffice
To be the heavenly court of paradise)."
The king replied: "What crack? Where is it? Where?
If you've come here for trouble, then take care!"
The man said: "Lord, it is the truth I tell –
And through that crack will enter Azra'el.
It may be you can block it, but if not,
Then throne and palace are not worth a jot!
Your palace now seems like some heavenly prize,
But death will make it ugly to your eyes;
Nothing remains for ever and you know –
Although you live here now – that this is so.
Don't pride yourself on things that cannot last;
Don't gallop your high-stepping horse so fast.
If one like me is left to indicate
Your faults to you, I pity your sad fate."

A merchant gives a party

To gratify his busy self-esteem,
A merchant built a mansion like a dream,
And when the preparations were all done,
He regally invited everyone
To an enormous entertainment there,
At which they'd feast and dutifully stare.
But running self-importantly around,
He met a begging fool, who stood his ground
And mocked the merchant's diligence. "My lord,"
He said, "I'm desolate (oh, rest assured!)
That I can't come and drink your health, but I'm
So busy that I really haven't time –
You will forgive me?" and he gave a grin.
"Of course," the merchant answered, taken in.

The spider

You've seen an active spider work – he seems
To spend his life in self-communing dreams;
In fact the web he spins is evidence
That he's endowed with some far-sighted sense.
He drapes a corner with his cunning snare
And waits until a fly's entangled there,
Then dashes out and sucks the meagre blood
Of his bewildered, buzzing, dying food.
He'll dry the carcass then, and live off it
For days, consuming bit by tasty bit –
Until the owner of the house one day
Will reach up casually to knock away
The cunning spider's home, and with her broom
She clears both fly and spider from the room.

Such is the world, and one who feeds there is
A fly trapped by that spider's subtleties;
If all the world is yours, it will pass by
As swiftly as the blinking of an eye;
And though you boast of kings and patronage,
You are a child, an actor on a stage.
Don't seek for wealth unless you are a fool;
A herd of cows is all that you can rule!
Whoever lives for banners, drums and glory
Is dead; the dervish understands this story
And calls it windy noise – winds vainly flap
The banners, hollowly the brave drums tap.
Don't gallop on the horse of vanity;
Don't pride yourself on your nobility.
They skin the leopard for his splendid pelt;
They'll flay you too before your nose has smelt
A whiff of danger. When your life's made plain,
Which will be better, death or chastening pain?
You cannot hold your head up then – obey!
How long must you persist in childish play?

Either give up your wealth or lay aside
The rash pretensions of your crazy pride.
Your palace and your gardens! They're your gaol,
The dungeon where your ruined soul will wail.
Forsake this dusty pride, know what it's worth;
Give up your restless pacing of the earth.
To see the Way, look with the eyes of thought;
Set out on it and glimpse the heavenly court –
And when you reach that souls' asylum, then
Its glory will blot out the world of men.

The restless fool and the dervish

A fool dashed onward at a reckless pace
Till in the desert he came face to face
With one who wore the ragged dervish cloak,
And asked: "What is your work?" The dervish
    spoke:
"Poor shallow wretch, can you not see I faint
With this strict pressure of the world's constraint?"
"Constraint? That can't be right," the man replied;
"The empty desert stretches far and wide."
The dervish said: "If there is no strict Way,
How has it led you to me here today?"

A myriad promises beguile your mind,
But flames of greed are all that you can find.
What are such flames? Tread down the world's
    desire,
And like a lion shun this raging fire.
Accomplish this, and you will find your heart;
There waits your palace, pure in every part.
Fire blocks the path, the goal is long delayed –
Your heart's a captive and your soul's afraid,
But in the midst of such an enterprise
You will escape this universe of lies.

lines 2195–2209

When worldly pleasures cloy, prepare to die –
The world gives neither name nor truth, pass by!
The more you see of it the less you see,
How often must I warn you to break free?

Seeing the world

A mourner following a coffin cried:
"You hardly saw the world, and yet you've died."
A fool remarked: "Such noise! You'd think that he
Had seen the world himself repeatedly!"

If you would take the world with you, you must
Descend with all the world unseen to dust;
You rush to savour life, and so life goes
While you ignore the balm for all its woes;
Until the Self is sacrificed your soul
Is lost in filth, divided from its goal.

A perfumed wood was burning, and its scent
Made someone sigh with somnolent content.
One said to him: "Your sigh means ecstasy;
Think of the wood, whose sigh means misery.'"

A bird who cannot leave his beloved

'Great hoopoe,' said another bird, 'my love
Has loaded me with chains, I cannot move.
This bandit, Love, confronted me and stole
My intellect, my heart, my inmost soul –
The image of her face is like a thief
Who fires the harvest and leaves only grief.
Without her I endure the pangs of hell,
Raving and cursing like an infidel;

How can I travel when my heart must stay
Lapped here in blood? And on that weary Way,
How many empty valleys lie ahead,
How many horrors wait for us? I dread
One moment absent from her lovely face;
How could I seek the Way and leave this place?
My pain exceeds all cure or remedy;
I've passed beyond both faith and blasphemy –
My blasphemy and faith are love for her;
My soul is her abject idolater –
And though companionless I weep and groan,
My friend is sorrow; I am not alone.
My love has brought me countless miseries,
But in her hair lie countless mysteries;
Without her face, blood chokes me, I am drowned,
I'm dust blown aimlessly across the ground.
Believe me, everything I say is true –
This is my state; now tell me what to do.'

The hoopoe answers him

The hoopoe said: 'You are the prisoner of
Appearances, a superficial love;
This love is not divine; it is mere greed
For flesh – an animal, instinctive need.
To love what is deficient, trapped in time,
Is more than foolishness, it is a crime –
And blasphemous the struggle to evade
That perfect beauty which can never fade.
You would compare a face of blood and bile
To the full moon – yet what could be more vile
In all the world than that same face when blood
And bile are gone? It is no more than mud.
This is the fleshly beauty you adore;
This is its being, this and nothing more.
How long then will you seek for beauty here?
Seek the unseen, and beauty will appear.

When that last veil is lifted neither men
Nor all their glory will be seen again,
The universe will fade – this mighty show
In all its majesty and pomp will go,
And those who loved appearances will prove
Each other's enemies and forfeit love,
While those who loved the absent, unseen Friend
Will enter that pure love which knows no end.

Shebli and a man whose friend had died

Once Shebli saw a poor wretch weeping. "Why
These tears?" the sheikh inquired. "What makes you cry?"
He said: "O sheikh, I had a friend whose face
Refreshed my soul with its young, candid grace –
But yesterday he died; since then I'm dead,
There's nothing that could dry the tears I shed."
The sheikh replied: "And is that all you miss?
Don't grieve, my friend, you're worth much more than
        this.
Choose now another friend who cannot die –
For His death you will never have to cry.
The friend from whom, through death, we must soon
        part
Brings only sorrow to the baffled heart;
Whoever loves the world's bright surfaces
Endures in love a hundred miseries;
Too soon the surface flees his groping hand,
And sorrow comes which no man can withstand."

A merchant who sold his favourite slave

There was a merchant once who had a slave
As sweet as sugar – how did he behave?
He sold that girl beyond comparison –
And oh, how he regretted what he'd done!

He offered her new master heaps of gold
And would have paid her price a thousandfold;
His heart in flames, his poor head in a whirl,
He begged her owner to resell the girl.
But he was adamant and would not sell;
The merchant paced the street, his mind in hell,
And groaned: "I cannot bear this searing pain –
But anyone who gives his love for gain,
Who stitches tight the eyes of common-sense
Deserves as much for his improvidence –
To think that on that fatal market-day
I tricked myself and gave the best away."

Your breaths are jewels, each atom is a guide
To lead you to the Truth, and glorified
From head to foot with His great wealth you stand;
Oh, if you could entirely understand
Your absence from Him, then you would not wait
Inured by patience to your wretched fate –
God nourished you in love and holy pride,
But ignorance detains you from His side.

A king and his greyhound

A royal hunt swept out across the plain.
The monarch called for someone in his train
To bring a greyhound, and the handler brought
A dark, sleek dog, intelligent, well-taught;
A jewelled gold collar sparkled at its throat,
Its back was covered by a satin coat –
Gold anklets clasped its paws; its leash was made
Of silk threads twisted in a glistening braid.
The king thought him a dog who'd understand,
And took the silk leash in his royal hand;
The dog ran just behind his lord, then found
A piece of bone abandoned on the ground –

He stooped to sniff, and when the king saw why,
A glance of fury flashed out from his eye.
"When you're with me," he said, "your sovereign king,
How dare you look at any other thing?"
He snapped the leash and to his handler cried:
"Let this ill-mannered brute roam far and wide.
He's mine no more – better for him if he
Had swallowed pins than found such liberty!"
The handler stared and tried to remonstrate:
"The dog, my lord, deserves an outcast's fate;
But we should keep the satin and the gold."
The king said: "No, do just as you are told;
Drive him, exactly as he is, away –
And when he comes back to himself some day,
He'll see the riches that he bears and know
That he was mine, a king's, but long ago."

And you, who had a King once as your friend,
And lost Him through your negligence, attend:
Give yourself wholly to the love of Truth;
Drink with this dragon like a reckless youth;
Now is the dragon's time – the lover must
Submit and see his throat's blood stain the dust;
What terrifies the human soul's so slight –
An ant at most – in this vast dragon's sight;
His lovers' thirst will not be quenched till they
Drink their own blood and take the selfless Way.

The martyrdom of Hallaj

Hallaj was taken to the gallows tree
And cried: "I am the Truth"; they could not see
The meaning of his words and hacked at him,
Tearing his bleeding carcass limb from limb.
Then as his face grew deathly pale he raised
The bleeding stumps of broken arms and glazed

His moon-like face with glittering blood. He said:
"Since it is blood which paints a man's face red,
I've painted mine that no one here may say:
'Hallaj turned pale on that last bloody day';
If any saw me pale they'd think that I
Felt fear to face my torturers and die –
My fear's of less than one hair's consequence;
Look on my painted face for evidence!
When he must die and sees the gallows near,
The hero's courage leaves no room for fear –
Since all the world is like a little 'o',
Why should I fear whatever it may show?
Who knows the seven-headed dragon's lair,
And sleeps and eats through summer's dog-days there,
Sees many games like this – the gallows seems
The least of all his transitory dreams."[12]
That sea of faith, Juneid, in Baghdad once
Discoursed with such persuasive eloquence
It seemed the stars bowed down to hear him speak.
This stalwart guide and comfort of the weak
Delighted in his son, a lovely child
Who as his father lectured was beguiled
And murdered by a gang – they tossed his head
In that assembly's midst and quickly fled.
Juneid looked steadfastly at this cruel sight
And did not weep but said: "What seems tonight
So strange was certain from eternity;
What happens happens from necessity."'

∽

A bird who fears death

Another bird spoke up: 'The Way is long,
And I am neither valiant nor strong.
I'm terrified of death; I know that I –
Before the first stage is complete – must die;

lines 2291–2307

I tremble at the thought; when death draws near,
I know I'll shriek and groan in snivelling fear.
Whoever fights death with his sword will meet
Inevitable, absolute defeat;
His sword and hand lie smashed. Alas! What grief
They grasp who grasp the sword as their belief!'

The hoopoe answers him

The hoopoe said: 'How feebly you complain!
How long will this worn bag of bones remain?
What are you but a few bones? And at heart
Each bone is soft and hastens to depart.
Aren't you aware that life, from birth to death,
Is little more than one precarious breath?
That all who suffer birth must also die,
Their being scattered to the windy sky?
As you are reared to live, so from your birth
You're also reared to one day leave this earth.
The sky is like some huge, inverted bowl
Which sunset fills with blood from pole to pole –
The sun seems then an executioner,
Beheading thousands with his scimitar.
If you are profligate, if you are pure,
You are but water mixed with dust, no more –
A drop of trembling instability,
And can a drop resist the surging sea?
Though in the world you are a king, you must
In sorrow and despair return to dust.

The phoenix

In India lives a bird that is unique:
The lovely phoenix has a long, hard beak
Pierced with a hundred holes, just like a flute –
It has no mate, its reign is absolute.

Each opening has a different sound; each sound
Means something secret, subtle and profound –
And as these shrill, lamenting notes are heard,
A silence falls on every listening bird;
Even the fish grow still. It was from this
Sad chant a sage learned music's artifice.
The phoenix' life endures a thousand years
And, long before, he knows when death appears;
When death's sharp pangs assail his tiring heart,
And all signs tell him he must now depart,
He builds a pyre from logs and massy trees
And from its centre sings sad threnodies:
Each plaintive note trills out, from each pierced hole
Comes evidence of his untarnished soul –
Now like a mourner's ululating cries,
Now with an inward care the cadence dies –
And as he sings of death, death's bitter grief
Thrills through him and he trembles like a leaf.
Then drawn to him by his heart-piercing calls
The birds approach, and savage animals –
They watch, and watching grieve; each in his mind
Determines he will leave the world behind.
Some weep in sympathy and some grow faint;
Some die to hear his passionate complaint.
So death draws near, and as the phoenix sings
He fans the air with his tremendous wings,
A flame darts out and licks across the pyre –
Now wood and phoenix are a raging fire,
Which slowly sinks from that first livid flash
To soft, collapsing charcoal, then to ash:
The pyre's consumed – and from the ashy bed
A little phoenix pushes up its head.
What other creature can – throughout the earth –
After death takes him, to himself give birth?
If you were given all the phoenix' years,
Still you would have to die when death appears.
For years he sings in solitary pain
And must companionless, unmated, reign;

lines 2324–2347

No children cheer his age and at his death
His ash is scattered by the wind's cold breath.
Now understand that none, however sly,
Can slip past death's sharp claws – we all must die;
None is immortal in the world's vast length;
This wonder shows no creature has the strength
To keep death's ruthless vehemence in check –
But we must soften his imperious neck;
Though many tasks will fall to us, this task
Remains the hardest that the Way will ask.

A mourning son

Before his father's coffin walked a son –
It seemed his tears would never cease to run.
"No day for me is like the day you died;
My wounded soul despairs," the poor man cried.
A passing Sufi said: "And such a day
Has never come your wretched father's way!"
The son knows sorrow, but do not compare
Such grief with all his father has to bear.
You come into the world a helpless child,
And spend your life by foolishness beguiled –
How your heart longs for sovereignty! – alas,
Like wind through outstretched fingers you will pass.

A viceroy at the point of death

A viceroy lingered close to death. One said:
"You are in sight of secrets all men dread –
What do you feel?" "There's nothing I can say,"
The man replied, "except that every day
I lived was wasted on what's trivial,
And now I shall be dust – and that is all."
To seek death is death's only cure – the leaf
Grows hectic and must fall; our life is brief.

Know we are born to die; the soul moves on;
The heart is pledged and hastens to be gone.
King Solomon, whose seal subdued all lands,
Is dust compounded with the desert sands,
And tyrants whose decrees spelt bloody doom
Decay to nothing in the narrow tomb:
How many sleep beneath the ground! And sleep
Like theirs is bitter, turbulent and deep.
Look hard at death – in our long pilgrimage
The grave itself is but the first grim stage;
How your sweet life would change if you could guess
The taste of death's unequalled bitterness!

Jesus and the stream

Once Jesus reached a clear stream's shaded bank –
He scooped up water in his palms and drank;
How sweet that water was! as if it were
Some rose-sweet sherbet or an elixir;
One with him filled a jug, and on they went.
When Jesus drank, to his astonishment,
The jug seemed filled with bitterness. "How strange,"
He said, "that water can so quickly change –
They were the same; what can this difference mean?
What tasted sweet is brackish and unclean!"
The jug spoke: "Lord, once I too had a soul
And was a man – but I have been a bowl,
A cruse, a pitcher of crude earthenware,
Remade a thousand times; and all forms share
The bitterness of death – which would remain
Though I were baked a thousand times again;
No water could be sweet which I contain."
O careless of your fate! From this jug learn,
And from your inattentive folly turn;
O pilgrim, you have lost yourself – before
Death takes you seek the hidden Way once more!

lines 2364–2380

If while you live and breathe you fail to see
The nature of your own reality,
How can you search when dead? The man who lives
And does not strive is lost; his mother gives
Him life but he cannot become a man –
He strays, a self-deluded charlatan.
How many veils obstruct the Sufi's quest,
How long his search till Truth is manifest!

The death of Socrates

When Socrates lay close to death, a youth –
Who was his student in the search for Truth –
Said: "Master, when we've washed the man we knew
And brought your shroud, where should we bury
       you?"
He said: "If you can find me when I've died,
Then bury me wherever you decide –
I never found myself; I cannot see
How when I'm dead you could discover me.
Throughout my life not one small particle
Had any knowledge of itself at all!"'

A bird complains of his bad luck

Another bird said: 'Hoopoe, it's no good.
Things never happen as I'd hoped they would;
I've spent my time in misery since birth,
The most unlucky wretch in all the earth –
My heart knows so much torment that it seems
Each atom of my body raves and screams;
My life has trodden out a hopeless way;
God damn me if I've had one happy day!
These sorrows lock me in myself – how can
I undertake this journey which you plan?

If I were happy I would gladly start;
What stops me is this sorrow in my heart.
What can I do? Look, I appeal to you –
I've told you everything, what can I do?'

The hoopoe answers him

The hoopoe said: 'How arrogant you are
To think your wretched Self so singular!
The disappointments of this world will die
In less time than the blinking of an eye,
And as the earth must pass, pass by the earth –
Don't even glance at it, know what it's worth;
What empty foolishness it is to care
For what must one day be dispersed to air!

The man who refused to drink

There was a man advanced along the Way
Who always, to his puzzled friends' dismay,
Refused to drink sweet sherbet. "Why is this?"
One asked. "What could explain this prejudice?"
He said: "I see a man who stands on guard
And notes who drinks – his eyes are cold and hard,
And if I drank, the sweetest sherbet would,
I know, act like a poison in my blood.
While he stands here the contents of the bowl
Are liquid fire to sear the drinker's soul."
Whatever lasts a moment's only worth
One barley grain – though it were all the earth;
How can I trust what has no rooted power
And holds existence for a transient hour?
If you achieve your every wish, why boast
Of glory insubstantial as a ghost?
If disappointments darken all your days,
You need not grieve, for nothing worldly stays –

lines 2395–2410

It is your passion for magnificence
That prompts your tears, not fancied indigence.
What is your grief compared with all the pain
God's martyrs suffered on Kerbela's plain?[13]
In His clear sight the hardships you endure
Show like a treasure, glittering and pure –
Each breath you breathe His kindness reaches you,
And untold love envelops all you do –
But you forget His grace, and negligence
Makes friendship look like meaningless pretence.

The king who gave his slave an apple

A good kind-hearted monarch one day gave
A rosy apple to his favourite slave,
Who seemed to eat the fruit with such delight
The laughing king said: "Here, give me a bite!"
The slave returned him half, but when the king
Bit into it it seemed a paltry thing,
Unripe and tart. Frowning, he said: "And how
Is what appeared so sweet so bitter now?"
The slave replied: "My lord, you've given me
Such proofs of constant generosity,
I could not find it in my grateful heart
To grumble just because one apple's tart –
I must accept whatever you bestow;
No harm can come to me from you, I know."
If you meet tribulations here be sure
That wealth will come from all you must endure;
The paths of God are intricate and strange –
What can you do? Accept what will not change!
The wise know every mouthful on this Way
Tastes bitter with their blood. Until that day
When as His guests they break their bread, they must
Consume in suffering each broken crust.

One asked a Sufi how he spent his time.
He said: "I'm thirsty, filthy, smeared with grime,
Burned in this stove men call the world, but I
Shall keep my courage up until I die."
If in this world you seek for happiness
You are asleep, your search is meaningless –
If you seek happiness you would do well
To think of that thin bridge arched over hell.[14]
The world's apparent joy cannot compare
With what we seek – it isn't worth a hair;
Here the Self rages like an unquenched fire,
And nothing satisfies the heart's desire –
Encompass all the earth, you will not find
One happy heart or one contented mind.

A *woman who wished to pray for happiness*

An old, sad woman talked to Mahna's sheikh:
"Teach me to pray for joy, for pity's sake –
I've suffered so much that I cannot bear
To think of future grief – give me some prayer
To murmur every day." The sheikh replied:
"How many years I wandered far and wide
Until I found the fortress that you seek –
It is the knee, bend it, accept, be meek;
I found no other way – this remedy,
And only this, will cure your misery."

One sat before Juneid. "You are God's prey,"
He said, "yet you are free in every way –
Tell me, when does a man know happiness?
When does his heart rejoice? I cannot guess."
Juneid replied: "That hour he finds the heart."
Unless we reach our King we must depart –
With all our courage wasted – into night.
We atoms are amazed, and lack the light

Of the immortal sun; what circumstance,
What suffering, could cleanse our ignorance?
An atom looked at from which way you will
Remains unalterably an atom still;
And one who has an atom's nature shows
That stubborn fact, no matter how he grows.
If he were lost within the blazing sun
He'd stay an atom till his life were done,
And, good or bad, no matter how he strains,
A tiny atom is what he remains.
O atom, weaving like a drunk until
You reach the sun – unsettled, never still –
My patience knows that one day you will see,
Beside the sun, your insufficiency.

The bat who wanted to see the sun

One night a bat said: "How is it that I
Have never seen the sun; I wonder why?
I long to lose myself in its pure light;
Instead my wretched life is one long night –
But though I travel with my eyes shut fast
I know I'll reach that promised blaze at last."
A seer had overheard and said: "What pride!
A thousand years might bring you to its side;
You are bewildered, lost – you could as soon
Attain the sun as could an ant the moon."
The unpersuaded bat said: "Never mind,
I'll fly about and see what I can find."
For years he flew in dismal ignorance,
Till he collapsed in an exhausted trance
And murmured as he tried in vain to fly:
"Where is the sun? Perhaps I've passed it by?"
The seer was there and said: "You've managed one
Short step, and yet you think you've passed the sun;

You live in dreams!" Shame crushed the bat; he felt
The last thin remnants of his courage melt.
Humble and wretched, he sought out the Way –
"He understands," he said. "I will obey."'

A bird accepts the hoopoe's leadership

Another bird said: 'Hoopoe, you're our guide.
How would it be if I let you decide?
I'm ignorant of right and wrong – I'll wait
For any orders that you stipulate.
Whatever you command I'll gladly do,
Delighted to submit myself to you.'

'Bravo!' the hoopoe cried. 'By far the best
Decision is the one that you suggest;
Whoever will be guided finds relief
From Fate's adversity, from inward grief;
One hour of guidance benefits you more
Than all your mortal life, however pure.
Those who will not submit like lost dogs stray,
Beset by misery, and lose their way –
How much a dog endures! and all in vain;
Without a guide his pain is simply pain.
But one who suffers and is guided gives
His merit to the world; he truly lives.
Take refuge in the orders of your guide,
And like a slave subdue your restive pride.

The king who stopped at the prison gates

A king returned once to his capital.
His subjects had prepared a festival,
And each to show his homage to the crown
Had helped to decorate the glittering town.

The prisoners had no wealth but iron gyves,
Chains, severed heads, racked limbs and ruined lives –
With such horrific ornaments they made
A sight to greet their monarch's cavalcade.
The king rode through the town and saw the way
His subjects solemnized the happy day,
But nothing stopped the progress of his train
Till he approached the prison and drew rein.
There he dismounted and had each man told
That he was free and would be paid in gold.
A courtier asked the king: "What does this mean?
To think of all the pageantry you've seen –
Brocade and satin shining everywhere,
Musk and sweet ambergris to scent the air,
Jewels scattered by the handful on the ground –
And not so much as once did you look round;
Yet here you stop – before the prison gate!
Are severed heads a way to celebrate?
What is there here to give you such delight?
Torn limbs and carcasses? A grisly sight!
And why did you dismount? Should you sit down
With all the thieves and murderers in town?"
The king replied: "The others make a noise
Like rowdy children playing with new toys;
Each takes his part in some festivity,
Careful to please himself as much as me –
They do their duty and are quite content,
But here in prison more than duty's meant.
My word is law here, and they've plainly shown
This spectacle was made for me alone.
I see obedience here; need I explain
Why it is here I'm happy to draw rein?
The others celebrate in pompous pride,
Conceited, giddy and self-satisfied,
But these poor captives sacrifice their will
And bow to my commands through good and ill;
They have no business but to spend each breath
In expectation of the noose and death,

Yet they submit – and to my grateful eyes
Their prison is a flower-strewn paradise."
Wisdom accepts authority and waits;
The king paused only at the prison gates.

A Sufi who surpassed Bayazid and Tarmazi

A master of the Way once said: "Last night
I saw a strange, unprecedented sight –
I dreamed that Bayazid and Tarmazi
Were walking, and they both gave way to me –
I was their guide! I sought to understand
How two such sheikhs were under my command,
And then remembered that one distant dawn
A sigh was from my very entrails torn;
That sigh had cleared the Way – a massive gate
Swung open, and I entered the debate
Of sheikhs and dervishes. All questioned me
But Bayazid, who was content to see
That I was there; he uttered no request
But said: 'I heard the sigh that tore your breast,
And knew I must accept you as you are,
Not seek for this or that particular –
Embrace the soul and disregard the pain,
Or weigh up what is loss and what is gain;
Your wish is my command, for who am I
To question those commands or to reply?
Your faithful slave cannot demur or tire;
I will perform whatever you desire.'
This shows why Bayazid and Tarmazi,
Though they are great, gave precedence to me."
When once a slave accepts his Lord's control
And hears Him whisper in his inmost soul
He does not boast, no outward signs are shown,
But when life's crises come – then he is known.

The death of Sheikh Kherghan

When Sheikh Kherghan lay near to death he cried:
"If men could split my heart and see inside,
They'd tell the world my misery and pain,
A wise man's secret doctrine would be plain:
Forsake idolatry; if you do this
You are His slave, and cannot go amiss;
All else is pride. If you are neither slave
Nor God you're substanceless, however brave –
I call you 'No-one'; turn now, No-one, seek
Devotion's path, be humbled, lowly, meek.
But when you bow the head in slavery,
Be resolute, bow down with dignity:
The king who sees a cringing, stupid slave
Who has no notion how he should behave
Expels him from his court, and Mecca's shrine
Is closed to louts and fools. If you combine
True servitude with dignity your Lord
Will not deny you your desired reward."

The slave who was given a splendid robe

A slave was given, from his sovereign's hand,
A splendid robe – and feeling very grand
He put it on to wander through the town.
By chance, as he paraded up and down,
Some mud splashed in his face, and with his sleeve
He quickly wiped it off: who should perceive
His action but a sneaking sycophant –
The king was told and hanged the miscreant.
From this unhappy story you can see
How kings treat those who have no dignity.'

lines 2525–2539

A bird questions the hoopoe about purity

Another bird spoke next: 'Dear hoopoe, say
What purity consists of on this Way,
It seems a settled heart's forbidden me –
All that I gain I lose immediately.
It's either scattered to the winds or turns
To scorpions in my hands; my being yearns
For this great quest, I'm bound to nothing here –
I smashed all worldly chains and knew no fear;
With purity of heart, who knows, I might
Behold His face with my unaided sight.'

The hoopoe answers him

The hoopoe said: 'Our Way does not belong
To anyone, but to the pure and strong –
To those who let go every interest
And give themselves entirely to our quest;
All your possessions are not worth a hair.
(Don't mend what's torn, what's sewn together
    tear!)
Consign them to the fire, and when its flash
Has burned them, rake together all the ash
And sit on it – then you will know their worth.
But you will curse the day that gave you birth
If you ignore my words. Until your heart
Is free of ownership you cannot start –
Since we must leave this prison and its pains,
Detach yourself from all that it contains;
Will what you own bribe death? Will death delay?
If you would enter on the pilgrim's Way,
Tie up your grasping hands: all you endure
Is valueless if you set out impure.

lines 2540–2554

A sheikh of Turkestan once said: "Above
All other things there are just two I love.
My swiftly trotting piebald horse is one –
The second is none other than my son;
If death should take my son I'd sacrifice
My horse in thanks – I know these two entice,
As idols would, my spirit from the Way."
Don't brag of purity until the day
You flare as candles do whose substance turns
To nothing as the flame leaps up and burns;
Whoever boasts a pure, unsullied name
Will find his actions contradict his claim,
When purity gives way to greed, the power
Of retribution strikes within the hour.

Sheikh Kherghani and the aubergine

One day Sheikh Kherghani's devout routine
Was spoilt by cravings for an aubergine.
His mother was unsure what should be done
But hesitantly gave him half a one –
The moment that he bit its flesh a crew
Of ruffians seized his son and ran him through.
That night, outside the sheikh's front door they laid
His boy's head hacked off by a cutlass blade.
The sheikh cried out: "How often I'd foreseen
Disaster if I tasted aubergine!"
The man who has been chosen by this Guide
Must follow Him and never swerve aside –
His service is more terrible than war,
Than shame that cringes to a conqueror.
It is not knowledge keeps a man secure –
With all his understanding, Fate is sure;
Each moment we receive a different guest,
And each that comes presents another test,
Although a hundred sorrows wring your soul,
The future will not bow to your control.

lines 2555–2573

But one who breaks illusion's hold will find
Misfortune will not always cloud his mind.
A hundred thousand of His lovers sigh
To sacrifice themselves for Him and die;
How many waste their idle lives until
They bleed and groan, subservient to His will!

A voice speaks to Zulnun

Zulnun said: "I was in the desert once.
Trusting in God, I'd brought no sustenance –
I came on forty men ahead of me,
Dressed all in rags, a closed community.
My heart was moved. 'O God,' I cried, 'take heed,
What wretched lives You make Your pilgrims lead!'
'We know their life and death,' a voice replied;
'We kill these pilgrims first; when they have died
We compensate them for the blood We shed.'
I asked: 'When will this killing stop?' He said:
'When My exchequer has no love to give;[15]
While I can pay for death they shall not live.
I drink My servant's blood and he is hurled
In frenzied turbulence about the world –
Then when he is destroyed and cannot find
His head, his feet, his passions or his mind,
I clothe him in the splendour he has won
And grace enfolds him, radiant as the sun:
Though I will have his face bedaubed by blood,
A starved ascetic smeared with dust and mud,
A denizen of shadows and the night –
Yet I will rise before him robed in light,
And when that sun, My countenance, is here
What can these shadows do but disappear?'"
Shadows are swallowed by the sun and he
Who's lost in God is from himself set free;

Don't chatter about loss – be lost! Repent,
And give up vain, self-centred argument;
If one can lose the Self, in all the earth
No other being can approach his worth.

I know of no one in the world profound
As Pharaoh's sorcerers: the wealth they found
Was faith's true Way, which is to sift apart
The grosser Self from the aspiring heart.
The world's known nothing of them since that day
They took this first short step along the Way –
And in the world no wisdom could provide
A surer path than this, a better guide!'

A bird who burns with aspiration

'O hoopoe,' cried another of the birds,
'What lofty ardour blazes from your words!
Although I seem despondent, weak and lame,
I burn with aspiration's noble flame –
And though I'm not obedient I feel
My soul devoured by an insatiate zeal.'

The hoopoe answers him

The hoopoe said: 'This strange, magnetic force
That holds God's ancient lovers to their course
Still shows the Truth: if you will but aspire
You will attain to all that you desire.
Before an atom of such need the sun
Seems dim and murky by comparison –
It is life's strength, the wings by which we fly
Beyond the further reaches of the sky.

The old woman who wanted to buy Joseph

When Joseph was for sale, the market-place
Teemed with Egyptians wild to see his face;
So many gathered there from dawn to dusk
The asking price was five whole tubs of musk.
An ancient crone pushed forward – in her hand
She held a few threads twisted strand by strand;
She brandished them and yelled with all her might:
"Hey, you, the seller of the Canaanite!
I'm mad with longing for this lovely child –
I've spun these threads for him, he drives me wild!
You take the threads and I'll take him away –
Don't argue now, I haven't got all day!"
The merchant laughed and said: "Come on, old girl,
It's not for you to purchase such a pearl –
His value's reckoned up in gold and jewels;
He can't be sold for threads to ancient fools!"
"Oh, I knew that before," the old crone said;
"I knew you wouldn't sell him for my thread –
But it's enough that everyone will say:
'She bid for Joseph on that splendid day.'"
The heart that does not strive can never gain
The endless kingdom's gates and lives in vain;
It was pure aspiration made a king
Set fire to all he owned – to everything –
And when his goods had vanished without trace
A thousand kingdoms sprang up in their place.
When noble aspiration seized his mind,
He left the world's corrupted wealth behind –
Can one who craves the sun be satisfied
With petty ignorance? Is this his guide?

The poverty of Ibrahim Adham

I know of one who whined unceasingly,
Complaining of his abject poverty,
Till Ibrahim Adham said: "Do you weep
Because you bought your poverty too cheap?"
The man replied: "What's that supposed to mean?
To purchase poverty would be obscene."
He said: "I gave a kingdom up for mine,
But for the earthly realm which I resign
I still receive, each moment that I live,
A hundred worlds: my realm was fugitive –
I said farewell to it, to all the earth,
And put my trust in goods of proven worth.
I know what value is; I praise His name –
And you know neither, to your lasting shame."
Those who aspire renounce both heart and soul,
Content through years to suffer for their goal;
The bird of aspiration seeks His throne,
Outsoaring faith and all the world, alone:
But if you lack this zeal, be off with you –
You're quite unfit for all we have to do.

Sheikh Ghuri and Prince Sanjar

When Sheikh Ghuri, an adept of the Way,
Took refuge underneath a bridge one day
Together with a group of crazy fools,
Sanjar rode by, resplendent in his jewels,
And said: "Who's huddled over there?" "O king,"
The sheikh replied, "we haven't got a thing,
But we've decided on a choice for you –
Be good to us, and bid the world adieu,
Or be our enemy, and you will find
It is your faith that you must leave behind.

If you will join us for a moment here,
Your pride and gorgeous pomp will disappear –
Look at our friendship and our enmity
And make your mind up; which is it to be?"
Sanjar replied: "I'm not the man for you.
It's not your kind my hate and love pursue;
You're not my enemy, you're not my friend;
My heart's directed to a different end.
In front of you I've neither pride nor shame
And have no business with your praise or blame."
The bird of aspiration spreads its wings
And quickly soars beyond terrestrial things –
Beyond the lower world's complacent guess
Of what is temperance, what drunkenness.

The feathers of the soul

One night a fool of God wept bitterly
And said: "The world, as far as I can see,
Is like a box, and we are locked inside,
Lost in the darkness of our sin and pride;
When death removes the lid we fly away –
If we have feathers – to eternal day,
But those who have no feathers must stay here,
Tormented in this box by pain and fear."
Give wings to aspiration; love the mind;
And if at death you'd leave this box behind,
Grow wings and feathers for the soul; if not,
Burn all your hopes, for you will die and rot.'

A bird questions the hoopoe about justice and loyalty

Another bird said: 'What are loyalty
And justice, put beside such majesty?
God gave me boundless loyalty and I've
Not been unjust to any man alive –
What is the ghostly rank of those who own
Such qualities, before our Sovereign's throne?'

The hoopoe answers him

The hoopoe said: 'Salvation's Lord is just,
And justice raises man above the dust;
To live with justice in your heart exceeds
A lifetime's earnest prayer and pious deeds;
And tales of lavish generosity
Are less than one just act done secretly
(Though justice given in a public place
Suggests deceit beneath the smiling face).
The just man does not argue for his rights;
It is for others that he stands and fights.

Ahmad Hanbal and the beggar

Ahmad Hanbal, a man renowned and wise,
Whose knowledge no one dared to criticize,
Would when he felt his mind inadequate
Consult a barefoot beggar at his gate.
If anyone discovered him they'd say:
"But you're our wisest man in every way;
When one of us is called upon to speak
You scarcely hear our words – yet here you seek

A barefoot beggar out; what can it mean?"
Ahmad Hanbal replied: "As you have seen,
My commentaries have carried off the prize;
In matters of *hadith*[16] and law I'm wise –
I know more worldly things than him, it's true,
But he knows God – much more than I can do."
Look at this action well before you claim
A justice that does not deserve the name.

An Indian king

As Mahmud's army moved through India,
They chanced to take an old king prisoner
Who learned the Muslim faith at Mahmud's court
And counted this world and the next as nought.
Alone, a hermit in a ragged tent,
He lived for prayer, an earnest penitent,
His face bathed day and night in scalding tears –
At last the news of this reached Mahmud's ears.
He summoned him and said: "I'll give to you
A hundred kingdoms and their revenue;
It's not for you to weep, you are a king;
I promise to return you everything!"
To this the Indian king replied: "My lord,
It's not my kingdom conquered by your sword
That makes me weep, but thoughts of Judgement Day;
For at the resurrection God will say:
'O faithless wretch, you had no thoughts of Me
Till you were crushed by Mahmud's cavalry –
It took an army's might to change your mind,
And till you stood defenceless you were blind –
Does this make you My friend or enemy?
How long did I treat you with loyalty
And in return endure your thankless hate?
Is this the friendship that you advocate?'
If God says this, what answer can I give
To contradict the damning narrative?

Young man, if you could understand my fears
You'd know the reason for an old man's tears."
Learn from these faithful words, and if your heart
Holds faith like this, prepare now to depart;
But if your heart is faithless, give up now,
Forget our struggle and renounce your vow;
The faithless have no place on any page
Within the volume of our pilgrimage.

The faithless Muslim and the faithful infidel

A Muslim fought an infidel one day
And as they fought requested time to pray.
He prayed and fought again – the infidel
Then asked for time to say his prayers as well;
He went aside to find a cleaner place
And there before his idol bowed his face.
The Muslim, when he saw him kneel and bow,
Said: "Victory is mine if I strike now."
But as he raised his sword for that last stroke,
A warning voice from highest heaven spoke:
"O vicious wretch – from head to foot deceit –
What promises are these, you faithless cheat?
His blade was sheathed when you asked him for time;
For you to strike him now would be a crime –
Have you not read in Our Qur'an the verse
'Fulfil your promises'? And will you curse
The word you gave? The infidel was true;
He kept his promises, and so should you.
You offer evil in return for good –
With others act as to yourself you would!
The infidel kept faith with you, and where
Is your fidelity, for all your prayer?
You are a Muslim, but false piety
Is less than this poor pagan's loyalty."
The Muslim heard this speech and went apart;
Sweat poured from him, remorse accused his heart.

lines 2684–2701

The pagan saw him as if spell-bound stand,
Tears in his eyes, his sword still in his hand,
And asked: "Why do you weep?" The man replied:
"My shame is not a matter I can hide" –
He told him of the voice that he had heard
Reproaching him when he would break his word,
And ending said: "My tears anticipate
The fury of your vengeance and your hate."
But when the infidel had heard this tale,
His eyes were filled with tears, his face turned pale –
"God censures you for your disloyalty
And guards the life of His sworn enemy –
Can I continue to be faithless now?
I'll burn my gods, to Allah I will bow,
Expound His law! Too long my heart has lain
In darkness bound by superstition's chain."
What infidelity you give for love!
But I shall wait until the heavens above
Confront you with the actions you have done
And number them before you, one by one.

Joseph and his brothers

Ten starving brothers left their home to stand
In Joseph's presence, in a foreign land,
And begged for some benevolent relief
To ease the torments of their wretched grief.
Now Joseph's face was veiled; he took a bowl
And struck it hard – a sound as if a soul
Cried out in misery was heard. He said:
"Do you know what this means?" Each shook his head.
"Lord, no one in the world, search far and wide,
Could give this noise a meaning," they replied.
Then Joseph said: "It speaks to you; it says
You had a brother once, in former days,
More precious than this bowl – he bore the name
Of Joseph; and it says that, to your shame,

His goodness overshadowed all of you."
Once more he struck the bowl. "It says you threw
This Joseph in a well, then stained his cloak
With wolf's blood; and it says the smeared rags broke
Poor Jacob's heart." He touched the bowl again:
"It says you brought your father needless pain
And sold the lovely Joseph. Is this true?
May God bestow remorse to chasten you!"
These brothers who had come to beg for bread
Stood speechless, faint with apprehensive dread:
When they gave Joseph for the merchant's gold,
It was themselves, and all the world, they sold –
And when they threw their brother in that well,
They threw themselves in the abyss of hell.
Whoever hears these words and cannot find
How they apply to him is truly blind.
There is no need to scrutinize my tale,
It is your own; when thoughtlessly you fail
To render loyalty its proper due,
How can the light of friendship shine for you?
But, till you're woken, sleep – too soon you'll see
Your shameful crimes, your infidelity,
And when you stand a prisoner in that place
They'll count them one by one before your face;
There, when the bowl is struck, you too will find
That fear dissolves your reason and your mind.
You're like a lame ant struggling for its soul,
Aimlessly sliding, caught inside this bowl –
Blood fills it, but a voice beyond its rim
Still calls to you – rise now, and fly to Him.'

A bird questions the hoopoe about audacity

Another bird said: 'Is audacity
Allowable before such majesty?
One needs audacity to conquer fear –
But is it right in His exalted sphere?'

The hoopoe answers him

The hoopoe said: 'Those who are worthy reach
A subtle understanding none can teach;
They guard the secrets of our glorious King
And therefore are not kept from anything –
But how could one who knows such secrets be
Convicted of the least audacity?
Since he is filled with reverence to the brim,
A breath of boldness is permitted him.
(The ignorant, it's true, can never share
The secrets of our King. If one should dare
To ape the ways of the initiate,
What does he do but blindly imitate?
He's like some soldier who kicks up a din
And spoils the ranks with his indiscipline.)
But think of some new pilgrim, some young boy,
Whose boldness comes from mere excess of joy;
He has no certain knowledge of the Way
And what seems rudeness is but loving play –
He's like a madman – love's audacity
Will have him walking on the restless sea.
Such ways are laudable; we should admire
This love that turns him to a blazing fire;

One can't expect discretion from a flame,
And madmen are beyond reproach or blame –
When madness chooses you to be its prey
We'll hear what crazy things you have to say.

The dervish who envied a king's slaves

Once Khorasan enjoyed great affluence
Beneath a prince of proved benevolence –
His slaves were lovely as the moon at dusk,
Straight-limbed and silver, scented with soft musk,
And in their ears shone pearls whose milky light
Reflected daytime in the darkest night.
Gold ornaments half hid and half revealed
Their silver limbs; each held a golden shield.
Bright gems adorned their belts; a white horse bore
Each slave as if he were a conqueror.
Whoever saw this shining army gave
His heart to them, the slaves' contented slave.
A barefoot, hungry dervish once, by chance,
Caught sight of this unique magnificence,
And wondering asked: "What houris might these
    be?"
The crowd exclaimed: "The splendid troop you see
Are slaves belonging to our noble lord."
The dervish writhed as if in pain, then roared:
"Great God, look down from Your exalted sphere –
Learn how to treat Your slaves from this man
    here!"
If you are mad like him, if you possess
Such leaves of Truth, forget all bashfulness,
Be bold! But if these leaves are not your style,
Control yourself, and wipe away your smile.
Boldness like this does not deserve our blame;
Such men are moths, ambitious for the flame –
They only see their goal and cannot say
What's good or bad along the pilgrims' Way.

lines 2757–2773

A madman seeks shelter

A naked madman, gnawed by hunger, went
Along the road – his shivering frame was bent
Beneath the icy sleet; no house stood there
To offer shelter from the wintry air.
He saw a ruined hut and with a dash
Stood underneath its roof; a sudden crash
Rang out – a tile had fallen on his head,
And how the gaping gash it cut there bled!
He looked up at the sky and yelled: "Enough!
Why can't you clobber me with better stuff?"

The poor man, the rich man and the ass

A poor man living in a drainage-ditch
Once borrowed from his neighbour (who was rich)
A valued ass, and rode it to the mill.
He slept there, and the ass made off at will –
A wolf devoured the beast; with indignation
The owner made a claim for compensation.
The poor man and his neighbour went to court,
Submitting an exhaustive, full report –
"Now who should pay?" they asked. The judge
    replied:
"Whoever[17] lets this wolf hunt far and wide,
Whoever put him here to roam about,
Should compensate you both without a doubt –
O God, who is the debtor, who can say?
It's certain that no mortal ought to pay."
As Egypt's noble maidens swooned to see
Dear Joseph's radiant face, so ecstasy
Is mirrored in the Sufi's maddened heart –
Then he has lost himself and moves apart
From all that we perceive – the world grows dim
As all the world resolves to follow him.

lines 2774–2791

A *famine in Egypt*

In Egypt once a baleful famine spread –
The people perished as they begged for bread.
Death filled the roads; the living gnawed the dead.
A crazy dervish saw their wretched plight
And cried: "O God, look down from Your great
    height –
If there's no food for them, make fewer men!"
A man who speaks like this asks pardon when
He comes back to himself – if he's to blame
He knows the ways to cancel all his shame.

A *dervish deceived by a hailstorm*

A dervish suffered bruises and sore bones
From children who continually threw stones.
He found a ruined hut and in he stole,
Not noticing its roof contained a hole.
A hailstorm started – through the leaky shed
The hail came bouncing on the old man's head.
The hail was stones for all that he could tell –
He lost his temper and began to yell.
Convinced that they were throwing stones once more,
He screamed out filthy names, fumed, stamped and
    swore –
Then thought: "This dark's so thick it's possible
It's not the children this time after all."
A door blew open and revealed the hail;
He saw his error and began to wail:
"The darkness tricked me, God – and on my head
Be all the foolish, filthy names I said."
If crazy dervishes behave like this
It's not for you to take their words amiss;
If they seem drunk to you, control your scorn –
Their lives are painful, savage and forlorn;

They must endure a lifetime's hopelessness
And every moment brings some new distress –
Don't meddle with their conduct; don't reprove
Those given up to madness and to love.
You would excuse them – nothing is more sure –
If you could share the darkness they endure.

Al-Vasati passes the Jewish cemetery

Al-Vasati, cast down by grief one day,
Proceeded on his troubled, weary way
Until he saw the Jewish cemetery
And said: "These souls are pardoned and go free;
But this is not a truth that can be taught."
His words were heard and he was haled to court,
Where angry judges asked him what he meant –
Al-Vasati replied: "Your government
Accuses them; their pardon's heaven-sent."'

A bird claims that he lives only for the Simorgh

Another bird spoke up: 'I live for love,
For Him and for the glorious world above –
For Him I've cut myself from everything;
My life's one song of love to our great King.
I've seen the world's inhabitants, and know
I could not worship any here below;
My ardent love's for Him alone; how few
Can manage to adore Him as I do!
But though I've struggled on with all my soul,
It seems I haven't quite achieved our goal.
The time has come – my Self will disappear;
I'll drink the wine of meekness and draw near;
His beauty will illuminate my heart;
His neck will know my touch; we shall not part.'

lines 2809–2825

The hoopoe answers him

The hoopoe said: 'The Simorgh isn't won
By boasts of who you are and what you've done –
Don't brag of love; He's not deceived by lies,
And no one pulls the wool across His eyes.
His call is like some lightly wafted breeze
Lifting the veil from hidden mysteries –
Then He will draw you to Himself, alone;
Your place will be with Him, beside His throne
(Though if mere pride of place prompts your desire,
Your love prepares you for eternal fire).

Bayazid after death

When Bayazid had left the world behind,
He came that night before the dreaming mind
Of one of his disciples, who in fear
Asked how he'd fared with Monkar and Nakir.
He said: "When those two angels questioned me
About the Lord, I told them I could see
No profit in our talk – if I should say:
'He is my God,' my answer would betray
A proud, ambitious heart; they should return
To God and ask Him what they wished to learn –
God says who is His slave; the slave is dumb,
Waiting for Him to say: 'Good servant, come!'"
If grace is given you from God above,
Then you are wholly worthy of His love;
And if He kindles joy in you, the fire
Will burst out and its flames beat ever higher –
It is His works that act, not yours, you fool;
When will these dunces understand His rule!

lines 2826–2846

A dervish in love with God

A dervish wept to feel the violence of
The inextinguishable fires of love.
His spirit melted, and his soul became
A seething mass of incandescent flame;
He wept as he proceeded on his way,
And through his scalding tears was heard to say:
"For how much longer must I weep? Desire
Has burned my life in its consuming fire."
"What's all this boasting for?" a voice replied.
"Can you approach Him with such senseless pride?"
"And when did I approach Him?" asked the saint.
"No, He approaches me; that's my complaint –
How could a wretched thing like me pretend
To have the worth to claim Him as my friend?
Look – I do nothing; He performs all deeds
And He endures the pain when my heart bleeds."
When He draws near and grants you audience
Should you hang back in tongue-tied diffidence?
When will your cautious heart consent to go
Beyond the homely boundaries you know?
O slave, if He should show His love to you,
Love which His deeds perpetually renew,
You will be nothing, you will disappear –
Leave all to Him who acts, and have no fear.
If there is any "you", if any wraith
Of Self persists, you've strayed outside our faith.

Shah Mahmud and the stoker at the public baths

Shah Mahmud, full of sorrow, went one night
To one who keeps the baths' huge fires alight;
The man made room among the ash and grime
(Feeding the furnace-mouth from time to time),

Then brought the king some stale, unwholesome bread.
"When he knows who I am," Shah Mahmud said,
"He'll beg to be allowed to keep his head!"
When, finally, the king prepared to go,
The poor man said: "I haven't much to show –
You've seen my home and food (I brought the best;
You were a rather unexpected guest),
But if in future you feel sorrow's pain
I hope you'll come and be my guest again.
If you weren't king you could be happy, sire;
I'm happy shovelling wood on this great fire –
So I'm not less than you or more, you see . . .
I'm nothing next to you, your majesty."
The king was so impressed that he returned,
And seven times saw how that furnace burned –
At last he said: "Stop stoking this great fire
And ask from me whatever you require."
"I am a beggar, lord," the man replied;
"And with a king all needs are satisfied."
Shah Mahmud said: "Speak up, ask anything –
You can forget the furnace and be king!"
He said: "My hope is this, that now and then
My king will visit me in this dark den –
The dust he treads on is a crown to me;
His presence here will be my monarchy.
Yours is the kingdom and the hand that gives,
But that's not how a bath attendant lives.
Better to sit with you in this foul place
Than reign in state and never see your face.
This spot has brought me luck, and I'd be wrong
To leave the furnace-mouth where I belong –
Besides, it's here I made friends with my king,
I wouldn't give this up for anything –
When you are here the bath-house shines anew;
What more could I desire from you than you?
May my perverse heart die if it should crave
Another fate than to remain your slave!

What's sovereignty to me? All I request
Is that from time to time you'll be my guest."
The bath attendant's love should teach you yours;
Learn from him all the loving heart endures –
And if this love has stirred in you, then cling
With passion to the garments of your King;
He too is moved; hold fast and do not stop –
He is a sea; He asks of you one drop.

Two water-sellers

A man who lived by selling water found
He'd very little left; he looked around
And saw another water-seller there –
"Have you got any water you could spare?"
He asked. "No, fool, I certainly have not,"
The other snapped; "make do with what you've
        got!"
"Oh, give me some," the man began to plead;
"I'm sick of what I have; it's yours I need."
When Adam's heart grew tired of all he knew,
He yearned for wheat, a substance strange and
        new –
He gave up all he owned for one small grain,
And naked suffered love's relentless pain;
He disappeared in love's intensity –
The old and new were gone and so was he;
He was annihilated, lost, made naught –
Nothingness swallowed all his hands had sought.
To turn from what we are, to yearn and die
Is not for us to choose or to deny.'

A bird who claims to be satisfied with his spiritual state

Another bird squawked: 'There can be no doubt
I've made myself unworldly and devout.
To reach this wise perfection which you see
I've lived a life of cruel austerity,
And as I've gained the sum of wisdom here,
I really couldn't move, I hope that's clear.
What fool would leave his treasury to roam
In deserts and dry mountains far from home?'

The hoopoe answers him

The hoopoe said: 'Hell's pride has filled your soul;
Lost in self-love, you dread our distant goal.
Your arrogance deceives you, and you stray
Further and further from the spirit's Way.
Your Self has trapped your soul and made it blind;
The devil's throne is your complacent mind.
The light that guides you is a fantasy,
Your love a self-induced absurdity –
All your austerities are just a cheat,
And all you say is nothing but deceit.
Don't trust the light which shows you where you go;
Your own Self sheds this dim, misleading glow –
It has no sword, but such an enemy
Will threaten any man's security.
If it's your Self's light which the road reveals,
It's like the scorpion's sting which parsley heals;
Don't be deceived by this false glow, but run
And be an atom since you're not the sun
(Don't grieve because the Way is dark as night,
Or strive to emulate the sun's pure light);

While you are locked within yourself your cares
Are worthless as your worthless cries and prayers.
If you would soar beyond the circling sky,
First free yourself from thoughts of "me" and "I";
If any thought of self-hood stains your mind
An empty void is all the Self will find;
If any taste of self-hood stays with you
Then you are damned whatever you may do.
If self-hood beckons you for but one breath
A rain of arrows will decide your death.
While you exist endure the spirit's pain;
A hundred times bow down, then bow again –
But if you cling to self-hood and its crimes,
Your neck will feel Fate's yoke a hundred times.

How Sheikh Abu Bakr's self-satisfaction was reproved

Sheikh Abu Bakr of Neishapur one day
Led his disciples through a weary way.
His donkey carried him, aloof, apart –
And then the beast let out a monstrous fart!
The sheikh began to tear his clothes and cry
Till one of his disciples asked him why.
The sheikh said: "When I looked I saw a sea
Of my disciples sworn to follow me;
They filled the roads and in my mind there slid
The thought: 'By God, I equal Bayazid!
So many praise me, can I doubt this sign
That heaven's boundless glories will be mine?'
Then as I triumphed in my inmost heart,
My donkey answered me – and with a fart;
My pompous, self-deceiving soul awoke,
And this is why I weep and tear my cloak."
How far away the Truth remains while you
Are lost in praise for all you say and do –
Destroy your arrogance, and feed the fire
With that vain Self you foolishly admire.

You change your face each moment, but deep down
You are a Pharaoh and you wear his crown;
While one small atom of this "you" survives
Hypocrisy enjoys a hundred lives.
If you put all your trust in "I" and "me"
You've chosen both worlds as your enemy –
But if you kill the Self, the darkest night
Will be illuminated with your light.
If you would flee from evil and its pain
Swear never to repeat this "I" again!

The devil's secret

God said to Moses once: "Go out and find
The secret truth that haunts the devil's mind."
When Moses met the devil that same day
He asked for his advice and heard him say:
"Remember this, repeat it constantly,
Don't speak of 'me', or you will be like me."
If life still holds you by a single hair,
The end of all your toil will be despair;
No matter how you prosper, there will rise
Before your face a hundred smirking "I"s.

A saint once said: "The novice ought to see
A door that opens on obscurity –
Then seas of love will inundate his mind,
And he will leave our earthly life behind;
If he sees anything but darkness there,
He is deceived and worships empty air."
Though others see them, you have not the art
To recognize the passions in your heart.
There is a den in you where dragons thrive;
Your folly keeps the prowling beasts alive –
By day and night you watch them sleep and eat
And cosset them, and toss them blood-soaked meat.

From dust and blood your earthly being grew –
Is it not strange that both should be taboo?
That blood, which flows within your every vein,
Is an impurity, an unclean stain?
What you most love defiles, and deep within
The chambers of your heart hide guilt and sin;
If you have seen this filth, why do you sit
Smiling as if you'd never heard of it?

The sheikh and the dog

A dog brushed up against a sheikh, who made
No move to draw his skirts in or evade
The filthy stray – a puzzled passer-by
Who'd noticed his behaviour asked him why.
He said: "The dog is filthy, as you see,
But what is outside him is inside me –
What's clear on him is hidden in my heart;
Why should such close companions stay apart?"
If inward filth is slight or if it's great,
The outcome is the same disgusting state –
If straws impede you, or a mountain-top,
Where is the difference if you have to stop?

The anchorite who loved his beard

In Moses' time there lived an anchorite
Who prayed incessantly by day and night,
And yet derived no pleasure from his quest;
No sun had risen in his troubled breast.
He had a beard, of which he took great care,
Loving to comb it hair by silky hair.
It happened that this pious man one day
Caught sight of Moses walking far away –
He ran to him and cried: "Mount Sinai's lord,
Ask God why he denies me my reward."

lines 2949–2964

When next on Sinai's slopes good Moses trod,
He put this poor man's question to his God,
Who answered: "Tell this would-be saint that he
Pays more attention to his beard than Me."
When Moses told the man of God's reply,
He tore his beard out with a piteous cry –
Then Gabriel appeared to them and said:
"Concern for that grey beard still fills his head;
He loved it then, and now he pulls it out,
His wretched love is even more devout."
Whatever stage you've reached, to spend one breath
Unmindful of your God is worse than death –
And what of you, still wrapped up in your beard,
For whom grief's ocean has not yet appeared?
Forget this beard and you will understand
How you can swim across and gain dry land –
But keep it as you enter that profound
Ungoverned sea, and with it you'll be drowned.

A *drowning fool*

A fool with an enormous beard once fell
Into a violent sea's tumultuous swell.
As he was struggling he heard someone shout:
"That bag tied on your collar – throw it out!"
"It's not a bag, it's my huge beard!" he cried.
"Well, that's just marvellous," the man replied,
"A splendid growth; but now the harvest's come."
Your goatish beards have made you quarrelsome,
Self-willed and vain, the devil's followers,
Strutting like Pharaoh and his ministers.
But beard this Pharaoh, as did Moses once,
And set out on the Way with confidence –
The pilgrim has no time to preen and comb;
Long suffering will attend his journey home.
If bleaching's his profession he'll complain
There is no sun – if crops, there is no rain.

A Sufi washing his clothes

Once, as a Sufi washed his clothes, a cloud
Filled all the heavens like a darkening shroud –
But though the world seemed plunged in deepest night,
The Sufi's clothes shone clean and strangely bright.
He'd been about to find a grocer's stall
To buy some soap – "I don't need soap at all,"
He told himself, and then he said aloud:
"I'll buy some raisins, thanks to you, O cloud –
You do far more than grocer's powders could,
I've washed my hands of earthly soap for good!"'

A bird asks for help and advice

Another bird spoke next: 'Dear hoopoe, say
What will sustain my heart along the Way –
To travel as I should I need your aid;
If you can help me I'll be less afraid –
To make me start this quest, then persevere,
I must be told how I can conquer fear.
I spurn the crowd's advice; I'm quite alone
And haven't any wisdom of my own.'

The hoopoe answers him

The hoopoe said: 'Trust Him, and while you live,
Avoid whoever seems too talkative.
With Him you will rejoice – when He is there
The saddest soul is freed from every care;
There is no sorrow He cannot console –
On Him depends the sky's revolving bowl.

lines 2988–3000

Let His joy teach you yours, as planets move
Within the orbit of sustaining love;
What is His equal? Say that nothing is,
Then happiness is yours, and you are His.

A dervish in ecstasy

A frenzied dervish, mad with love for God,
Sought out bare hills where none had ever trod.
Wild leopards kept this madman company –
His heart was plunged in restless ecstasy;
He lived within this state for twenty days,
Dancing and singing in exultant praise:
"There's no division; we two are alone –
The world is happiness and grief has flown."
Die to yourself – no longer stay apart,
But give to Him who asks for it your heart;
The man whose happiness derives from Him
Escapes existence, and the world grows dim;
Rejoice for ever in the Friend, rejoice
Till you are nothing, but a praising voice.

"For seventy years my happy heart has led
A life of constant bliss," a Sufi said.
"My God has been so good to me that I
Am bound to Him until the day I die."
You seek for faults to censure and suppress
And have no time for inward happiness –
How can you know God's secret majesty
If you look out for sin incessantly?
To share His hidden glory you must learn
That others' errors are not your concern;
When someone else's failings are defined,
What hairs you split – but to your own you're blind!
Grace comes to those, no matter how they've strayed,
Who know their own sin's strength, and are afraid.

A drunkard accuses a drunkard

A sot became extremely drunk – his legs
And head sank listless, weighed by wine's thick
    dregs.
A sober neighbour put him in a sack
And took him homewards hoisted on his back.
Another drunk went stumbling by the first,
Who woke and stuck his head outside and cursed.
"Hey, you, you lousy dipsomaniac,"
He yelled as he was borne off in the sack,
"If you'd had fewer drinks, just two or three,
You would be walking now as well as me."
He saw the other's state but not his own,
And in this blindness he is not alone;
You cannot love, and this is why you seek
To find men vicious, or depraved, or weak –
If you could search for love and persevere
The sins of other men would disappear.

The lover who saw a blemish in his beloved's eye

A lion-hearted hero met defeat –
Five years he loved, and slavery was sweet.
The girl for whom he was content to sigh
Had one small blemish lurking in her eye,
And though, as often as she would permit,
He gazed at her he never noticed it.
(How could a man possessed by frenzy see
This unimportant, faint deformity?)
Then imperceptibly love ceased to reign;
A balm was found to ease his aching pain –
The pretty girl and all her blandishments
Became a matter of indifference;
And now the blemish in her eye was clear –
He asked her: "When did that white speck appear?"

lines 3018–3034

She answered: "As your love began to die,
This speck was brought to being in my eye."
How long will others' faults distract your mind?
Your own accuse you, but your heart is blind.
Your sins are heavy, and while they are there,
Another's guilt is none of your affair.

The drunk and the constable

A man whose job it was to keep the peace
Beat up a drunk, who fought for his release
And cried: "It's you who's tippled too much wine;
Your rowdiness is ten times worse than mine –
Who's causing this disturbance, you or me?
But yours is drunkenness that men can't see;
Leave me alone! Let justice do its worst –
Enforce the law and beat yourself up first!"'

A bird wonders what gift he should ask for from the Simorgh

Another bird said: 'Leader of my soul,
What shall I ask for if I reach our goal?
His light will fill the world, but I'm not sure
What special gift I should be looking for –
I'll ask Him for whatever you suggest.'

The hoopoe answers him

The hoopoe said: 'Poor fool, make one request;
Seek only Him – of all things He is best;
If you're aware of Him, in all the earth
What could you wish for of a greater worth?

Whoever joins Him in that secret place
Is step by step admitted to His grace –
No bribe can turn aside the penitent
Who knows the fragrance of His threshold's scent.

The death of Bu Ali Rudbar

When Bu Ali Rudbar drew near to death,
He said: "Impatience hastens my last breath.
I see the gates of heaven part and rise;
A throne of glory shines before my eyes –
Angelic voices fill the glistening dome;
Like nightingales they call my ardour home.
'Rejoice!' they sing, 'no man has ever known
This radiant splendour which is yours alone.'
Though I believe in this refulgent state,
It's not for this my soul and spirit wait;
They murmur to me: 'What is this to you?
Was it for this you bid the world adieu?'
I cannot share the cravings of that tribe
Who sneak and bow and snatch each petty bribe –
Infuse my soul with Your sustaining love,
And I know neither hell nor heaven above;
I know but You; no faith or blasphemy
Could make me swerve from my fidelity;
I love but You; to You I must resign
My thirsting soul and take Your soul for mine –
Both worlds for me are You; You are my creed;
I recognize no other hope or need;
A hair's breadth lies between us now – remove
This last impediment to perfect love,
And if my wayward soul attempts to stir
Our mingled whispers will admonish her."

lines 3049–3065

God said to David: "Tell My servants prayer
Should be creation's all-consuming care;
Though hell were not his fear nor heaven his goal,
The Lord should wholly occupy man's soul.
But if the sun did not light up the day,
They would not think of Me, nor ever pray –
Their prayers know nothing of love's selfless pain;
Not love inspires them but mere lust for gain.
True prayer seeks God alone; its motives start
Deep in the centre of a contrite heart.
Tell them to turn from all that is not Me;
To worship none but God continuously;
To heap together all the world can show;
To break it piece by piece and blow by blow;
To burn these fragments in one vivid flash,
And scatter on the winds the swirling ash –
When they have done this they will understand
The ash they grasped for with each greedy hand."
If it is paradise for which you pray
You can be sure that you have lost your way.

A story of Mahmud and Ayaz

Shah Mahmud called Ayaz to him and gave
His crown and throne to this bewitching slave,
Then said: "You are the sovereign of these lands;
I place my mighty army in your hands –
I wish for you unrivalled majesty,
That you enslave the very sky and sea."
But when the soldiers heard of this, their eyes
Grew black with envy they could not disguise.
"What emperor in all the world," they said,
"Has heaped such honours on a servile head?"
Though even as they murmured Ayaz wept
That what the king decreed he must accept;
The courtiers said to him: "You are insane
To change from slave to king and then complain!"

But Ayaz answered them: "Oh, rather say
My king desires me to be far away,
To lead the army and be occupied
In almost any place but by his side.
What he commands I'll do, but in my heart
We shall not – for one instant – live apart;
And what have I to do with majesty?
To see my king is realm enough for me."
If you would be a pilgrim of the Truth,
Learn how to worship from this lovely youth.
Day follows night – you argue and protest
And cannot pass the first stage of our quest;
Each night you chatter as the hours pass by
And send Orion down the dawning sky,
And still you linger – though another day
Has broken, you're no further on your way.
From highest heaven they came to welcome you,
And you made lame excuses and withdrew!
Alas! You're not the man for this; your thoughts
See hell's despair and heaven's wondrous courts –
Forget these two, and glory's radiant light
Will stage by stage emerge from darkest night;
The pilgrim does not long for paradise –
Keep back your heart; He only will suffice.

Rabe'eh's prayer

This was the common hymn of Rabe'eh:
"O God, who knows all secrets," she would pray,
"May fortune favour all my enemies,
And may my friends taste heaven's ecstasies;
It is not this world or the next I crave
But, for one moment, to be called Your slave –
With passion I embrace this poverty;
Such endless blessings flow from You to me
If I desire this world or shrink from hell,
I am no better than an infidel."

lines 3086–3107

A man has everything who knows his Lord –
The world and all its seven seas afford.
All that the universe has ever shown
Can find its match but God, who is alone;
And only He, wherever you may seek,
Is absolute, abiding and unique.

God counselled David: "There is nothing here
Of good or bad, unseen or far or near,
Which does not have some cunning complement;
For only I have no equivalent.
I am alone; make Me your single goal –
My presence is sufficient for your soul;
I am your God, your one necessity –
With every breath you breathe remember Me;
Make God your one desire, for only I
Shall live eternally and never die."
And you – obsessed with what the world contains,
Subjected day and night to envy's pains –
Turn now and put our journey to the test;
In this world and the next make Him your quest;
To choose what is not God is to prefer
To be some worthless idol's worshipper,
And if this idol is your soul, your creed
Is nothing more than irreligious greed.

Shah Mahmud at Somnat

When Mahmud's army had attacked Somnat
They found an idol there that men called "Lat".[18]
Its worshippers flung treasure on the ground
And as a ransom gave the glittering mound;
But Mahmud would not cede to their desire
And burned the idol in a raging fire.
A courtier said: "Now if it had been sold
We'd have what's better than an idol – gold!"

Shah Mahmud said: "I feared God's Judgement
    Day;
I was afraid that I should hear Him say:
'Here two – Azar and Mahmud – stand, behold!
One carved his idols, one had idols sold!'"
And as the idol burned, bright jewels fell out –
So Mahmud was enriched but stayed devout;
He said: "This idol Lat has her reward,
And here is mine, provided by the Lord."
Destroy the idols in your heart, or you
Will one day be a broken idol too –
First burn the Self, and as its fate is sealed
The gems this idol hides will be revealed.
Your soul has heard the Lord's commanding call;
Accept, and at His threshold humbly fall.
Your soul and God have formed a covenant;
Do not turn back from that first firm assent –
Will you object to what you once averred,
Swear true allegiance and then break your word?
Your soul needs only Him – through good and ill
Keep faith, and what you promised Him fulfil.

Another story of Shah Mahmud in India

Mahmud began his Indian campaign
And saw before him, drawn up on the plain,
The massive army of his enemy –
In fear he prayed to God for victory
And said: "If I should win this doubtful day,
The dervishes will bear the spoils away."
They fought, and Mahmud's conquest was
    complete –
His captives piled their treasures at his feet.
The king declared: "I will fulfil my vow;
The dervishes shall have this booty now."
But all his courtiers cried: "Can gold and jewels
Be given to that crowd of cringing fools?

lines 3125–3147

Reward the soldiers who have won this war,
Or have it piled up in the royal store."
What should he do? Shah Mahmud was unsure.
Just then his eye caught sight of Bul-Hussein,
A pious fool whom many thought insane;
He said: "Whatever that man says, I'll do –
No kings or armies influence his view."
They called the madman over to the king,
Who welcomed him and told him everything.
The madman said: "O king, these anxious pains
Are not worth more than two small barley grains –
If all your dealings with the Lord cease here,
Forget the vow you made and never fear;
But if you think you might need Him again
Then keep your promise to the final grain.
God gave the victory to you; now where
In this agreement is your lordship's share?"
So Mahmud gave the gold where it was owed,
And took his way along the royal road.'

A bird asks what gifts he should take the Simorgh

Another bird said: 'You have seen our King –
What gifts would it be right for me to bring?
I'll gladly get whatever you advise;
What would be welcome to our Sovereign's eyes?
A king deserves a quite distinctive gift;
Only a miser would be ruled by thrift!'

The hoopoe answers him

'Be ruled by me,' the hoopoe said. 'Take care
To offer something which is lacking there –
Where is the point in dragging all that way
A costly present common there as day?

There mystery resides and confidence,
Pure knowledge and the soul's obedience –
But take the torment of a heart alone,
The soul's distress, for these are there unknown,
And let the anguish you endure arise
Borne upward to the King in bitter sighs;
If one sigh rises from the inmost soul,
That man is saved, and has attained our goal.

Zuleikha has Joseph whipped

Zuleikha used her great authority
To have poor Joseph kept in custody –
She gave her callous orders to the guard:
"Give that man fifty lashes, good and hard!
Deal with this Joseph's body so that I
From far away can hear him groan and sigh."
But when the guard saw Joseph's face he felt
The cold indifference of his calling melt.
There was a leather coat left on the ground,
And with his whip he made this skin resound –
As every blow descended on the coat,
A scream of pain went up from Joseph's throat.
But when Zuleikha heard his voice she cried:
"You are too soft; whip harder, break his pride!"
The guard said: "What, dear Joseph, can I do?
Zuleikha only has to look at you
And see no weals or bruises on your back,
And I'll be torn to pieces on the rack –
So bare your shoulders to the lash; some sign
Must mar your skin if I'm to rescue mine."
When Joseph stripped in readiness, a sound
Of mourning spread from heaven to the ground;
The guard's right arm was raised, and its descent
Produced a cry that split the firmament –

Zuleikha said: "Now Joseph cannot bluff;
This sigh is from his inmost soul – enough!
This sigh was real and from his essence came –
His former groans were nothing but a game."

The mourners at a funeral

A hundred mourners at a funeral grieved;
One truly sighed – the man who was bereaved.
They were a ring, but only one of them
Was set within that circle as a gem –
Till you have truly mourned beside the grave,
You cannot take your place among the brave.
Love drives the wandering pilgrim on his quest;
And where by day or night will he find rest?

The devout slave

A negro had a slave devout and wise
Who at an early hour would wake and rise,
Then pray until the sun came peeping through.
His master said: "Wake me up early too,
And we can pray together till the dawn."
The slave said: "Just before a baby's born,
Who tells the mother: 'Now your time draws near'?
She knows it does – her pain has made it clear;
If you have felt this pain you are awake –
No other man can feel it for your sake.
If someone has to rouse you every day,
Then someone else instead of you should pray."
The man without this pain is not a man;
May grief destroy the bragging charlatan!
But one who is entangled in its spell
Forgets all thoughts of heaven or of hell.

A vision of heaven and hell

Sheikh Bu Ali Tusi's long pilgrimage
(He was the wisest *savant* of his age)
Conducted him so far that I know none
Who could draw near to what this man has done.
He said: "The wretches damned in hell will cry
To those in paradise: 'Oh, testify
To us the nature of your happiness;
Describe the sacred joys which you possess!'
And they will say: 'Ineffable delight
Shines in the radiance of His face; its light
Draws near us, and this vast celestial frame –
The eightfold heaven – darkens, bowed by shame.'
And then the tortured souls in hell will say:
'From joys of paradise you turn away;
Such lowly happiness is not for you –
All that you say is true, we know how true!
In hell's accursèd provinces we reign
Clothed head to foot in fire's devouring pain;
But when we glimpse that radiant face and know
That we must live for ever here below,
Cut off through all eternity from grace –
Such longing seizes us for that far face,
Such unappeasable and wild regret,
That in our anguished torment we forget
The pit of hell and all its raging fire;
For what are flames to comfortless desire?'"
The man who feels such longing takes no part
In public prayers; he prays within his heart.
Regret and sighs should be your portion here;
In sighs rejoice, in longing persevere –
And if beneath the sky's oppressive dome
Wounds scar you, you draw nearer to your home;
Don't flinch from pain or search here for its cure.
Uncauterized your wounds must bleed; endure!

The man who wanted a prayer-mat

Once someone asked the Prophet to provide
A prayer-mat, and the best of men replied:
"The desert's arid sands are burning now.
Pray there; against the hot dust press your brow
And feel it sear your flesh; the wounded skin
Will be an emblem of the wound within."
If no scar marks your heart, the countenance
Of love will pass you by without a glance;
But heart's wounds show that on the battlefield
Your friends have found a man who will not yield.'

A bird asks how long the journey is, and the hoopoe describes the seven valleys of the Way

Another bird said: 'Hoopoe, you can find
The way from here, but we are almost blind –
The path seems full of terrors and despair.
Dear hoopoe, how much further till we're there?'

'Before we reach our goal,' the hoopoe said,
'The journey's seven valleys lie ahead;
How far this is the world has never learned,
For no one who has gone there has returned –
Impatient bird, who would retrace this trail?
There is no messenger to tell the tale,
And they are lost to our concerns below –
How can men tell you what they do not know?
The first stage is the Valley of the Quest;
Then Love's wide valley is our second test;
The third is Insight into Mystery,
The fourth Detachment and Serenity –
The fifth is Unity; the sixth is Awe,
A deep Bewilderment unknown before,

The seventh Poverty and Nothingness,
And there you are suspended, motionless,
Till you are drawn – the impulse is not yours –
A drop absorbed in seas that have no shores.

The Valley of the Quest

When you begin the Valley of the Quest
Misfortunes will deprive you of all rest,
Each moment some new trouble terrifies,
And parrots there are panic-stricken flies.
There years must vanish while you strive and grieve;
There is the heart of all you will achieve –
Renounce the world, your power and all you own,
And in your heart's blood journey on alone.
When once your hands are empty, then your heart
Must purify itself and move apart
From everything that is – when this is done,
The Lord's light blazes brighter than the sun,
Your heart is bathed in splendour and the quest
Expands a thousandfold within your breast.
Though fire flares up across his path, and though
A hundred monsters peer out from its glow,
The pilgrim driven on by his desire
Will like a moth rush gladly on the fire.
When love inspires his heart he begs for wine,
One drop to be vouchsafed him as a sign –
And when he drinks this drop both worlds are gone;
Dry-lipped he founders in oblivion.
His zeal to know faith's mysteries will make
Him fight with dragons for salvation's sake –
Though blasphemy and curses crowd the gate,
Until it opens he will calmly wait,
And then where is this faith, this blasphemy?
Both vanish into strengthless vacancy.

lines 3222–3249

Eblis and God's curse

God breathed the pure soul into Adam's dust,
And as He did so said the angels must,
In sight of Adam, bow down to the ground
(God did not wish this secret to be found).
All bowed, and not one saw what God had done,
Except Eblis, who bowed himself to none.
He said: "Who notices if I don't bow?
I don't care if they cut my head off now;
I know this Adam's more than dust – I'll see
Why God has ordered all this secrecy."
He hid himself and kept watch like a spy.
God said: "Come out – I see you peer and pry;
You know My treasure's home and you must die.
The kings who hide a treasure execute
Their secret's witnesses to keep them mute –
You saw the place, and shall the fact be spread
Through all the world? Prepare to lose your head!"
Eblis replied: "Lord, pity me; I crave
For mercy, Lord; have mercy on Your slave."
God answered him: "Well, I will mitigate
The rigour and the justice of your fate;
But round your neck will shine a ring to show
Your treachery to all the world below –
For fraudulence and guile you will be known
Until the world ends and the last trump's blown."
Eblis replied: "And what is that to me?
I saw the treasure and I now go free!
To curse belongs to You and to forgive,
All creatures of the world and how they live;
Curse on! This poison's part of Your great scheme
And life is more than just an opium-dream.
All creatures seek throughout the universe
What will be mine for ever now – Your curse!"

Search for Him endlessly by day and night,
Till victory rewards your stubborn fight;
And if He seems elusive He is there –
Your search is incomplete; do not despair.

The death of Shebli

As Shebli's death approached his eyes grew dim;
Wild torments of impatience troubled him –
But strangest was that round his waist he tied
A heathen's belt,[19] and weeping sat beside
Heaped ash, with which he smeared his hair and head.
"Why wait for death like this?" a stranger said,
And Shebli cried: "What will become of me?
I melt, I burn with fevered jealousy,
And though I have renounced the universe
I covet what Eblis procured – God's curse."
So Shebli mourned, uncaring if his Lord
Gave other mortals this or that reward;
Bright jewels and stones are equal from His hand,
And if His gems are all that you demand,
Ours is a Way you cannot understand –
Think of the stones and jewels He gives as one;
They are not yours to hope for or to shun.
The stone your angry lover flings may hurt,
But others' jewels compared with it are dirt.
Each moment of this quest a man must feel
His soul is spilled, and unremitting zeal
Should force him onward at whatever cost –
The man who pauses on our path is lost.

Majnun searches for Leili

Once someone saw Majnun, oppressed with pain,
Sifting the dusty highway grain by grain,
And asked: "What are you searching for, my friend?"
He cried: "My search for Leili has no end."
The man protested: "Leili is a girl,
And dust will not conceal this precious pearl!"
Majnun replied: "I search in every place;
Who knows where I may glimpse her lovely face?"
Yusef of Hamadan, a learnèd seer,
Once said: "Above, below, in every sphere,
Each atom is a Jacob fervently
Searching for Joseph through eternity."
By pain and grief the pilgrim is perplexed
But struggles on through this world and the next –
And if the goal seems endlessly concealed,
Do not give up your quest; refuse to yield.
What patience must be theirs who undertake
The pilgrim's journey for salvation's sake!
Now, like a baby curled inside the womb,
Wait patiently within your narrow room;
Ignore the world – blood is your element;
Blood is the unborn child's sole nourishment.[20]
What is the world but wretchedness and fear?
Endure, be steadfast till your time draws near.

Sheikh Mahna and the peasant

In deep despair Sheikh Mahna made his way
Across the empty desert wastes one day.
A peasant with a cow came into sight,
And from his body played a lambent light –
He hailed the man and started to narrate
The hopeless turmoil of his wretched state.

lines 3288–3305

The old man heard, then said: "O Bu Sa'id,
Imagine someone piled up millet seed
From here to highest heaven's unknown climes,
And then repeated this a hundred times;
And now imagine that a bird appears
And pecks one grain up every thousand years,
Then flies around the earth's circumference
A hundred times – from heaven's eminence
In all those years no sign would come to show
Sheikh Bu Sa'id the Truth he longs to know."
Such is the patience that our pilgrims need,
And many start our quest, but few succeed;
Through pain and blood their journey lies – blood hides
The precious musk the hunted deer provides;
And he who does not seek is like a wall,
Dead, blank and bland, no living man at all;
He is, God pardon me, a walking skin,
A picture with no life or soul within.
If you discover in your quest a jewel,
Do not, like some delighted doting fool,
Gloat over it – search on, you're not its slave;
It is not treasures by the way you crave.
To make an idol of the gems you find
Is to be drunk, to cloud the searching mind –
At this first glass your soul should not submit;
Seek out the wine-press of the infinite.

Shah Mahmud and the sweeper

Shah Mahmud rode without a guard one night.
A man who swept the streets came into sight,
Sifting through dust-heaps pile by filthy pile.
The king drew rein and with a gracious smile
Flung down his bracelet on the nearest heap;
Then like the wind he left the searching sweep.
Some later night the king returned and saw
The man engaged exactly as before.

He said: "I threw a bracelet on the ground;
You could redeem the world with what you found!
You could be like a king, a lord of men,
And yet I find you sifting dust again!"
The sweep replied: "The treasure that you gave
Made me a hidden, greater treasure's slave –
I have perceived the door to wealth and I
Shall sift through dust-heaps till the day I die."
Search for the Way! The door stands open, but
Your eyes that should perceive the door are shut!
Once someone cried to God: "Lord, let me see
The door between us opened unto me!"
And Rabe'eh said: "Fool to chatter so –
When has the door been closed, I'd like to know?"

The Valley of Love

Love's valley is the next, and here desire
Will plunge the pilgrim into seas of fire,
Until his very being is enflamed
And those whom fire rejects turn back ashamed.
The lover is a man who flares and burns,
Whose face is fevered, who in frenzy yearns,
Who knows no prudence, who will gladly send
A hundred worlds toward their blazing end,
Who knows of neither faith nor blasphemy,
Who has no time for doubt or certainty,
To whom both good and evil are the same,
And who is neither, but a living flame.
But you! Lukewarm in all you say or do,
Backsliding, weak – oh no, this is not you!
True lovers give up everything they own
To steal one moment with the Friend alone –
They make no vague, procrastinating vow,
But risk their livelihood and risk it now.

Until their hearts are burned, how can they flee
From their desire's incessant misery?
They are the falcon when it flies distressed
In circles, searching for its absent nest –
They are the fish cast up upon the land
That seeks the sea and shudders on the sand.
Love here is fire; its thick smoke clouds the head –
When love has come the intellect has fled;
It cannot tutor love, and all its care
Supplies no remedy for love's despair.
If you could seek the unseen you would find
Love's home, which is not reason or the mind,
And love's intoxication tumbles down
The world's designs for glory and renown –
If you could penetrate their passing show
And see the world's wild atoms, you would know
That reason's eyes will never glimpse one spark
Of shining love to mitigate the dark.
Love leads whoever starts along our Way;
The noblest bow to love and must obey –
But you, unwilling both to love and tread
The pilgrim's path, you might as well be dead!
The lover chafes, impatient to depart,
And longs to sacrifice his life and heart.

A lord who loved a beer-seller

Love led a lord through paths of misery.
He left his splendid house and family
And acted like a drunkard to be near
The boy he loved, who lived by selling beer –
He sold his house and slaves and all he had
To get the means to buy beer from this lad.
When everything was gone and he grew poor
His love grew stronger, more and then yet more –
Though food was given him by passers-by,
His endless hunger made him long to die

lines 3342–3359

(Each morsel that he had would disappear,
Not to be eaten but exchanged for beer,
And he was happy to endure the pain,
Knowing that soon he could buy beer again).
When someone asked: "What is this love?" he cried:
"It is to sell the world and all its pride –
A hundred times – to buy one drop of beer."
Such acts denote true love, and it is clear
That those who cannot match this devotee
Have no acquaintance with love's misery.

Majnun's love for Leili

When Leili's tribe refused Majnun, he found
They would not let him near their camping-ground.
Distraught with love, he met a shepherd there
And asked him for a sheepskin he could wear,
And then, beneath the skin, began to creep
On hands and knees as if he were a sheep.
"Now lead your flock," he cried, "past Leili's tent;
It may be I shall catch her lovely scent
And hidden by this matted fleece receive
From untold misery one hour's reprieve."
And so Majnun, disguised beneath the skin,
Drew near his love unnoticed by her kin –
Joy welled in him and in its wild excess
The frenzied lover lost all consciousness;
Love's fire had dried the fluids of his brain –
He fainted and lay stretched out on the plain;
The shepherd bore him to a shaded place
And splashed cold water on his burning face.
Later, Majnun was talking with some friends
When one said: "What a tattered fleece defends
Your body from the cold; but trust in me
I'll bring you all you need immediately."
Majnun replied: "No garment's worthy of
Dear Leili, but I wear this skin for love –

I know how fortune favours me, and I
Burn rue to turn away the Evil Eye."
The fleece for him was silk and rare brocade;
With what else should a lover be arrayed?
I too have known love scent the passing air –
What other finer garment could I wear?
If you would scour yourself of each defect,
Let passion wean you from the intellect –
To leave such toys and sacrifice the soul
Is still the first small step towards our goal.
Begin, if you can set aside all shame –
To risk your life is not some childish game.

The beggar who fell in love with Ayaz

A beggar fell in love once with Ayaz –
The news soon spread through markets and bazaars,
And when he rode about the gaping town
There was the beggar running up and down;
Or if Ayaz once halted in the square,
His eyes would meet the beggar's hungry stare.
But someone gossiped to Mahmud, who went
To try and apprehend the miscreant –
Ayaz rode out; Mahmud was horrified
To see the beggar running at his side,
And from his hiding-place the monarch saw
The beggar's face, wasted like yellow straw,
His back bent like a polo-mallet's curve –
From side to side he watched him duck and swerve,
As if he had no self-control at all
But moved when hit just like a polo-ball.
He summoned him, then said: "And so you thought
A beggar could be equal to the court?"
The man replied: "In matters of desire,
A beggar is his monarch's equal, sire –
You cannot sunder love from pauper's rags;
They're like a rich man and his money bags –

And poverty in love resembles salt:
It gives love taste; you can't call that a fault!
You have the world and love your sovereignty –
You should leave passion to the likes of me!
Your love is with you; you need never know
The pains of absence love should undergo.
Oh, you are proud to have him, but love's trial
Would come if you should lose him for a while."
The king said: "You are ignorant, that's all –
Staring as if he were a polo-ball!"
"It's me who is the ball," the man replied;
"Look – both of us are struck from side to side;
Each shares the other's pain, each feels the force
Of Ayaz when he rides by on his horse –
We're both bewildered by his mallet's blows,
And where we're going neither of us knows.
But if we share the same predicament
And seem in grief to be equivalent,
Yet still the ball does more than I can do
And sometimes gets to kiss his horse's shoe.
Though both are hurt, mine is the grimmer part –
Its skin is scarred, my scars are in my heart.
Ayaz pursues the ball he hits – but I
In unregarded agony must sigh;
The ball will sometimes land at Ayaz' feet,
But when shall Ayaz and a beggar meet?
The ball will know the scent of victory
But all such joys have been denied to me!"
The king cried: "You may boast that you are poor,
But where's your witness? How can I be sure?"
"I don't belong here, sire," the beggar said,
"But I'm not poor and you have been misled;
You want a witness – if I sacrifice
My living soul for love, will that suffice?
O Mahmud, love like yours is meaningless;
Die if you want to boast of your distress!"
Then, in the silence after he replied,
He sank at his belovèd's feet and died –

And when he saw the lifeless body there
The world was darkened by Mahmud's despair.
Prepare to risk your being while you live,
And know the glory sacrifice will give –
If you are summoned by that distant call,
Pursue the fading sound until you fall;
And as you fall the news you longed to find
Will break at last on your bewildered mind.

The Arab in Persia

Through Persia once an Arab took his way,
Where foreign customs filled him with dismay –
He met a group of dervishes, who had
Renounced the world and seemed to him quite mad
(But don't be fooled – if they seem filthy thieves
They are far purer than the world believes,
And though in drunkenness they seem to sink
The ecstasy they know is not from drink).
The Arab saw these men; without a sound
He fainted and lay stretched out on the ground –
They quickly splashed his face to bring him round
And then cried: "Enter, no-one, enter here!"
And in he went, though torn by doubt and fear.
They made him drunk, he lost himself, and soon
His mind had foundered in a vacant swoon;
His gold, his jewels, his very livelihood
Were stolen there and disappeared for good –
A dervish gave him more to drink, and then
They pushed him naked out of doors again.
Dry-lipped and poor the man was forced to roam,
A naked beggar, till he reached his home,
And there the Arabs said: "But what's gone wrong?
Where is your wealth, where have you been so long?
Your gold and silver's gone, what can you do?
This Persian expedition's ruined you!"

lines 3422–3440

Did thieves attack you? You don't say a word –
You seem so different; tell us what occurred."
He said: "I went as usual – full of pride –
Then saw a dervish by the highway's side.
But then what happened next I can't be sure;
My gold and silver went and now I'm poor!"
They said: "Describe this man who blocked your
      way."
He said: "I have; there's nothing more to say."
His mind was still elsewhere and all he heard
Seemed idle chatter, empty and absurd.
Enter the Way or seek some other goal,
But do so to the utmost of your soul;
Risk all, and as a naked beggar roam
If you would hear that "Enter" call you home.

The lover who wanted to kill his beloved

A selfless youth had lost his heart to one
Whose beauty beggared all comparison,
But then the girl grew sick (as Fate decreed),
As thin and yellow as a rotten reed.
Now death approached – she seemed to waste away;
Dark night descended on the brightest day.
When he was told his love despaired of life,
The youth ran riot, brandishing a knife,
And cried: "If death – which no man can withstand –
Has come, then let her perish by my hand!"
But someone grabbed the wild youth's arm and said:
"What point is murder, fool? Why should you shed
Her blood when in the hour she will be dead?"
"But if I kill her," came the youth's reply,
"The law decrees that I too have to die,
And at the resurrection hell will be
My burning doom through all eternity;
Thus I shall die for her today and light
A candle for her in the future's night –

To die for her is my supreme desire,
To die, and burn for her in endless fire."
True lovers tread this path and turn aside
From this world and the next unsatisfied;
Their souls rise up from death and seek above
The undiscovered, secret home of love.

The death of Abraham

As Abraham approached his life's last breath,
He fought with Azra'el and parried death.
"Go back," he cried, "and tell my King to wait;
The King's friend will arrive a little late."
God answered him: "But if you are My friend,
You are prepared, and glad, to reach life's end."
Then someone said: "What makes your soul rebel
And seek to hide itself from Azra'el?
True-hearted lovers risk their lives; so why
Are you reluctant or afraid to die?"
And he replied: "How can I give my soul
When Azra'el obscures the longed-for goal?
When Gabriel himself appeared in fire
And asked me to describe my heart's desire,
I did not glance at him; the path I trod
Had then as now no other goal but God –
I turned my head aside from Gabriel,
And shall I hand my soul to Azra'el?
I shall not give this soul until I hear
The word of God command me to draw near;
And when I hear His voice this life will be
Less use than half a barley grain to me –
How could I give my soul to anyone
But Him? Enough, my explanation's done!"

The Valley of Insight into Mystery

The next broad valley which the traveller sees
Brings insight into hidden mysteries;
Here every pilgrim takes a different way,
And different spirits different rules obey.
Each soul and body has its level here
And climbs or falls within its proper sphere –
There are so many roads, and each is fit
For that one pilgrim who must follow it.
How could a spider or a tiny ant
Tread the same path as some huge elephant?
Each pilgrim's progress is commensurate
With his specific qualities and state
(No matter how it strives, what gnat could fly
As swiftly as the winds that scour the sky?).
Our pathways differ – no bird ever knows
The secret route by which another goes.
Our insight comes to us by different signs;
One prays in mosques and one in idols' shrines –
But when Truth's sunlight clears the upper air,
Each pilgrim sees that he is welcomed there.
His essence will shine forth; the world that seemed
A furnace will be sweeter than he dreamed.
He will perceive the marrow, not the skin –
The Self will disappear; then, from within
The heart of all he sees, there will ascend
The longed-for face of the immortal Friend.
A hundred thousand secrets will be known
When that unveiled, surpassing face is shown –
A hundred thousand men must faint and fail
Till one shall draw aside the secrets' veil –
Perfected, of rare courage he must be
To dive through that immense, uncharted sea.

If you discern such hidden truths and feel
Joy flood your life, do not relax your zeal;
Though thirst is quenched, though you are bathed in
    bliss
Beyond all possible hypothesis,
Though you should reach the throne of God, implore
Him still unceasingly: "Is there yet more?"
Now let the sea of gnosis drown your mind,
Or dust and death are all that you will find.
If you ignore our quest and idly sleep,
You will not glimpse the Friend; rise now and weep.
And if you cannot find His beauty here,
Seek out Truth's mysteries and persevere!
But shame on you, you fool! Bow down your head;
Accept a donkey's bridle and be led!

The stone man

A man in China has become a stone;
He sits and mourns, and at each muffled groan
Weeps melancholy tears, which then are found
Congealed as pebbles scattered on the ground
(What misery the world would know, what pain,
If clouds should shed such adamantine rain!).
This man is Knowledge (sensible, devout;
If you should go to China seek him out),
But he has turned to stone from secret grief,
From lack of zeal, indifference, unbelief.
The world is dark, and Knowledge is a light,
A sparkling jewel to lead you through the night –
Without it you would wander mystified,
Like Alexander lost without a guide;
But if you trust its light too much, despair
Will be the sequel of pedantic care,
And if you underestimate this jewel
Despair will mark you as a righteous fool

(Ignore or overvalue this bright stone,
And wretchedness will claim you for her own).
If you can step outside the stage we know,
The dark confusions of our life below,
And reach man's proper state, you will possess
Wisdom at which the world can never guess.
The path brings sorrow and bewildered fear,
But venture on until the Way is clear,
And neither sleep by night nor drink by day,
But give your life – completely – to the Way.

The lover who slept

A lover, tired out by the tears he wept,
Lay in exhaustion on the earth and slept;
When his belovèd came and saw him there,
Sunk fast in sleep, at peace, without a care,
She took a pen and in an instant wrote,
Then fastened to his sleeve, a little note.
When he awoke and read her words his pain
(Increased a thousandfold) returned again –
"If you sell silver in the town," he read,
"The market's opened, rouse your sleepy head;
If faith is your concern, pray through the night –
Prostrate yourself until the dawning light;
But if you are a lover, blush with shame;
Sleep is unworthy of the lover's name!
He watches with the wind throughout the day;
He sees the moon rise up and fade away –
But you do neither, though you weep and sigh;
Your love for me looks like an empty lie.
A man who sleeps before death's sleep I call
A lover of himself, and that is all!
You've no idea of love, and may your sleep
Be like your ignorance – prolonged and deep!"

lines 3513–3530

A *watchman in love*

A watchman fell in love – the poor man kept
Love's vigil day and night and never slept.
A friend reproved this lover. "Sleep!" he cried.
"Sleep for one moment!" But the man replied:
"I am a lover and a watchman; how
Could I know sleep and break this double vow?
How can a watchman sleep, especially
A wretched watchman who's in love like me?
My earthly duties and my love unite
To ward off sleep throughout the longest night.
There's no sleep in me – can I ask a friend
For sleep? It's not a substance you can lend!
Each night love puts his watchman to the test,
Watching to see the watchman has no rest,
Beating a drum as if to wake the dead,
Or slapping me about the face and head –
And if I slept a moment, sleepless love
Would raise a tumult to the skies above."
His friend said: "But you never even blink;
All night you burn and cannot sleep a wink!"
He answered him: "A watchman never sleeps;
He knows no water but the tears he weeps –
A watchman's duty is to stay awake,
And lovers parch with thirst for passion's sake;
Since lovers' eyes are filled with flowing tears
Sweet sleep is driven out and disappears –
A lover and a watchman should agree,
Since neither sleeps through all eternity.
Love helps the watchman's vigilance; its pain
Will banish slumber from his fevered brain."
Shun sleep if you would be this sentinel
(Though if your vigil is mere talk, sleep well!).
Pace the heart's streets; thieves lurk in ambush there,
Waiting for you to waver in your care;

But as you scan the darkness you will find
New love and insight wake within your mind;
The man who suffers, who will watch and wait,
Is given insight by his sleepless state,
And sleepless nights enable him to bring
A tried and wakeful heart before his King.
Since sleepless watches nourish vigilance,
Sleep little, guard your heart with diligence –
What shall I say? What words have ever found
A means to save the sinking? You are drowned!
But lovers journey on before us all;
Intoxicated by their love, they fall –
Strive, drink as they have drunk, discover love,
The key to this world and the world above;
A woman will become a man, a man
A sea whose depths no mortal mind may scan.

Abbasseh told a wandering scholar once:
"The man who's kindled by love's radiance
Will give birth to a woman; when love's fire
Quickens within a woman this desire,
She gives birth to a man; is it denied
That Adam bore a woman from his side,
That Mary bore a man? Until this light
Shines out, such truths are hidden from your sight;
But when its glory comes you will receive
Blessings far greater than you can conceive.
Count this as wealth; here is the faith you need.
But if the world's base glory is your creed,
Your soul is lost – seek the wealth insight gives;
In insight our eternal kingdom lives.
Whoever drinks the mystics' wine is king
Of all the world can show, of everything –
Its realms are specks of his authority,
The heavens but a ship on his wide sea;

If all the sultans of the world could know
That shoreless sea, its mighty ebb and flow,
They'd sit and mourn their wretched impotence
With eyes ashamed to meet each other's glance."

Mahmud and a dervish

Once in a ruined palace Mahmud met
A dervish bowed by sorrow and regret,
Who when he saw his noble sovereign cried:
"Get out of here or I shall tan your hide –
You call yourself a king; you're just a lout,
A thankless, selfish infidel – get out!"
The king said: "I am Mahmud; I suggest
That 'infidel' is not how I'm addressed!"
The dervish answered him: "O splendid youth,
If you but knew how far you are from Truth,
You would not smear your humbled head and face
With dust and ash; live coals would take their
    place."

∿

The Valley of Detachment

Next comes the Valley of Detachment; here
All claims, all lust for meaning disappear.
A wintry tempest blows with boisterous haste;
It scours the land and lays the valley waste –
The seven planets seem a fading spark,
The seven seas a pool, and heaven's arc
Is more like dust and death than paradise;
The seven burning hells[21] freeze cold as ice.
More wonderful than this, a tiny ant
Is here far stronger than an elephant;
And, while a raven feeds, a caravan
Of countless souls will perish to a man.

lines 3569–3583

A hundred thousand angels wept when light
Shone out in Adam and dispelled the night;
A hundred thousand drowning creatures died
When Noah's ark rode out the rising tide;
For Abraham, as many gnats were sent
To humble Nimrod's vicious government;
As many children perished by the sword
Till Moses' sight was cleansed before the Lord;
As many walked in wilful heresy
When Jesus saw Truth's hidden mystery;
As many souls endured their wretched fate
Before Mohammad rose to heaven's gate.
Here neither old nor new attempts prevail,
And resolution is of no avail.
If you should see the world consumed in flame,
It is a dream compared to this, a game;
If thousands were to die here, they would be
One drop of dew absorbed within the sea;
A hundred thousand fools would be as one
Brief atom's shadow in the blazing sun;
If all the stars and heavens came to grief,
They'd be the shedding of one withered leaf;
If all the worlds were swept away to hell,
They'd be a crawling ant trapped down a well;
If earth and heaven were to pass away,
One grain of gravel would have gone astray;
If men and fiends were never seen again,
They'd vanish like a tiny splash of rain;
And should they perish, broken by despair,
Think that some beast has lost a single hair;
If part and whole are wrecked and seen no more,
Think that the earth has lost a single straw;
And if the nine revolving heavens stop,
Think that the sea has lost a single drop.

lines 3584–3600

A youth who tumbled into a well

A fine youth living in our village fell
Into a deep and dangerous, dark well –
His fall dislodged the dust; a long time passed
Before they got the young man out at last,
But he had suffered underneath the grime –
It seemed his rescuers were just in time
(Mohammad was the poor boy's name); his breath
Was laboured and he lingered close to death.
His father whimpered: "O my pride and joy,
Mohammad, speak to me, my precious boy."
"Where is Mohammad now?" the youth replied;
"Where is your son? Or anyone?" and died.
Good pilgrim, ask: Where is Mohammad, where?
And where is Adam and his every heir?
Where are the earth, the mountains and the sea?
Where are the angels and humanity?
Where are the bodies buried underground,
Where are their minds so subtle and profound?
Where is the pain of death? Where is the soul?
Where are the sundered parts? Where is the whole?
Sift through the universe, and it will seem
An airy maze, an insubstantial dream.

Yusef of Hamadan, that learnèd seer,
Whose heart and knowledge were uniquely clear,
Said: "Travel to the throne of majesty,
Then to the ends of all the earth, and see
That all that is, will be, has ever been,
Is but one atom when correctly seen."
The world is but a drop – what will be missed
If one son prospers or does not exist?
This valley is not easy, child – your mind
Knows nothing of the dangers you will find,
And when the Way flows blood, your pilgrimage
Has only journeyed through a single stage.

Traverse the world from place to distant place;
What have you managed but a single pace?
No pilgrim sees his journey's end; no cure
Has yet been found for all he must endure.
If you stand petrified with grief and dread,
You are no better than the senseless dead;
And if you hasten on you cannot hear
The bell that summons you sound loud and clear.
Hope lies neither in motion nor in rest;
Neither to live nor yet to die is best.
What profit have your labours brought? What gain
The teachers you pursued with so much pain?
What difference have these constant efforts made?
Be silent now and seek another trade.
Strive not to strive; withdraw and concentrate
On that small region you can cultivate.
The remedy is labour – this is true,
But not that labour which is known to you –
Renounce the work you know, the tasks you've done,
And learn which tasks to work at, which to shun.
What words can guide you where you ought to turn?
It may be you will have the wit to learn;
But whether you lament or idly sing,
Act with detachment now in everything.
Detachment is a flame, a livid flash,
That will reduce a hundred worlds to ash;
Its valley makes creation disappear,
And if the world has gone, then where is fear?

A horoscope drawn on sand

Astrologers can help you understand
With fine configurations traced in sand –
You've seen one draw the heaven's calendar
And indicate each fixed and moving star,
Set out the zodiac sign by mighty sign,
The zenith of the sun and its decline –

The complex forms that influence the earth,
The house of mournful death, the house of birth,
Which will enable him to calculate
Your happiness, your grief, your final fate . . .
Then brush the sand – and all that you have seen
Has gone, as though the marks had never been.
Such is the solid world we live in here,
A subtle surface which will disappear.
You cannot bear this truth, that all must die –
Seek out some corner; watch the world pass by!
When men and women enter here they own
No trace of either world, they are alone.
When mountains weigh as little as a straw
You have the strength required, but not before.

Once someone said: "The veil was drawn aside;
I saw the secret world its shadows hide –
In bliss I heard a voice that seemed to say:
'Name what you wish and it is yours today.'
But then I saw that from eternity
God's prophets have endured adversity,
That, everywhere disaster takes its course,
They are the first to feel its crushing force –
And how can I expect contentment when
Such miseries beset the best of men?
Their glory and their grief could not be mine!
Since pain is theirs who set forth God's design,
How can a wretch desire beatitude?
Oh, leave me to my helpless solitude!
The prophets led the world, but I am weak –
Oh, let me mourn alone, I cannot speak!"
My words must come from my experience,
And till you share it they will make no sense.
You know the dangers that this ocean brings,
But flounder like a partridge without wings –

lines 3639–3656

The whirlpool waits, the monstrous whale, the
    shark,
And are you still determined to embark?
Imagination makes you waver – think,
How will you save yourself if you should sink?

The fly in the beehive

A hungry fly once saw a hive of bees;
Transported by delicious fantasies,
He buzzed: "What noble friend will be my guide?
I'd give a barley grain to get inside –
How marvellous if I could just contrive
To find myself in this delightful hive."
A passer-by took pity on his pain,
Lifted him in and took the barley grain.
But when he reached the honey-store at last,
He found his wings and hairy joints stuck fast –
His sticky, struggling legs began to tire,
Encumbered by the honey's clammy mire.
He cried: "When free I didn't know my luck;
This honey's worse than poison. Help! I'm stuck!
To get into this mess I gave a grain;
I'd offer double to get out again!"
Within this valley no man can be free –
Your life has passed in thoughtless liberty;
But only adults can traverse this waste:
Let childhood go; a new life must be faced!
The valley waits; prepare now to depart;
Relinquish your belovèd, selfish heart –
That pagan idol, that deceptive guide
Which turns detachment harmlessly aside.

A sheikh in love

A dervish sheikh became enamoured of
A girl whose father traded dogs. His love
Was like a surging sea that has no shore –
He slept among the dogs outside their door.
Her mother saw him lying there and said:
"Good sheikh, it seems my daughter's turned your
      head!
Well, if you want her you will have to be
A man who markets dogs, who lives like me.
Take up the dog trade; do it for a year
And then we'll have the wedding, never fear."
This love-lorn sheikh was not a man to shirk –
He tore his dervish cloak and set to work,
Leading the dogs to market every day
Until the promised year had passed away.
He saw a Sufi there who said: "Dear friend,
Whatever led you to this wretched end?
For thirty years you were a man – what fate
Has brought you to this ludicrous, sad state?"
The sheikh replied: "Idiot, no sermons, please –
If you could see into these mysteries,
If God should show these secret truths to you,
You'd do exactly as you see me do.
When God unveils your shame, you'll understand
What kind of dog-leash dangles from your hand!"

How much must I describe this journey's pain?
Who heeds my talk? How long must I explain?
What is the point of all these words I say?
Not one of you has set out on the Way,
And till you set out you cannot perceive
The truth of all I urge you to believe –
Who shares the patient vigil that I keep?
What good's a leader? You are all asleep!

                                          lines 3674–3690

The pupil who asked for advice

There was a pupil once who begged his sheikh:
"Give me some good advice, for pity's sake!"
The sheikh cried: "Leave me – go on, get away,
And if you itch for what I've got to say,
First wash your face – musk can't drive out a stink;
Words are no good to someone sick with drink!"

~

The Valley of Unity

Next comes the Valley of pure Unity,
A place of lonely, long austerity,
And all who enter on this waste have found
Their various necks by one tight collar bound –
If you see many here or but a few,
They're one, however they appear to you.
The many here are merged in one; one form
Involves the multifarious, thick swarm
(This is the oneness of diversity,
Not oneness locked in singularity);
Unit and number here have passed away;
Forget For-ever and creation's day –
That day is gone; eternity is gone;
Let them depart into oblivion.

The world compared to a wax toy

Once someone asked a dervish to portray
The nature of this world in which we stray.
He said: "This various world is like a toy –
A coloured palm-tree given to a boy,
But made of wax – now knead it in your fist,
And there's the wax of which its shapes consist;

The lovely forms and colours are undone,
And what seemed many things is only one.
All things are one – there isn't any two;
It isn't me who speaks; it isn't you."

Bu Ali and the old woman

An ancient crone once went to Bu Ali
And said: "This gold-leaf is a gift from me."
The sheikh replied: "Since first this Way I trod,
I've taken gifts from no one except God."
The woman laughed: "Well said, and no mistake!
How many can you see, O reverend sheikh?
The man who treads the Way sees one alone
And counts a temple as the ka'aba's stone."
Listen! Attend to all He has to say,
For His existence cannot pass away;
The pilgrim sees no form but His and knows
That He subsists beneath all passing shows –
The pilgrim comes from Him whom he can see,
Lives in Him, with Him, and beyond all three.
Be lost in Unity's inclusive span,
Or you are human but not yet a man.
Whoever lives, the wicked and the blessed,
Contains a hidden sun within his breast –
Its light must dawn though dogged by long delay;
The clouds that veil it must be torn away –
Whoever reaches to his hidden sun
Surpasses good and bad and knows the One.
This good and bad are here while you are here;
Surpass yourself and they will disappear.
You come from nothing but lie caught within
The cumbersome entanglements of sin –
Would that your first blank state were with you yet,
Before existence trapped you in its net.
First free yourself from sin's adhesive loam,
Then be dispersed in dust and wind-swept foam.

lines 3705–3723

How could you guess what ills within you lurk,
The foulness of their haunts, the dripping murk,
Where snake and scorpion slither through the deep,
Then undiscovered lose themselves in sleep?
Wake them, encourage them, and they will swell
Into a hundred monsters loosed from hell.
All men contain this evil in their hearts,
And hell is yours till every snake departs –
Work free of each insinuating coil;
Your soul's salvation will reward your toil.
If not, you are the hidden scorpion's prey,
The quick snake's quarry till God's Judgement Day;
And those who will not seek this freedom crawl
Like worms who have no higher life at all . . .'
(Attar! Enough of all this oratory;
Resume your tale, you'd got to 'Unity'.)
'When once the pilgrim has attained this stage,
He will have passed beyond mere pilgrimage;
He will be lost and dumb – for God will speak,
The God whom all these wandering pilgrims seek –
Beyond all notions of the part, the Whole,
Of qualities and the essential soul.
All four of them will rise up from all four;
A hundred thousand states will rise and more.
In this strange school the inward eye detects
A hundred thousand yearning intellects,
But failure dogs the analytic mind,
Which whimpers like a child born deaf and blind.
To glimpse this secret is to turn aside
From both worlds, from all egocentric pride –
The pilgrim has no being, yet will be
A part of Being for eternity.

A slave's freedom

Loghman of Sarrakhs cried: "Dear God, behold
Your faithful servant, poor, bewildered, old –
An old slave is permitted to go free;
I've spent my life in patient loyalty,
I'm bent with grief, my black hair's turned to snow;
Grant manumission, Lord, and let me go."
A voice replied: "When you have gained release
From mind and thought, your slavery will cease;
You will be free when these two disappear."
He said: "Lord, it is You whom I revere;
What are the mind and all its ways to me?"
And left them there and then – in ecstasy
He danced and clapped his hands and boldly cried:
"Who am I now? The slave I was has died;
What's freedom, servitude, and where are they?
Both happiness and grief have fled away;
I neither own nor lack all qualities;
My blindness looks on secret mysteries –
I know not whether You are I, I You;
I lose myself in You; there is no two."

The lover who saved his beloved from drowning

A girl fell in a river – in a flash
Her lover dived in with a mighty splash,
And fought the current till he reached her side.
When they were safe again, the poor girl cried:
"By chance I tumbled in, but why should you
Come after me and hazard your life too?"
He said: "I dived because the difference
Of 'I' and 'you' to lovers makes no sense –
A long time passed when we were separate,
But now that we have reached this single state

When you are me and I am wholly you,
What use is it to talk of us as two?"
All talk of two implies plurality –
When two has gone there will be Unity.

Mahmud offers Ayaz the command of his armies

One day Mahmud's unconquered armies made
A splendid pageant drawn up on parade;
And on a mountain-side to watch the show
Of elephants and soldiers spread below,
The king and his two favourite courtiers stood,
Hasan, the slave Ayaz and Shah Mahmud.
The serried soldiers, jostling elephants,
Seemed like a plague of locusts or of ants;
More armies at that moment filled the plain
Than all the world has seen or will again,
And Mahmud said: "Ayaz, my child, look down –
All this is yours, dear boy; accept the crown."
The great king spoke – Ayaz seemed quite unmoved,
Lost in his private thoughts; Hasan reproved
The youth and said: "Where are your manners, slave?
Think of the honour that our king just gave!
And yet you stand there like an imbecile,
And do not even murmur thanks or kneel –
How can you justify such gross neglect?
Is this the way you show your king respect?"
Ayaz was silent till this sermon's end,
Then said: "Two answers come to me, my friend.
First then, a slave could grovel on the ground
Or gabble thanks and have the heavens resound
With some self-advertising, long address –
And climb above the king or say far less;
But who am I to interpose my voice
Between the king and his asserted choice?
The slave is his, and regal dignity
Demands that he decide and act, not me.

If in his praise I see both worlds unite,
It is no more than such a monarch's right;
Can I – unworthy to be called his slave –
Comment on how he chooses to behave?"
And when Hasan had heard him speak he said:
"Ayaz, a thousand blessings on your head;
Your words convince me and I now believe
That you deserve the favours you receive –
But what's the second of your answers, pray?"
Ayaz replied: "Hasan, I cannot say
While you are here – you do not share the throne.
This mystery is for the king alone."
The king dismissed Hasan. "There's no one here,"
He said; "now make your hidden secret clear."
Ayaz replied: "When generosity
Persuades my sovereign lord to glance at me,
My being vanishes in that bright light
Which radiates from his refulgent sight;
His splendour shines, and purified I rise,
Dispersed to nothing by his sun-like eyes.
Existence has deserted me, so how
Could I prostrate myself before you now?
If you see anyone or anything,
It is not me you see – it is the king!
The honours you continually renew
Are offered, given and received by you;
And from a shadow lost within the sun
What kind of service could you hope for? None!
That shadow called Ayaz must disappear –
Do what you wish; you know he is not here."

The Valley of Bewilderment

Next comes the Valley of Bewilderment,
A place of pain and gnawing discontent –
Each second you will sigh, and every breath
Will be a sword to make you long for death;
Blinded by grief, you will not recognize
The days and nights that pass before your eyes.
Blood drips from every hair and writes "Alas"
Beside the highway where the pilgrims pass;
In ice you fry, in fire you freeze – the Way
Is lost, with indecisive steps you stray –
The Unity you knew has gone; your soul
Is scattered and knows nothing of the Whole.
If someone asks: "What is your present state;
Is drunkenness or sober sense your fate,
And do you flourish now or fade away?"
The pilgrim will confess: "I cannot say;
I have no certain knowledge any more;
I doubt my doubt, doubt itself is unsure;
I love, but who is it for whom I sigh?
Not Muslim, yet not heathen; who am I?
My heart is empty, yet with love is full;
My own love is to me incredible."

The story of the princess who loved a slave

A great king had a daughter whose fair face
Was like the full moon in its radiant grace,
She seemed a Joseph, and her dimpled chin
The well that lovely youth was hidden in –
Her face was like a paradise; her hair
Reduced a hundred hearts to love's despair;

Her eyebrows were two bows bent back to shoot
The arrows of love's passionate dispute;
The pointed lashes of her humid eyes
Were thorns strewn in the pathway of the wise;
The beauty of this sun deceived the train
Of stars attendant on the moon's pale reign;
The rubies of her mouth were like a spell
To fascinate the angel Gabriel –
Beside her smile, her sweet, reviving breath,
The waters of eternal life seemed death;
Whoever saw her chin was lost and fell
Lamenting into love's unfathomed well;
And those she glanced at sank without a sound –
What rope could reach the depths in which they
    drowned?
It happened that a handsome slave was brought
To join the retinue that served at court,
A slave, but what a slave! Compared with him
The sun and moon looked overcast and dim.
He was uniquely beautiful – and when
He left the palace, women, children, men
Would crowd into the streets and market-place,
A hundred thousand wild to see his face.
One day the princess, by some fateful chance,
Caught sight of this surpassing elegance,
And as she glimpsed his face she felt her heart,
Her intellect, her self-control depart –
Now reason fled and love usurped its reign;
Her sweet soul trembled in love's bitter pain.
For days she meditated, struggled, strove,
But bowed at last before the force of love
And gave herself to longing, to the fire
Of passionate, insatiable desire.

Attendant on the daughter of the king
Were ten musicians, slave girls who could sing
Like nightingales – whose captivating charms
Would rival David's when he sang the psalms.

The princess set aside her noble name
And whispered to these girls her secret shame
(When love has first appeared who can expect
The frenzied lover to be circumspect?),
Then said: "If I am honest with this slave
And tell my love, who knows how he'll behave?
My honour's lost if he should once discover
His princess wishes that she were his lover!
But if I can't make my affection plain
I'll die, I'll waste away in secret pain;
I've read a hundred books on chastity
And still I burn – what good are they to me?
No, I must have him; this seductive youth
Must sleep with me and never know the truth –
If I can secretly achieve my goal
Love's bliss will satisfy my thirsting soul."
Her girls said: "Don't despair; tonight we'll bring
Your lover here and he won't know a thing."
One of them went to him – she simpered, smiled,
And, oh, how easily he was beguiled!
He took the drugged wine she'd prepared – he drank,
Then swooned – unconscious in her arms he sank,
And in that instant all her work was done;
He slept until the setting of the sun.
Night came and all was quiet as the grave;
Now, stealthily, the maidens brought this slave,
Wrapped in a blanket, to their mistress' bed
And laid him down with jewels about his head.
Midnight: he opened his dazed, lovely eyes
And stared about him with a mute surprise –
The bed was massy gold; the chamber seemed
An earthly paradise that he had dreamed;
Two candles made of ambergris burned there
And with their fainting fragrance filled the air;
The slave girls made such music that his soul
Seemed beckoned onward to some distant goal;
Wine passed from hand to hand; the candles' light
Flared like a sun to drive away the night.

But all the joys of this celestial place
Could not compare with her bewitching face,
At which he stared as if struck senseless, dumb,
Lost both to this world and the world to come –
His heart acknowledged love's supremacy;
His soul submitted to love's ecstasy;
His eyes were fixed on hers, while to his ears
The girls' song seemed the music of the spheres;
He smelt the burning candles' ambergris;
His mouth burned with the wine, then with her kiss;
He could not look away, he could not speak,
But tears of eloquence coursed down his cheek –
And she too wept, so that each kiss was graced
With salty sweetness mingled in one taste,
Or he would push aside her stubborn hair
And on her lovely eyes in wonder stare.
Thus, in each other's arms, they passed the night
Until, worn out by sensual delight,
By passion, by the vigil they had kept,
As dawn's cool breeze awoke, the young man slept.

Then, as he slept, they carried him once more
And laid him gently on his own hard floor.
He woke, he slowly knew himself again –
Astonishment, regret, grief's aching pain
Swept over him (though what could grief achieve?
The scene had fled and it was vain to grieve).
He bared his body, ripped his tattered shirt,
Tore out his hair, besmeared his head with dirt –
And when his friends asked what assailed his heart,
He cried: "How can I say? Where could I start?
No dreamer, no, no seer could ever see
What I saw in that drunken ecstasy;
No one in all the world has ever known
The bliss vouchsafed to me, to me alone –
I cannot tell you what I saw; I saw
A stranger sight than any seen before."

They said: "Try to remember what you've done,
And of a hundred joys describe just one."
He answered: "Was it me who saw that face?
Or did some other stand there in my place?
I neither saw nor heard a thing, and yet
I saw and heard what no man could forget."
A fool suggested: "It's some dream you had;
Some sleepy fantasy has sent you mad."
He asked: "Was it a dream, or was it true?
Was I drunk or sober? I wish I knew –
The world has never known a state like this,
This paradox beyond analysis,
Which haunts my soul with what I cannot find,
Which makes me speechless speak and seeing blind.
I saw perfection's image, beauty's queen,
A vision that no man has ever seen
(What is the sun before that face? God knows
It is a mote, a speck that comes and goes!).
But did I see her? What more can I say?
Between this 'yes' and 'no' I've lost my way!"

The grieving mother and the Sufi

Beside her daughter's grave a mother grieved.
A Sufi said: "This woman has perceived
The nature of her loss; her heart knows why
She comes to mourn, for whom she has to cry –
She grieves, but knowledge makes her fortunate:
Consider now the Sufi's wretched state!
What daily, nightly vigils I must keep
And never know for whom it is I weep;
I mourn in lonely darkness, unaware
Whose absence is the cause of my despair.
Since she knows what has caused her agony,
She is a thousand times more blessed than me –
I have no notion of what makes me weep,
What prompts the painful vigils I must keep.

My heart is lost, and here I cannot find
That rope by which men live, the rational mind –
The key to thought is lost; to reach this far
Means to despair of who and what you are.
And yet it is to see within the soul –
And at a stroke – the meaning of the Whole."

The man who had lost his key

A Sufi heard a cry: "I've lost my key;
If it's been found, please give it back to me –
My door's locked fast; I wish to God I knew
How I could get back in. What can I do?"
The Sufi said: "And why should you complain?
You know where this door is; if you remain
Outside it – even if it is shut fast –
Someone no doubt will open it at last.
You make this fuss for nothing; how much more
Should I complain, who've lost both key and door!"
But if this Sufi presses on, he'll find
The closed or open door which haunts his mind.
Men cannot understand the Sufis' state,
That deep Bewilderment which is their fate.
To those who ask: "What can I do?" reply:
"Bid all that you have done till now goodbye!"
Once in the Valley of Bewilderment
The pilgrim suffers endless discontent,
Crying: "How long must I endure delay,
Uncertainty? When shall I see the Way?
When shall I know? Oh, when?" But knowledge here
Is turned again to indecisive fear;
Complaints become a grateful eulogy
And blasphemy is faith, faith blasphemy.

lines 3903–3920

The old age of Sheikh Nasrabad

Sheikh Nasrabad made Mecca's pilgrimage
Twice twenty times, yet this could not assuage
His yearning heart. This white-haired sheikh became
A pilgrim of the pagans' sacred flame,
A naked beggar in whose heart their fire
Was mirrored by the blaze of his desire.
A passer-by said: "Shame on you, O sheikh,
Shame on these wretched orisons you make;
Have you performed the Muslims' pilgrimage
To be an infidel in your old age?
This is mere childishness; such blasphemy
Can only bring the Sufis infamy.
What sheikh has followed this perverted way?
What is this pagan fire to which you pray?"
The sheikh said: "I have suffered from this flame,
Which burned my clothes, my house, my noble name,
The harvest of my life, all that I knew,
My learning, wisdom, reputation too –
And what is left to me? Bewilderment,
The knowledge of my burning discontent;
All thoughts of reputation soon depart
When such fierce conflagrations fire the heart.
In my despair I turn with equal hate
Both from the ka'aba and this temple's gate –
If this Bewilderment should come to you
Then you will grieve, as I am forced to do."

A novice sees his dead master

A novice in whose heart the faith shone bright
Met with his teacher in a dream one night
And said: "I tremble in bewildered fear;
How is it, master, that I see you here?

My heart became a candle when you went,
A flame that flickers with astonishment;
I seek Truth's secrets like a searching slave –
Explain to me your state beyond the grave!"
His teacher said: "I cannot understand –
Amazed, I gnaw the knuckles of my hand.
You say that you're bewildered – in this pit
Bewilderment seems endless, infinite!
A hundred mountains would be less to me
Than one brief speck of such uncertainty!"

The Valley of Poverty and Nothingness

Next comes that valley words cannot express,
The Vale of Poverty and Nothingness:
Here you are lame and deaf, the mind has gone;
You enter an obscure oblivion.
When sunlight penetrates the atmosphere
A hundred thousand shadows disappear,
And when the sea arises what can save
The patterns on the surface of each wave?
The two worlds are those patterns, and in vain
Men tell themselves what passes will remain.
Whoever sinks within this sea is blessed
And in self-loss obtains eternal rest;
The heart that would be lost in this wide sea
Disperses in profound tranquillity,
And if it should emerge again it knows
The secret ways in which the world arose.
The pilgrim who has grown wise in the Quest,
The Sufi who has weathered every test,
Are lost when they approach this painful place,
And other men leave not a single trace;
Because all disappear, you might believe
That all are equal (just as you perceive

That twigs and incense offered to a flame
Both turn to powdered ash and look the same).
But though they seem to share a common state,
Their inward essences are separate,
And evil souls sunk in this mighty sea
Retain unchanged their base identity;
But if a pure soul sinks, the waves surround
His fading form, in beauty he is drowned –
He is not, yet he is; what could this mean?
It is a state the mind has never seen.

One night that sea of secrets, that loved seer
Of Tus, said to a pupil standing near:
"When you are worn out by love's fierce despair
And in your weakness tremble like a hair,
You will become that hair and take your place
In curls that cluster round the loved one's face –
Whoever wastes away for love is made
A hair concealed within those tresses' shade –
But if you will not waste away, your soul
Has made the seven gates of hell its goal."

A frenzied lover wept; a passer-by
Inquired the cause, and this was his reply:
"They say that when at last the Lord appears,
He will receive, for forty thousand years,
The men who are deserving in this place;
Then from that summit of celestial grace
They will return and know themselves once more
Bereft of light, the poorest of the poor.
I will be shown myself – I weep to think
That from such heights to such depths I must sink;
I have no need of my identity –
I long for death; what use is 'I' to me?"
I live with evil while my Self is here;
With God both Self and evil disappear.
When I escape the Self I will arise
And be as God; the yearning pilgrim flies

From this dark province of mortality
To Nothingness and to eternity.
And though, my heart, you bid the world farewell
To cross the bridge that arches over hell,
Do not despair – think of the oil-lamp's glow
That sends up smoke as black as any crow;
Its oil is changed and what was there before
The shining flame flared up exists no more.
So you, my quaking heart, when you endure
These threatening flames, will rise up rare and pure."

First put aside the Self, and then prepare
To mount Boraq[22] and journey through the air;
Drink down the cup of Nothingness; put on
The cloak that signifies oblivion –
Your stirrup is the void; absence must be
The horse that bears you into vacancy.
Destroy the body and adorn your sight
With kohl of insubstantial, darkest night.
First lose yourself, then lose this loss and then
Withdraw from all that you have lost again –
Go peacefully, and stage by stage progress
Until you gain the realms of Nothingness;
But if you cling to any worldly trace,
No news will reach you from that promised place.

The moths and the flame

Moths gathered in a fluttering throng one night
To learn the truth about the candle's light,
And they decided one of them should go
To gather news of the elusive glow.
One flew till in the distance he discerned
A palace window where a candle burned –
And went no nearer; back again he flew
To tell the others what he thought he knew.

lines 3972–3990

The mentor of the moths dismissed his claim,
Remarking: "He knows nothing of the flame."
A moth more eager than the one before
Set out and passed beyond the palace door.
He hovered in the aura of the fire,
A trembling blur of timorous desire,
Then headed back to say how far he'd been,
And how much he had undergone and seen.
The mentor said: "You do not bear the signs
Of one who's fathomed how the candle shines."
Another moth flew out – his dizzy flight
Turned to an ardent wooing of the light;
He dipped and soared, and in his frenzied trance
Both Self and fire were mingled by his dance –
The flame engulfed his wing-tips, body, head;
His being glowed a fierce translucent red;
And when the mentor saw that sudden blaze,
The moth's form lost within the glowing rays,
He said: "He knows, he knows the truth we seek,
That hidden truth of which we cannot speak."
To go beyond all knowledge is to find
That comprehension which eludes the mind,
And you can never gain the longed-for goal
Until you first outsoar both flesh and soul;
But should one part remain, a single hair
Will drag you back and plunge you in despair –
No creature's Self can be admitted here,
Where all identity must disappear.

The Sufi who thought he had left the world

A Sufi once, with nothing on his mind,
Was – without warning – struck at from behind.
He turned and murmured, choking back the tears:
"The man you hit's been dead for thirty years;
He's left this world!" The man who'd struck him said:
"You talk a lot for someone who is dead!

But talk's not action – while you boast, you stray
Further and further from the secret Way,
And while a hair of you remains, your heart
And Truth are still a hundred worlds apart."
Burn all you have, all that you thought and knew
(Even your shroud must go; let that burn too),
Then leap into the flames, and as you burn
Your pride will falter, you'll begin to learn.
But keep one needle back and you will meet
A hundred thieves who force you to retreat
(Think of that tiny needle which became
The negligible cause of Jesus' shame).[23]
As you approach this stage's final veil,
Kingdoms and wealth, substance and water fail;
Withdraw into yourself, and one by one
Give up the things you own – when this is done,
Be still in selflessness and pass beyond
All thoughts of good and evil; break this bond,
And as it shatters you are worthy of
Oblivion, the Nothingness of love.

The dervish who loved a prince

A great king had a son whose slender grace
Recalled the comely Joseph's form and face –
He had no rival; none could emulate
This prince's dignified and splendid state.
Lords were his slaves; beauty bowed in defeat;
The loveliest were dust beneath his feet,
And if he walked the desert's wastes at night
It seemed a second sun diffused its light.
That he eclipsed the moon's magnificence
Is scant praise for his lovely countenance;
The darkness of his curls was like a well
In which a hundred thousand lovers fell;
The beauty of that hair was like a fire –
A flame that tantalized the world's desire

(But fifty years and more could not suffice
To paint the tumbling curls of paradise).
A glance from those narcissus eyes was like
The searing fire when bolts of lightning strike.
His laugh was honey and his smile could bring
A hundred thousand blossoms news of spring –
But of his wondrous mouth I cannot speak:
There self-hood vanishes; I am too weak.
When he appeared it seemed that every hair
Reduced a hundred hearts to love's despair –
He was far lovelier than words convey;
The world adored him, what more can I say?
When he rode out toward the market-place,
A naked sword was held before his face;
Another followed him; and those who tried
To stand and stare were quickly pushed aside.

There was a dervish, a poor simpleton,
Who fell in love with this great monarch's son –
Too weak to chatter, he would sit and sigh,
Beyond all help and hope, prepared to die.
He sat outside the palace night and day,
But closed his eyes to all who passed that way;
He had no friend, no comrade who could share
Love's pain, or sympathize with his despair.
His heart was broken; tears of silver rolled
Down sunken cheeks that looked like sallow gold;
And what kept him alive? At times he'd see
The prince ride by in distant majesty.
Then crowds of people ran from near and far
To gather in the noisy, packed bazaar –
They pushed and shoved; shouts filled the atmos-
     phere,
You'd think that resurrection day was here;
Distracted heralds tried to clear the way,
Raging at stragglers who would not obey –
The ushers yelled, then called the army in,
To clear a mile or so and quell the din.

lines 4028–4046

And when our dervish heard the heralds' sound,
He fainted and lay stretched out on the ground;
It seemed he left himself, and ecstasy
Was strangely mingled with his misery
(Though no one noticed him, there should have been
A hundred thousand mourners at the scene).
His body would turn blue, or to his eyes
Great gouts of blood instead of tears would rise;
His tears would freeze with grief, and then desire
Would make them scald his face like liquid fire.
But how could such a wretch (who begged for bread,
A skinny wraith half living and half dead,
A man with half a shadow, which the sun
Appeared determined to reduce to none)
Expect to be befriended by a prince
Whose like has not been seen before or since?

It happened that one day the prince rode out.
The beggar sent up an ecstatic shout:
"Love's conflagration fills my heart and head;
All patience, reason, strength have turned and fled!"
He raved and ranted, and at every groan
Dashed his bewildered head against a stone,
Until unconsciousness had quenched his sighs
And thick blood spurted from his ears and eyes.
A herald of the prince saw everything,
And hurried to denounce him to the king.
"My lord," he panted, "something must be done;
A filthy libertine adores your son!"
The monarch felt his honour was at stake,
And for his injured reputation's sake
Cried: "Chain his feet and drag him through the
         town,
Then from the gibbet hang him upside-down."
The royal guards set off at once and made
A ring around the hapless renegade –
They dragged him to the public gibbet, where
A huge, blood-thirsty mob had filled the square,

And no one knew his pain, or thought to plead
On his behalf, or tried to intercede.
A courtier brought him to the gallows tree,
Where he screamed out in mortal agony:
"Grant me the time to worship God before
The gallows claims me; let me pray once more."
The angry courtier signalled his assent
And gave him time to make his testament.
But halfway through his prayers he groaned: "Oh, why
Should kings decree that guiltless men must die?
Before I'm murdered in this wretched place,
Lord, let me see that boy's seductive face,
And when he stands here I will gladly give
My soul for him and have no wish to live.
I'd give a hundred thousand lives to see
That princely pattern of nobility;
O God, this is your servant's last request –
I love, and those who die for love die blessed,
And though for him I bid the world farewell,
Love cannot make love's slave an infidel.
How many countless prayers you grant, dear Lord –
Grant mine; grant my life's vigil its reward!"

This arrow reached its mark; the courtier felt
His adamantine heart begin to melt –
He hurried to the king and there made plain
The secret causes of this Sufi's pain;
Weeping, he told how halfway through his prayer
The Sufi had succumbed to love's despair.
The monarch's anger passed, and clemency
Made him revoke his former harsh decree.
He turned then to his son and gently said:
"Do not distress this wretch who hangs half dead
Beneath the gibbet's arm – go to him now,
And speak to him as only you know how.
His heart is in your hands; use all your art
To comfort him and give him back his heart.

lines 4066–4084

You were the poisoned draught that seared his throat;
Drink with him now, be poison's antidote!
Let happiness replace his misery;
Renew his life, then bring him here to me."
Oh, clap your hands, dance, stamp your nimble feet,
Rejoice, prosperity is now complete!
This prince sought out a beggar; this bright sun
Sought out the unregarded simpleton;
This ocean of rich treasures did not stop
Until he had united with a drop!
The prince sped like an angel through the town
And saw the beggar hanging upside-down –
The body shuddered, swayed and fought for breath,
Clinging half conscious at the edge of death.
Beneath the gallows tree his tears and blood
Had clogged the swirling dust to viscid mud,
And seeing him the prince's noble eyes
Flooded with tears that he could not disguise.
He wished to hide them from his army's sight,
But tears in princes are a sign of might.
They flowed like rain and in that moment he
Increased a hundred times his sovereignty.
Endure in love, be steadfast and sincere –
At last the one you long for will appear;
Act as this beggar did, lament and sigh
Until the glorious prince gives his reply.
He saw the prince approach from far away
But could not catch the words he tried to say;
He twisted, struggled, raised his face and there
The prince's weeping eyes returned his stare.
He trembled, weak as water with desire;
He shuddered, burned by love's consuming fire,
And with his last laborious, hoarse breath
Gasped: "Prince, you see me at the point of death –
Your words can kill me now; you did not need
Guards and a gibbet to perform this deed."
Then as a dying candle flares he cried
The last exultant laugh of death and died;

Made one with his belovèd he became
The Nothingness of an extinguished flame.
True pilgrims fathom, even as they fight,
The passion of annihilation's night –
Your Being here is mixed with Nothingness,
And no joy comes to you without distress;
If you cannot endure, how will you find
The promised peace that haunts your troubled mind?

You leapt like lightning once, yet now you stand
Like marshy water clogged with desert sand –
Renew your courage, put aside your fear
And in love's fire let reason disappear.
To be unsure, to pine for liberty,
Is to resist our journey's alchemy.
How long will caution make you hesitate?
Fly beyond thought before it is too late!
To reach that place where true delight is won,
Accept the dervish path as I have done –
I speak of "I"; in truth there is no "I"
Where logic falters and the mind must die.
I lose myself within myself; I seek
For strength in being poor, despised and weak.
When poverty's bright sun shines over me,
A window opens on reality;
I see both worlds and in that light I seem
Like water lost in water's moving stream.
All that I ever lost or ever found
Is in the depths of that black deluge drowned.
I too am lost; I leave no trace, no mark;
I am a shadow cast upon the dark,
A drop sunk in the sea, and it is vain
To search the sea for that one drop again.
This Nothingness is not for everyone,
Yet many seek it out as I have done;
And who would reach this far and not aspire
To Nothingness, the pilgrim's last desire?

lines 4108–4125

Nuri was questioned by one pure in soul:
"How far is it until we reach our goal?"
And said: "We pass through fire and splendour first;
Then seven oceans have to be traversed.
A fish[24] (now listen carefully to me,
And I will show you how to cross this sea)
Will draw you by its breath – a mighty whale,
Vast but invisible from head to tail,
Who deep in solitude delights to swim
And by his breathing draws the world to him."'

The journey

The hoopoe paused, and when the group had heard
His discourse, trembling fear filled every bird.
They saw the bow of this great enterprise
Could not be drawn by weakness, sloth or lies,
And some were so cast down that then and there
They turned aside and perished in despair.
With fear and apprehension in each heart,
The remnant rose up ready to depart.
They travelled on for years; a lifetime passed
Before the longed-for goal was reached at last.
What happened as they flew I cannot say,
But if you journey on that narrow Way,
Then you will act as they once did and know
The miseries they had to undergo.
Of all the army that set out, how few
Survived the Way; of that great retinue
A handful lived until the voyage was done –
Of every thousand there remained but one.
Of many who set out no trace was found.
Some deep within the ocean's depths were drowned;
Some died on mountain-tops; some died of heat;
Some flew too near the sun in their conceit,

Their hearts on fire with love – too late they learned
Their folly when their wings and feathers burned;
Some met their death between the lion's claws,
And some were ripped to death by monsters' jaws;
Some died of thirst; some hunger sent insane,
Till suicide released them from their pain;
Some became weak and could no longer fly
(They faltered, fainted, and were left to die);
Some paused bewildered and then turned aside
To gaze at marvels as if stupefied;
Some looked for pleasure's path and soon confessed
They saw no purpose in the pilgrims' quest;
Not one in every thousand souls arrived –
In every hundred thousand one survived.

The birds arrive and are greeted by a herald

A world of birds set out, and there remained
But thirty when the promised goal was gained,
Thirty exhausted, wretched, broken things,
With hopeless hearts and tattered, trailing wings,
Who saw that nameless Glory which the mind
Acknowledges as ever-undefined,
Whose solitary flame each moment turns
A hundred worlds to nothingness and burns
With power a hundred thousand times more bright
Than sun and stars and every natural light.
The awe-struck group, bewildered and amazed,
Like insubstantial, trembling atoms, gazed
And chirmed: 'How can we live or prosper here,
Where if the sun came it would disappear?
Our hearts were torn from all we loved; we bore
The perils of a path unknown before;
And all for this? It was not this reward
That we expected from our longed-for Lord.'
It seemed their throats were cut, as if they bled
And weakly whimpered until left for dead,

Waiting for splendour to annihilate
Their insubstantial, transitory state.
Time passed; then from the highest court there flew
A herald of the starry retinue,
Who saw the thirty birds, trembling, afraid,
Their bodies broken and their feathers frayed,
And said: 'What city are you from? What race?
What business brings you to this distant place?
What are your names? You seem destroyed by fear;
What made you leave your homes and travel here?
What were you in the world? What use are you?
What can such weak and clumsy creatures do?'
The group replied: 'We flew here for one thing,
To claim the Simorgh as our rightful King;
We come as suppliants and we have sought
Through grievous paths the threshold of His court –
How long the Way was to complete our vow;
Of thousands we are only thirty now!
Was that hope false which led us to this place,
Or shall we now behold our Sovereign's face?'

The herald tells the birds to turn back

The herald said: 'This King for whom you grieve
Governs in glory you cannot conceive –
A hundred thousand armies are to Him
An ant that clambers up His threshold's rim,
And what are you? Grief is your fate – go back;
Retrace your steps along the pilgrims' track!'
And when they heard the herald's fearsome words,
A deathly hopelessness assailed the birds;
But they replied: 'Our King will not repay
With sorrow all the hazards of the Way;
Grief cannot come to us from majesty;
Grief cannot live beside such dignity.
Think of Majnun, who said: "If all the earth
Should every passing moment praise my worth,

I would prefer abuse from Leili's heart
To all creation's eulogizing art –
The world's praise cannot equal Leili's blame;
Both worlds are less to me than Leili's name."
We told you our desire – if grief must come,
Then we are ready and shall not succumb.'

The herald said: 'The blaze of majesty
Reduces souls to unreality,
And if your souls are burned, then all the pain
That you have suffered will have been in vain.'
They answered him: 'How can a moth flee fire
When fire contains its ultimate desire?
And if we do not join Him, yet we'll burn,
And it is this for which our spirits yearn –
It is not union for which we hope;
We know that goal remains beyond our scope.'

The birds narrated then the moth's brief tale:
'They told the moth: "You are too slight, too frail
To bear the vivid candle-flame you seek –
This game is for the noble, not the weak;
Why die from ignorance?" The moth replied:
"Within that fire I cannot hope to hide –
I know I could not penetrate the flame;
Simply to reach it is my humble aim."'

Though grief engulfed the raggèd group, love made
The birds impetuous and unafraid;
The herald's self-possession was unmoved,
But their resilience was not reproved –
Now, gently, he unlocked the guarded door;
A hundred veils drew back, and there before
The birds' incredulous, bewildered sight
Shone the unveiled, the inmost Light of Light.
He led them to a noble throne, a place
Of intimacy, dignity and grace,

Then gave them all a written page and said
That when its contents had been duly read
The meaning that their journey had concealed,
And of the stage they'd reached, would be revealed.

Joseph's brothers read of their treachery

When Malek Dar bought Joseph as a slave,
The price agreed (and which he gladly gave)
Seemed far too low – to be quite sure he made
The brothers sign a note for what he'd paid;
And when the wicked purchase was complete
He left with Joseph and the sealed receipt.
At last when Joseph ruled in Egypt's court
His brothers came to beg and little thought
To whom it was each bowed his humbled head
And as a suppliant appealed for bread.
Then Joseph held a scroll up in his hand
And said: 'No courtier here can understand
These Hebrew characters – if you can read
This note I'll give you all the bread you need.'
The brothers could read Hebrew easily
And cried: 'Give us the note, your majesty!'
(If any of my readers cannot find
Himself in this account, the fool is blind.)
When Joseph gave them that short document
They looked – and trembled with astonishment.
They did not read a line but in dismay
Debated inwardly what they should say.
Their past sins silenced them; they were too weak
To offer an excuse or even speak.
Then Joseph said: 'Why don't you read? You seem
Distracted, haunted by some dreadful dream.'
And they replied: 'Better to hold our breath
Than read and in so doing merit death.'

The birds discover the Simorgh

The thirty birds read through the fateful page
And there discovered, stage by detailed stage,
Their lives, their actions, set out one by one –
All that their souls had ever been or done:
And this was bad enough, but as they read
They understood that it was they who'd led
The lovely Joseph into slavery –
Who had deprived him of his liberty
Deep in a well, then ignorantly sold
Their captive to a passing chief for gold.
(Can you not see that at each breath you sell
The Joseph you imprisoned in that well,
That he will be the king to whom you must
Naked and hungry bow down in the dust?)
The chastened spirits of these birds became
Like crumbled powder, and they shrank with shame.
Then, as by shame their spirits were refined
Of all the world's weight, they began to find
A new life flow towards them from that bright
Celestial and ever-living Light –
Their souls rose free of all they'd been before;
The past and all its actions were no more.
Their life came from that close, insistent sun
And in its vivid rays they shone as one.
There in the Simorgh's radiant face they saw
Themselves, the Simorgh of the world[25] – with awe
They gazed, and dared at last to comprehend
They were the Simorgh and the journey's end.
They see the Simorgh – at themselves they stare,
And see a second Simorgh standing there;
They look at both and see the two are one,
That this is that, that this, the goal is won.
They ask (but inwardly; they make no sound)
The meaning of these mysteries that confound

Their puzzled ignorance – how is it true
That 'we' is not distinguished here from 'you'?
And silently their shining Lord replies:
'I am a mirror set before your eyes,
And all who come before My splendour see
Themselves, their own unique reality;
You came as thirty birds and therefore saw
These selfsame thirty birds, not less nor more;
If you had come as forty, fifty – here
An answering forty, fifty, would appear;
Though you have struggled, wandered, travelled far,
It is yourselves you see and what you are.'
(Who sees the Lord? It is himself each sees;
What ant's sight could discern the Pleiades?
What anvil could be lifted by an ant?
Or could a fly subdue an elephant?)
'How much you thought you knew and saw; but
          you
Now know that all you trusted was untrue.
Though you traversed the Valleys' depths and
          fought
With all the dangers that the journey brought,
The journey was in Me, the deeds were Mine –
You slept secure in Being's inmost shrine.
And since you came as thirty birds, you see
These thirty birds when you discover Me,
The Simorgh, Truth's last flawless jewel, the light
In which you will be lost to mortal sight,
Dispersed to nothingness until once more
You find in Me the selves you were before.'
Then, as they listened to the Simorgh's words,
A trembling dissolution filled the birds –
The substance of their being was undone,
And they were lost like shade before the sun;
Neither the pilgrims nor their guide remained.
The Simorgh ceased to speak, and silence reigned.

The ashes of Hallaj

Hallaj's corpse was burned and when the flame
Subsided, to the pyre a Sufi came
Who stirred the ashes with his staff and said:
'Where has that cry "I am the Truth"[26] now fled?
All that you cried, all that you saw and knew,
Was but the prelude to what now is true.
The essence lives; rise now and have no fear,
Rise up from ruin, rise and disappear –
All shadows are made nothing in the one
Unchanging light of Truth's eternal sun.'

A hundred thousand centuries went by,
And then those birds, who were content to die,
To vanish in annihilation, saw
Their Selves had been restored to them once more,
That after Nothingness they had attained
Eternal Life, and self-hood was regained.
This Nothingness, this Life, are states no tongue
At any time has adequately sung –
Those who can speak still wander far away
From that dark Truth they struggle to convey,
And by analogies they try to show
The forms men's partial knowledge cannot know.
(But these are not the subject for my rhyme;
They need another book, another time –
And those who merit them will one day see
This Nothingness and this eternity;
While you still travel in your worldly state,
You cannot pass beyond this glorious gate.)
Why do you waste your life in slothful sleep?
Rise up, for there is nothing you can keep;
What will it profit you to comprehend
The present world when it must have an end?
Know He has made man's seed and nourished it
So that it grows in wisdom until fit

To understand His mysteries, to see
The hidden secrets of eternity.
But in that glorious state it cannot rest –
In dust it will be humbled, dispossessed,
Brought back to Nothingness, cast down, destroyed,
Absorbed once more within the primal void –
There, lost in non-existence, it will hear
The truths that make this darkness disappear,
And, as He brings man to blank vacancy,
He gives man life to all eternity.
You have no knowledge of what lies ahead;
Think deeply, ponder, do not be misled –
Until our King excludes you from His grace,
You cannot hope to see Him face to face;
You cannot hope for Life till you progress
Through some small shadow of this Nothingness.
First He will humble you in dust and mire,
And then bestow the glory you desire.
Be nothing first! and then you will exist,
You cannot live while life and Self persist –
Till you reach Nothingness you cannot see
The Life you long for in eternity.

The king who ordered his beloved to be killed

There was a monarch once of seven lands,
A second Alexander, whose commands
Sent armies forth from pole to pole, whose might
Eclipsed the splendour of the moon at night.
He had a minister whose wise advice
Was well-informed, sagacious and precise.
This minister was father to a son,
A beauteous youth, a peerless paragon;
No man has ever seen such comely grace
As glanced out from that boy's bewitching face
(He dared not leave the palace save at night
For fear of causing some tumultuous fight;

Since all the world began no youth has known
The love, the adoration, he was shown).
His face was like the sun; his curls like dusk,
A twilight scented with delicious musk;
His little mouth was fresher than the brook
That gives eternal life, and in his look
A hundred stars seemed gathered as a guide
To tempt whoever saw him to his side;
His thick, spell-binding hair spilled down his back
In twisted tresses, glistening smooth and black;
And round his face the clustered ringlets seemed
Like little miracles a saint had dreamed;
His eyebrows' curve was like a bow (what arm
Could ever draw it or resist its charm?),
The eyes themselves a sorcery to quell
A hundred hearts with their hypnotic spell;
His lips were like the freshet that bestows
A sweet, new life on spring's reviving rose;
His youthful beard was like the fledgling grass
That re-emerges where spring's runnels pass;
His serried teeth were like . . . oh, who but fools
Would try to represent such shining jewels!
And on his cheek there was a musk-like mole,
That seemed a portent of Time's hidden soul;
What can I say? No eloquence conveys
A beauty that surpassed all mortal praise.
His king caught sight of him – and passion made
This monarch like a drunken renegade.
That full moon caused his sovereign to appear
As thin as is the new moon, wan with fear.
His love obsessed the king; a moment spent
Without that youth was torture, banishment –
He could not rest away from him; desire
Destroyed his patience in its raging fire.
He sat the boy beside him day and night,
Whispering secrets till the last dim light
Left that belovèd face – when darkness fell,
Sleep did not touch this sovereign sentinel;

And when the boy's head drooped the monarch kept
A guardian vigil while his servant slept,
The face lit by a candle's softening light
Watched by the weeping king throughout the night.
The king threw blossoms in his loved one's hair,
Or combed it hour by hour with tender care,
And then for sudden love would cry aloud,
Weep tears like raindrops scattered from a cloud,
Or make a public banquet for the boy,
Or drink with him alone, in secret joy –
He could not bear to be without his face,
To see him absent for a moment's space.
The youth chafed inwardly, but he was tied
By terror to his royal master's side,
Afraid that if he went away but once
The king would hang him for his impudence
(Even his parents were afraid to say
They wished to see their son from day to day –
They dared not offer succour or support
To one who seemed the prisoner of the court).

There was a girl at court, a lovely child
Who filled the room with sunlight when she smiled.
This youth caught sight of her, and like a fire
Love kindled his impetuous desire.
One night (the king was drunk) he slipped away
And in her room the two together lay.
At midnight, though the king could hardly stand,
He staggered out, a dagger in his hand,
And searched the court, prowling from place to place,
Until he found them locked in love's embrace.
Then hate and love could not be held apart;
Wild flames of jealousy swept through his heart.
'How could you choose another love?' he cried.
'What idiocy is this, what selfish pride?
To think of all that I have done for you
(Far more than any other man would do!).

Is this then my reward? Continue, please!
You're expert at it, everyone agrees!
But think – my coffer's key was in your hand;
My noblemen were under your command;
I ruled with your assistance and consent;
You were my closest friend, my confidant;
And yet you sneak in secret to this whore –
Foul slave, you are my confidant no more!'
He paused, then ordered that the youth be bound
And dragged in chains along the filthy ground –
The silver pallor of his lovely back
Was at the king's commandment beaten black,
And where his throne had been the soldiers built
The gibbet that would show the world his guilt.
'First flay the faithless wretch,' their monarch said,
'Then hang him upside-down until he's dead –
And then those chosen for my love will see
Their eyes should glance at no one else but me.'
The monarch's courtiers hurried to comply –
Gasping, head down, the youth was left to die.

But when the minister, his father, heard
The punishment this lover had incurred,
He wept and cried: 'What harsh necessity
Has made the king my son's sworn enemy?'
Two slaves had seized the boy – to them he went,
To them he made his fatherly lament,
And as he gave them each a pearl he said:
'Drink has confused our noble monarch's head;
He will regret my son's uncalled-for fate,
But when he's sober it will be too late;
Whoever kills my son will then be killed.'
They said: 'If his commands are not fulfilled,
It's we who'll die – if he comes here and sees
No bloody corpse, the next deaths he decrees
Are ours!' The wily minister then brought
A murderer, convicted by the court,

Who waited in a prison-cell for death –
They stripped the villain, flayed him, stopped his breath,
Then hanged him upside-down until the mud
Beneath the gibbet reddened with his blood
(The boy was hidden in a private place
Till it was safe for him to show his face).

The next day dawned; the king was sober now,
But anger still stamped furrows on his brow.
He called the slaves and asked: 'What did you do
With that abhorrent dog I gave to you?'
They said: 'We flayed the wretch, then hanged him where
The court could witness his last, cruel despair –
He hangs there now, my lord, head down and dead.'
The king rejoiced to hear the words they said
(He there and then made each of them a lord,
And gave them presents as a fit reward).
'Let him hang there,' he cried, 'till late tonight –
There is a lesson in this shameful sight!'
But when his people heard the tale they felt
Their hearts in surreptitious pity melt;
They came to stare, but none could recognize
The youth in that hacked corpse which met their eyes.
They saw the beaten, blood-stained flesh but kept
Their thoughts a secret and in secret wept;
All day the city mourned with smothered cries,
Tears hastily suppressed and inward sighs.

A few days passed; the king's rage vanished too,
And as his anger went his sorrow grew –
Love made him weak; this lion-hearted king
Became an ant, afraid of everything.
Then he remembered how they used to sit
For days and nights, when love seemed infinite,
Drinking their wine in homely privacy,
And more drunk with each other's company –
He could not bear the thought; he felt tears rise
To overflow his weeping, downcast eyes.

Regret consumed him; reason, patience fled,
And in the dust he bowed his noble head.
He dressed in mourning, neither ate nor slept,
But, shut away in lonely anguish, wept.
Night came; he drove off that still-gaping crowd
Which stood beneath the gallows tree, and, bowed
By lonely grief, told over one by one
The actions of his absent paragon.
Then as each loved, lost deed was called to mind,
He groaned that he had been so rash, so blind.
Pain gripped his heart; his tears flowed like a flood;
He smeared his features with the corpse's blood,
Grovelled in dust, clawed at his pampered skin,
Wept countless storms for his unthinking sin –
He raved, and, as a candle burns away,
Wasted with grief until the break of day,
And when dawn's gentle breeze arose returned
To his apartments' hearth, and still he burned.

For forty nights the ashes of despair
Reduced him to the stature of a hair;
For forty nights none dared approach the throne
Or speak to him, and he was left alone.
For forty days he fasted, then one night
He dreamed he saw the boy – his face was white
And smeared with trickling tears; from foot to head
Were blood-stains where his gaping wounds had bled.
The king cried: 'Comfort of my soul, what chance
Reduced you to this evil circumstance?'
'I am like this,' the weeping boy replied,
'Because of your ingratitude and pride –
Is this fidelity, to flay my skin
For some imagined slight, some paltry sin?
Is this how lovers act? No infidel
Would make his lover undergo such hell;
What have I done that I should hang and die,
A shameful spectacle to passers-by?

God will revenge my death; I turn away
But I shall face you on His Judgement Day!'
The king woke trembling from his troubled sleep;
Grief overwhelmed him; he began to weep
And in his wretched agony he saw
Insanity swing open like a door.
He cried: 'Dear heart and soul, your shameful death
Bereaves my heart and soul of vital breath –
You loved me and you died for me; what fool
Would smash, as I did, his most precious jewel?
Oh, I have killed my only love, and I
Deserve to suffer torture and to die!
Wherever you are now, my child, do not
Let all our vows of friendship be forgot;
It was myself I killed! Do not give back
The blackness of my deeds with deeds as black;
It is for you I grieve, for you I groan,
For you I bow down in the dust alone –
Take pity on me now; where can I find
Some trace of you to comfort my poor mind?
I tricked you, but be bountiful and true –
Do not serve me as once I dealt with you.
I spilt your body's blood, but you have spilt
My spirit's blood to expiate my guilt –
The deed was done when I was drunk; some fate
Conspired against me and my sovereign state.
If you have left the world before me, how
Can I endure the world without you now?
One moment's absence kills my life and heart;
One moment more, my life and body part –
Your king's soul hovers ready now to pay
Blood-vengeance for your death and die away!
Oh, it is not my death which troubles me,
But my unthinking, vicious treachery;
However long I beg and sue and plead,
I know that nothing can forgive this deed.
O God, that you had cut my throat, that I
Untouched by grief had been condemned to die!

My soul is burned with passion and despair;
There is no part of me that does not bear
The scars of wild regret – how long, O Lord,
Must absence be my fate and my reward?
Just God, destroy me now; I gladly give
My soul to death; I have no will to live.'
He fell bewildered in a strengthless faint,
And silence closed his passionate complaint.
But help was near; the minister had heard
Each conscience-stricken and repentant word –
He slipped out from his hiding-place and dressed
His son as if he were some honoured guest,
Then sent him to the king. The youth appeared
Like moonlight when the heaven's clouds have cleared;
Dressed all in white he knelt before the king,
And wept as clouds weep raindrops in the spring.
Then, when the wakened monarch saw the boy,
There were no words that could express his joy.
They knew that state of which no man can speak;
This pearl cannot be pierced;[27] we are too weak.
The absence that the king endured was gone
And they withdrew, united now as one.

No stranger followed them, or could unfold
The secrets they to one another told –
Alone at last, together they conferred;
Blindly they saw themselves and deaf they heard –
But who can speak of this? I know if I
Betrayed my knowledge I would surely die;
If it were lawful for me to relate
Such truths to those who have not reached this state,
Those gone before us would have made some sign;
But no sign comes, and silence must be mine.
Here eloquence can find no jewel but one,
That silence when the longed-for goal is won.

lines 4434–4453

The greatest orator would here be made
In love with silence and forget his trade,
And I too cease: I have described the Way –
Now, you must act – there is no more to say.

EPILOGUE

The poet and his work

O Attar, with these mysteries' musky scent[1]
You've filled the wide world and its firmament –
The earth's horizons are scent-soaked by you,
And lovers' longings are provoked by you.
Sigh then the breath of purest love, and play
The lovers' mode that steals men's hearts away.
Your poem is the lovers' source, to guide them,
And may they always have this source beside them!
Your *Conference of the Birds* is like the sun,
An endless fount of light for everyone;
Amazement haunts its stages of ascent
Or it's a book that's all bewilderment.

Embark upon this book with longing, give
Your soul up as a shield that you may live
(And once your soul is lost to sight, then know
The stage where you've arrived will also go).
If you don't start with longing, you won't see
A single dust grain of its mystery,
But mount the mule of longing, give it rein,
Let it, unhindered, pace across the plain.
Unless you feed on discontent and strife
How will your anguished heart recover life?
Harvest your longing, since it is the cure,
In both worlds, for the pain our souls endure.

If you're a pilgrim of the Way, don't look
For pleasing tales and tropes within my book;
No, look with longing, credit one per cent
Of all my longing, longing's what is meant!
The man who looks with longing on my story
Will strike the ball,[2] and with that stroke win glory!

Leave your ascetic piety, and find
Longing's required here, and a humble mind.
May he who longs acquire no cure, and may
The soul of he who seeks cures fade away –
A man must thirst, and fast, and sleepless spend
Each night as though his thirst could have no end;
Those with no feeling for my words can know
Nothing of how or where true lovers go.
The man who's read my book will act, and he
Who's learned its lessons knows reality;
Those who love surface beauty love its art,
Those who love inwardness seek out its heart.
This book's an ornament to all the ages,
Both high and low find something in its pages,
And if a man were ice-bound, once he'd felt
Its truth he'd burn, and all his ice would melt.
My verse has something wonderful within it,
Which is, it gives new meanings every minute,
And if you read it often I'm quite sure
Each time you do so you'll enjoy it more,
Since you can only gradually prevail
Upon this bashful bride to lift her veil.
Until the end of time there'll be no one
Who'll write about these things as I have done;
I bring pearls from Truth's sea, and poetry –
This book's the proof – has found its seal in me!
And if I praise myself (since who approves
Of one who shows that it's himself he loves?),
The just acknowledge what I say is right;
My full moon doesn't try to hide her light.

I've said but little of myself, although
All those who grasp what discourse is will know
The jewels I've scattered guarantee that I
Will live till Judgement Day, and when I die
I'll live on men's tongues, and this memory
Among mankind will be enough for me.
If the nine spheres should perish, this account
Will not diminish by the least amount,
And if its words remove the veil, and show
Even one man the Way that he must go
So that he's comforted by what he's read,
Then may he pray for me when I am dead.
I've strewn my roses here; remember me,
My friends, when I am gone, with sympathy!
Since, after his own fashion, each man shows
A little of himself, then quickly goes,
Like those who've gone before, I, with my words,
Have shown to sleeping men their souls as birds.
And if these words can prompt one heart to wake
From lifelong stupor for their mystery's sake,
I'll know, I'll have no doubt, that all my pain
And grief are over, and were not in vain –
I will have been a lamp, a candle's light
That burns itself, and makes the whole world bright.

My brain's smoke-blackened like a lamp, how long
Before I shine in heaven, where I belong?
I cannot eat or sleep, such heartfelt fire
Consumes my inner being with desire
That to my heart I cry: 'How much you say!
Silence! Seek out the mysteries of the Way!'
My heart replies: 'Don't blame my speeches, I
Am drowned in fire, if I don't speak I'll die –
My soul's a sea, tumultuous and violent,
How for one moment can the sea stay silent?'

But I don't boast of this to others, no;
My faith is my concern, it's not for show;
My heart's not void of pain, but I'm not one
To talk of what I feel and what I've done.
All this is merely pointless fantasies,
A man should filter out such vanities;
The heart that cares for such things will produce
Tired, worn-out words that are of little use.
The hard things must be done, to cast aside
The soul, and to repent of foolish pride;
How long will turmoil drown the soul? But cast
Aside this burden, and find peace at last.

Listening and talking

A man of faith declared, as death drew near:
'If I had known that listening matters here
Much more than talking, I would not have spent
My life in endless, wasted argument.
If speech is golden, speech that is suppressed,
Speech that is never said out loud, is best.'

Men who are men will act, but as for you,
Your trouble is you talk, and never do!
And if you were a man of faith, you'd see
The certain truth of all you hear from me –
But you don't know your own heart; all I say
To you seems fabulous and far away.
Sleep softly then, my friend, while I wait here
Whispering these sweet tales in your stubborn ear;
If Attar's tales are sweet to you, it seems
Your sleep is sweeter; may you have sweet dreams!
How often we've poured oil on porous sands,
Hung pearls around pigs' necks in glistening strands,
Set out a splendid feast, and then departed
As hungry as we were when we first started.

I reprimand my Self and it betrays me,
I give it medicines and it disobeys me;
Since I can't tame my Self, as I admit,
I've stepped aside, and washed my hands of it.
I'm helpless here, unless I am inspired
And drawn by God; it's this that is required,
And since the Self grows grosser by the hour,
Improvement's clearly not within its power –
All that it hears just makes it worse than ever,
My wasted words do no good whatsoever!
As God's my refuge, till my dying day
It won't accept a word of what I say!

Alexander the Great[3] facing death

Aristotle was at Alexander's side;
'Faith's king,' he said, as Alexander died,
'You've led your people well, and now, my friend,
They see your wisdom has achieved its end.'

Be warned, my heart, death's whirlpool is close by,
Let life be heartfelt, all too soon you'll die!
I've told you of the birds' great conference,
But now you must extract my story's sense.
The birds are lovers too, since like a lover
Each fled his cage before his life was over;
Each has a special meaning, each one shows
A special way, each in the tongue he knows,
And there is Someone, when the Simorgh's won,
Whose elixir makes all these tongues as one.

How will you know the truths religion speaks
While you're philosophizing with the Greeks?
How can you be a man of faith while you're
Still wrapped up in their philosophic lore?
If someone travelling on love's Way should say
'Philosophy', he doesn't know love's Way;

lines 4546–4561

Better, by God, the 'B' for blasphemy,
Than 'P' that stands for their Philosophy:
Once blasphemy's thin veil is torn, you'll find
It easy to dispel it from your mind;
Philosophy, though, snares you with its 'why's
And 'how's, and mostly it ensnares the wise.
Is this the light within your heart? Disdain it,
As Omar burned the volumes that contain it;[4]
Faith's candle burned Greek wisdom, and since then
It lights no candles in the hearts of men.
Medina's wisdom is enough, my friend,
Throw dirt on Greece, and all that Greece might send.

'O Attar, how long will you talk?' I ask;
You're not the man for such a mighty task.
Step out from what you are, be dust upon
The dust, know Nothingness, and so be gone.
While you exist, you're kicked, downcast; but when
You're nothing, you're the diadem of men!
Be void, so that the birds may lead you to
That court where endless being waits for you.

My words are everyone's best guide since they
Embody here the wisdom of the Way;
For me, although I'm nothing to the birds,
Is it enough they live here in my words?
Their journey's dust clouds reach me, and my heart
Aches for those travellers, since we had to part.

The Sufi who liked to tell stories

An old man asked a Sufi: 'Why do you say
So much about the travellers on Truth's Way?'
He answered: 'Women like a talker when
He's always chatting to them about men.

I'm not a traveller, but it never fails
To give me pleasure when I tell their tales;
It's just a taste of sweetness, I'm aware,
But better that than having poison there.'

My book's all madness, Reason won't appear
Within its pages, she's a stranger here,
And till the soul breathes in this madness she
Remains a stranger to eternity.
But how long must I talk, how long go on
Searching for something that was never gone?
I turned my back on luck, and like a fool
Learned what I know in carelessness's school,
And when they say: 'Lost wanderer, it's you
You must ask pardon from for what you do,'
I don't know where to turn, since who could give
Forgiveness to the hundred lives I live?
If I were on His Way now, would I be
Drowned as I am in all this poetry?
If I were there, not here composing verse,
Would 'P' mean 'Poetry' then, or 'Perverse'?
This writing poetry's a vanity,
This peering in oneself's idolatry,
But since I am alone here, I recite
These verses quietly, and stay out of sight.

If you're a person who can seek, do so,
Give up your soul, find what you long to know,
But I weep tears of blood for verse, and bleed them
To shed blood in the hearts of those who read
    them,
And if you sniff my ocean, in this flood
Of poetry you'll certainly smell blood;
And people falsehood poisons need but look
For poison's antidote within my book.

I'm Attar, one who deals in drugs,[5] but my
Own heart's as dark as any musky dye,
Grieving in solitude for people who
Lack salt and sense in everything they do.
I spread the cloth, and wet my crust of bread
With all the copious salty tears I shed;
It is my heart I cook, and I am blessed
From time to time when Gabriel is my guest,[6]
And since an angel dines with me how can
I break the bread of every foolish man?
I don't want evil wretches' food; with bread,
And this accompaniment, I'm amply fed;
My heart's hoard feeds my soul, my soul's content
Suffices as eternal nourishment –
How could a man who has such wealth descend
To dine with any vile fool as his friend?

Thanks be to God, I say, I don't consort
With worthless dupes, or hang around a court;
Why pawn my heart like this? Why eulogize
Some idiotic fool as great and wise?
No tyrant feeds me, and I've never sold
The dedication of a book for gold.
My praise is for the virtues that sustain me;
My body's strength, my soul's strength – these
        maintain me!
My predecessors welcome me, why then
Should I seek out self-centred, vapid men?
My privacy has brought a kind of joy
That endless crowding cares cannot destroy;
Good riddance to that slanderous crowd; I'm free,
And they can praise me now or censure me.
I've turned my back upon the world, my mind
And its concerns are all that I can find;
And if you learned of all the grief I've known
Your wild confusion would exceed my own.
My body and my soul dissolve, I am bereft
Of both, and grief and pain are all that's left.

A Sufi's death

A Sufi traveller in his death throes said:
'I've no provisions for the way ahead;
But with my sweat I've made the mud here thick
And from it fashioned for myself a brick;
And I've a phial of tears; these rags can be
A patched-up shroud that's suitable for me.
First, use the tears to wash me when I'm dead,
Then place the brick I've made beneath my head;
I've wept upon the shroud, and written there
From end to end: "Alas for my despair!"
It's this with which my body should be bound;
Then place me simply, quickly, in the ground.
When this is done, till Judgement Day appears,
The clouds will soak my grave in sorrow's tears.'

D'you know what all this grief is for, and why?
Because a gnat can't scale the windy sky!
A shadow wants to join the sun; it fails,
And hence these endless sorrows and travails –
It's clear this is impossible, but still
This is the goal it struggles to fulfil;
Whoever thinks in this way will not find
A nobler thought to occupy his mind.
I see my problems grow each moment – how
Can my poor heart be emptied of them now?
Who is like me, alone, in solitude,
Parched in the ocean's watery plenitude?
I've no one with me who might comprehend
My confidences, no one who's a friend;
I've no encouragement, and no defence
Against the darkness's malevolence,
No heart to help (not even mine), no mind
That's either good or bad or cruel or kind.
I don't want scraps from royal tables, nor
The blows they'd give me at the royal door;

lines 4611–4627

I'm neither patient in my loneliness
Nor free from others in my heart's distress,
My mental state seems upside-down, my mind
Is in that shape an old man once defined:

The wise old man

A pure soul once remarked: 'Well, it appears
I've lived outside myself for thirty years,
Like Esmail, watching, grieving for his life,
As his own father stood there with the knife.'
And as that moment was for Esmail, he
Lived all his life in that strange misery.[7]

Who knows what I must suffer, who can say
What I endure confined here night and day?
I flare up like a candle, then I weep as though
I were a spring cloud that's consumed by woe;
You see the lantern's light cast far and wide
But do not see the fire that burns inside,
And how can someone who's outside surmise
What lies within, what's hidden from his eyes?
I'm like a polo-ball that's struck here, there,
Backwards and forwards and I don't know where.
I've had no profit from my life, and all
I've said and done here is contemptible.
Alas, I have no friends to help me, and I've spent
My life in indolence and discontent.
When I was able I was ignorant;
Now I have Knowledge, and it's strength I want.
These days my only help is helplessness,
My misery, and my extreme distress.

Shebli after death

A young man dreamed and saw Shebli, when he
Had left this vile place for eternity,
And asked: 'Dear sheikh, how has God treated you?'
Shebli said: 'My account was overdue!
God saw my Self and me still fighting there,
He saw my weakness, frailty and despair,
And pitied me, and cancelled my account,
And at a stroke annulled the whole amount.'

O my Creator, in Your eyes I must
Be like a lame ant toiling in the dust;
I don't know where I'm from, and I don't know
Who 'I' is here, or where I have to go –
I have no body, strength or stored-up food,
No joy, no wealth, no heart, no fortitude;
My life's been blood and suffering, and I've got
No profit from this business, not a jot!
I've lived my life in fear, and now a fine
Mulcts from me everything I thought was mine.
My heart is lost, the world too, and my being,
Both outwardly and inwardly, is fleeing,
And neither Muslim now, nor heathen either,
Bewildered I'm between them, and I'm neither,
Not one and not the other, dazed, bemused,
I'm helpless, hopeless, baffled and confused.
I'm trapped now in a doorway blocked by all
The daydreams I've erected as a wall –
Open this doorway up to me, and show
A wretch that's gone astray where he should go!
A slave with no provisions can still cry
His way along the Way, and groan and sigh,
And with his sighs You'll burn his sins, and look –
His tears will cleanse the blackness of his book.

lines 4642–4657

To those whose tears fall like an ocean say:
'Come, enter, you are worthy of the Way,'
And tell the dried-eyed: 'Go now, disappear!'
Since they can have no reason to be here.

Tears

Once, as a Sufi sheikh was travelling, he
Caught sight of a celestial company –
A group of angels squabbling where they'd found
A hoard of gold coins scattered on the ground.
So the sheikh asked the group: 'But what's all this?
What are these coins? And why this avarice?'
A wingèd being said: 'Good master, know
One of the holy sufferers here below
Passed on this way, and heaved a noble sigh
And wept warm tears as he went sadly by;
It is his sigh we're seeking, and each tear;
They're what we snatch from one another here.'

O Lord, I've copious tears and sighs; although
I've nothing else, I've these at least to show.
If tears are current where I go, and sighs,
These are the goods I'll bring as merchandise.
Cleanse my soul's courtyard with my heartfelt sighs,
My record with the tears dropped from my eyes.

I wander lost, and cannot find the Way,
And with a blackened heart I wildly stray.
Oh, guide me, wash my record clean, and in
Both worlds cleanse all my soul of ancient sin!
My heart is filled with endless longing for You,
If I've a soul it is ashamed before You;
My life is grief as long as I shall live,
Would that I had a hundred lives to give,

And I could pass them all in endless pain
Suffered for You, then suffered yet again.
Left in my own hands, how can I withstand
My hundred sorrows? Save me, grasp my hand!

Abu Sa'id and the drunk

Abu Sa'id was sitting down one day
With his companions of the Sufi Way
When at the door a roaring drunk appeared,
Dishevelled, weeping, with his eyes all bleared,
Crying his drunken heart out, stumbling, moaning,
Shamelessly lurching here and there, and groaning.
When the sheikh saw him he felt pity for him
And gently went to him, and stood before him,
And said: 'Now what's all this? You're drunk; don't
    shout!
Just let me take your hand and lead you out.'
The drunk replied: 'God help you, sheikh, it's not
A job for you, to lead a drunken sot;
Hold your head high and be a man! Leave me
To Him; I've bowed my head, now let me be!
If everyone could lend a helping hand
An ant could greet a prince, and be as grand;
You're not the man to lend a hand, just go!
Get out now, you don't care for me, I know.'
The sheikh fell to the ground, blushing to see
The pallor of this drunkard's agony.

You are to me the Indispensable;
Come, take my hand, O perfect All-in-All!
My feet are fettered in this prison's pit;
If you don't raise me, who can manage it?
My body is a prisoner's, soiled and stinking,
My heart's worn out with grief, it's frail and sinking,
And though I come here soiled like this, forgive
My filth, since prison's where I've had to live.

lines 4673–4688

What have you brought?

A saint said: 'If tomorrow God should say
To me upon the plain of Judgement Day,
"What have you brought here from the path you
     trod?"
I'll say: "What can men bring from prison, God?"'
I come from prison, broken by defeat,
My head as lost and wandering as my feet.
With nothing in my hands, I'm at Your door,
A slave, a prisoner, dust, and nothing more.
Ah, do not sell Your slave – be gracious, clothe me
In robes of honour, cherish me, don't loathe me!
Cleanse me of all my filth, and let me be
Interred within a Muslim cemetery,
And when my body's buried don't recall
My good deeds or my bad – forget them all!
You made me freely, as was just; if You
Forgive me freely this is justice too!

The prayer of Nezam al-Molk

Nezam al-Molk, when he was dying, said:
'I'll come with empty hands when I am dead,
O my Creator. This, though, I have done:
I always helped whenever anyone
Would speak of You, and I did not neglect
Their needs, but treated them with real respect.
I was their pupil, keen to learn about You,
And never willing to betray or doubt You;
I bought You fervently, and I can tell You
That unlike some men I would never sell You.
So, as I die, I pray that You buy me,
O matchless Friend, for all eternity.'

lines 4689–4702

And when death comes, befriend me, Lord, since then
I cannot look for any help from men.
You'll be my Friend when weeping friends surround
My body there, and lay me in the ground;
Extend Your hand to me in that dread place
And let me grasp the garment of Your grace.

Solomon and the ant

Great Solomon inquired once from an ant
Whose leg was lame (he was his confidant):
'More mired in mud than I am, tell me now
Which is the mud most mixed with grief, and how?'
'That mud's the final brick,' the lame ant said,
'Placed in the narrow grave, when someone's dead.'

When that last brick is placed, the act makes plain
That absolutely no hope can remain.
O God, when I'm beneath the earth, and when
All hope's exhausted in my fellow men,
And when they place that brick, don't turn Your face
Away from me, vouchsafe me then Your grace.
Do not confront me in the grave with all
I've done that's wrong and reprehensible;
My hope is still that You will turn away
Your face from all my sins, Lord, on that day.
You are all mercy; may what's past be past,
And pardon for my sins be mine at last.

Abu Sa'id at the public bath

A foolish masseur in the bath-house once
Attended Abu Sa'id there, by chance.
The man scraped all the grime he scrubbed off on
The sheikh's forearm, to show him what he'd done,

And asked the sheikh: 'What would you recommend
As good behaviour then, my pure-souled friend?'
The sheikh said: 'I'd say hiding filth and grime,
Not showing it to people all the time!'
The masseur was abashed, and knelt before
Abu Sa'id there on the bath-house floor,
And since he was so ready to confess
His fault, the sheikh forgave his foolishness.

O God, Accomplisher of everything,
Creator and Preserver, mighty King,
All our fine acts are but one drop of dew
Within the sea of grace here that is You.
You are the world's stay, Absolute in essence,
And out of chivalry withhold Your presence;
Forgive our filth and grime; don't scrutinize
Our foolish failings – hide them from our eyes.

Notes

PROLOGUE

1. *He made the nine spheres*: in medieval Islamic cosmology, the universe consisted of nine spheres. The same figure can be found in Christian cosmology during the Middle Ages (e.g. Beatrice leads Dante through nine celestial spheres in *The Divine Comedy*).

2. *He made flowers bloom in fire*: in the Qur'an, God transforms a fire into which Abraham has been thrown into a bed of roses.

3. *He cleared . . . held the ocean back*: the parting of the waters of the Red Sea for Moses.

4. *He caused a gnat . . . sent His foe insane*: in the Qur'an, a punishment for Nimrod (see the Biographical Index), who opposed Abraham's leadership.

5. *He made a spider . . . within a cave*: an allusion to the Prophet Mohammad hiding in a cave to escape his enemies (see also note 1 to 'The Conference of the Birds' below); a spider wove a web over the cave entrance, so that it seemed no one had entered the place.

6. *He made an ant . . . Solomon in argument*: in the Qur'an, the leader of a group of ants converses with Solomon. (See also 'Solomon and the ant' in the Epilogue, lines 4706–14.)

7. *Abbasid caliphs*: the Abbasid caliphs, descended from an uncle of the Prophet Mohammad, were the leaders of the Islamic community, from their capital in Baghdad, from 750 to 1258, when the city was sacked by the Mongols.

8. *Ta and Sin's mysterious story*: certain suras (chapters or sections) of the Qur'an begin with letters whose meaning is unknown. The sura concerning the ants and Solomon begins with the Arabic letters *ta* and *sin*.

9. *He saw the needle (Jesus' robes concealed it)*: a story recounts Jesus reaching the fourth sphere of heaven (beyond which no

earthly goods can journey) with a needle, thereby breaking God's
prohibition on earthly possessions.

10. *He makes a staff take on a snake-like form*: a reference to Moses'
staff, which was transformed into a snake.

11. *Or from an oven He can start a storm*: in the Qur'an, the storm
that caused Noah's flood burst forth from an old woman's oven.

12. *He makes a camel come out from a stone*: a miracle alluded to in
the Qur'an (17:59).

13. *Or makes a golden calf cry out and groan*: another reference to
the Qur'an (20:90–100).

14. *From fish to moon*: a common expression in medieval Persian
verse, meaning 'from the depths to the heights'.

15. *Earth rests upon a cow . . . The cow upon a fish*: see previous
note.

16. *And he who did not bow*: in the Qur'an, Satan refuses to acknowl-
edge Adam's sovereignty over creation.

17. *poor Hindu*: 'Hindu' is generally a pejorative term in medieval
Persian, and usually indicates a dark-skinned Indian slave or serv-
ant. Medieval Persian literature is very conscious of skin colour,
with pale skin being seen as beautiful and dark skin as unattrac-
tive.

18. *have me wear / Your earring*: slaves wore earrings indicating to
whom they belonged.

19. *This light appeared . . . the faithful prayed*: here light is described
as performing the Muslim postures of prayer.

20. *Demonic djinns*: evil supernatural beings, mentioned in the
Qur'an.

21. *The holy ka'aba*: the black stone in Mecca towards which Muslims
pray. The stone, which predates Islam, is incorporated in a cube-
shaped building at the centre of the great mosque in Mecca,
circumambulated by every pilgrim seven times. The building (also
referred to as the ka'aba) is the geographical centre of Islam.

22. *Simorgh*: originally, a fabulous bird from pre-Islamic Persian
mythology.

23. *palm-tree groaned . . . beneath the tree*: in Islamic tradition, a
particular palm-tree, beneath which Mohammad had habitually
preached, groaned in sorrow when the Prophet no longer preached
there.

24. *the name we share*: one of Attar's names was Mohammad.

25. *One as your confidant and your vizier*: Abu Bakr, the first of the
four 'rightly guided' caliphs of Sunni Islam (see the Biographical
Index).

26. *One as a sun of justice, bright and clear*: Omar, the second caliph (see the Biographical Index).

27. *One as a sea of patient modesty*: Osman, the third caliph (see the Biographical Index).

28. *One as a lord of generosity*: Ali, the fourth caliph (see the Biographical Index).

29. *Companion of the Prophet in the cave*: Abu Bakr was with Mohammad in the cave referred to in note 5 above. (See also note 1 to 'The Conference of the Birds' below.)

30. *Hu*: a pronoun, meaning 'He', used by Sufis to refer to God.

31. *God sent Ta Ha to begin / His chapter*: the letters *ta ha* at the beginning of Sura 20 of the Qur'an, which was instrumental in Omar's conversion to Islam; the letters' meaning is unknown.

32. *master twice illuminated*: because he married two daughters of the Prophet in succession.

33. *A second Joseph*: in Islamic tradition, Joseph is the ideal of male beauty (see the Biographical Index for more on this), and Osman was said to have been extremely handsome.

34. *favouring his own . . . cut his body from his head*: Osman was accused of nepotism, and this is one of the reasons he was murdered. Attar interprets this as a kind of self-sacrifice.

35. *The Prophet vouched . . . oath of loyalty*: Osman was absent from a crucial swearing of loyalty to the Prophet, known as 'The Oath of the Tree', but the Prophet affirmed his loyalty despite his absence.

36. *His daughter's husband*: Ali married the Prophet's daughter Fatima.

37. *Ali's restored . . . severed by a sword*: there are two separate legends attesting to this miracle, one during a battle, the other after a man's hand had been severed as a judicial punishment.

38. *The mighty zulfiqar*: Ali's famous sword; it was a curved sword, or scimitar, one of the principal symbols of Islam.

39. *faction*: by 'faction' Attar here means the Shi'a rejection of the legitimacy and authority of the first three caliphs recognized by Sunni Muslims. For more on this, see the Introduction (pp. xi, xx).

40. *Thirty-three thousand*: the number of the followers and Companions of the Prophet.

41. *Hobbling the camel*: someone is said to have asked the Prophet if he could let his camel wander freely and trust in God that it wouldn't stray. Mohammad replied, 'Hobble the camel', which became proverbial for taking sensible precautions.

42. *whipped his guilty son to death*: there is a tradition that Omar allowed his son to be whipped to death for his dissipation.

43. *Omar . . . justice was his trade*: Omar was famous for his austerity, which was as stringent against himself as against others.

44. *so many heathen lands . . . at his hands*: the most spectacular conquest during Omar's reign was that of Iran, and it is probably this to which Attar is chiefly referring.

45. *No poison killed him*: Omar was killed by a Persian slave.

46. *When Fate decreed . . . lay him low*: Ali was killed by a man called Ibn Moljam, a member of the Kharijite sect, which began by supporting Ali but then turned against him.

47. *When Aysha moved against him*: Aysha (see the Biographical Index) was involved in armed opposition to Ali becoming the fourth caliph.

48. *They*: i.e. the four caliphs.

49. *Your heart rejected . . . remained unproved*: Mohammad had seemed inclined to credit gossip about Aysha and another man, until a revelation proclaimed her innocence.

THE CONFERENCE OF THE BIRDS

1. *Unity's black cave . . . your companion there*: a reference to the Companion of the Cave. During a period of danger the Prophet Mohammad and a close companion, Abu Bakr, hid for a while in a cave on Mount Thaur. In mystical poetry this episode became a symbol of withdrawal from the world.

2. *Simorgh*: see note 22 to the Prologue above.

3. *Bismillah*: 'In the name of God', the opening words of the Qur'an.

4. *Kaf's mountain peak*: a mythological sacred mountain.

5. *half-dang*: a *dang* is a sixth of a *mesqal* (a *mesqal* being about 4.6 grams). Colloquially, it indicates something that weighs virtually nothing.

6. *homa . . . his shadow heralds majesty*: a mythical bird whose shadow, when it falls on a man, indicates that he is destined to be king.

7. *mourning robes of darkest blue*: blue was the colour of mourning in ancient Persia; the epic poet Ferdowsi (see note 3 to the Introduction) mentions it as being worn by the first of the legendary kings, Keyumars, when in mourning for his son Siyamak.

8. *Kausar's cleansing stream*: a stream that flows through paradise.

9. *ka'aba*: see note 21 to the Prologue above.

10. *The Christian's belt*: the *zonnar*, a belt or cord worn by Eastern
    Christians and Jews; thus a symbol of heresy.

11. *A ragged cloak made up of scraps and shreds*: i.e. the dervish
    cloak.

12. *Who knows . . . transitory dreams*: the last four lines of this
    passage are Attar's paraphrase of a poem by Hallaj (see the Intro-
    duction, p. xiii). In this and the following anecdote Attar juxtaposes
    the attitude to death of the 'ecstatic' mystic (Hallaj) and that of
    the 'sober' mystic (Juneid – see the Biographical Index).

13. *all the pain . . . Kerbela's plain*: it was at Kerbela that Hussein,
    the son of Ali and grandson of the Prophet Mohammad, was
    killed. Hussein refused to swear allegiance to the Caliph Yazid;
    he and his followers were surrounded at Kerbela, and a swift
    decisive battle resulted in victory for Yazid's troops. It is Hussein's
    death which is remembered with such fervour by Shi'a Muslims
    through the mourning month of Moharram. Before the battle
    Hussein's water-supply was cut off, and he and his followers
    suffered greatly from thirst. During Moharram, and particularly
    on the anniversary of Hussein's death, many Muslims will refuse
    to drink, in commemoration of this thirst. It is this memory which
    is behind the otherwise rather obscure anecdote about the Sufi
    who refused to touch sherbet, which precedes the mention of
    Kerbela.

14. *that thin bridge arched over hell*: Sirat, a hair-thin bridge over the
    pit of hell. The good will be able to cross it; the wicked will slip
    and plunge into the pit.

15. *When My exchequer has no love to give*: the metaphor is based
    on the notion of blood-money. A murder could be compensated,
    if the victim's relatives agreed, by payment of a sum of money;
    God destroys the dervishes, then pays for this 'crime' with His
    love; He will continue to do this until He has no more love to
    give, i.e. for ever.

16. *hadith*: actions or (more particularly) sayings of the Prophet
    Mohammad. The scholar's task is to sort out which are genuine.

17. *Whoever*: i.e. God.

18. *Lat*: Lat was the name of an Arabian pre-Islamic goddess.
    Mahmud attacked and conquered Somnat in north-west India in
    1026 and destroyed the Hindu temple there; Attar has either
    confused the Arabian and Indian deities, or used the name 'Lat'
    generically to mean 'idol', or has been seduced by the fortuitous
    rhyme.

19. *A heathen's belt*: the *zonnar* (see note 10 above).

20. *Blood is the unborn child's sole nourishment*: the comparison depends on a pun; to 'feed on blood' is to 'suffer'.

21. *The seven planets . . . seven seas . . . seven burning hells*: Seven was a sacred number in both medieval Islam and medieval Christianity, and cosmic and natural phenomena were counted in sevens where possible.

22. *Boraq*: the fabulous beast the Prophet mounted on the night of his ascent to heaven.

23. *that tiny needle . . . cause of Jesus' shame*: see note 9 to the Prologue above.

24. *A fish*: it is possible that this refers to Jesus. Jesus' breath is an important element in Muslim stories about Him (it was reputed to have vivifying powers), and it may be that Attar had heard of the Christian use of the fish to signify Jesus.

25. *There in the Simorgh's . . . the Simorgh of the world*: this crucial moment depends on a pun: *si* means 'thirty', *morgh* means 'bird(s)'; the *si morgh* see the 'Simorgh'. It was probably this pun which suggested the idea of the poem to Attar.

26. *I am the Truth*: Hallaj was executed for, among other things, crying out 'I am the Truth' while in a state of religious exaltation (see the Introduction, p. xiii).

27. *This pearl cannot be pierced*: the stringing of pearls on a necklace is a stock metaphor in Persian verse for the writing of poetry; Attar is suggesting that this particular 'pearl' is beyond the scope of his, or any, poem – it is too difficult for him to 'pierce'.

EPILOGUE

1. *O Attar . . . musky scent*: see the Introduction, p. x.

2. *strike the ball*: the metaphor is from polo.

3. *Alexander the Great*: Alexander in the Islamic tradition is regarded as a kind of proto-Sufi. But Attar's rejection of Philosophy, which was seen as 'Greek' knowledge, makes his anecdote about him more ambiguous.

4. *Omar burned the volumes that contain it*: an allusion to the tradition that Omar ordered the destruction of the library at Alexandria (which had in reality been destroyed long before the Arab conquest of Egypt).

5. *I'm Attar, one who deals in drugs*: see the Introduction, p. x.

6. *Gabriel is my guest*: Attar has already implicitly compared himself to the Prophet by saying he is the 'seal' of poets (as Mohammad

was the 'seal' of the prophets – see the Introduction, p. xxi); saying that Gabriel (who revealed the Qur'an to Mohammad) has been his guest is another suggestion that he is like the Prophet.

7.   *Like Esmail . . . in that strange misery*: the old man has spent his life in the same state of bewildered terror as Esmail when he knew his father was about to kill him (see the Biographical Index).

Biographical Index

This includes most of the characters unfamiliar to western readers to whom Attar refers, together with entries on one or two well-known figures (e.g. Joseph) whose role in Islamic literature differs slightly from the western conception of their legends. It has not been possible to trace a few characters; some of these (e.g. Sheikhs Abu Bakr, Bu Ali and Nughani) probably had a purely local fame in Neishapur. Attar may have invented Abbasseh – he gives her no provenance and reports no anecdotes about her.

Abu Bakr: (c.573–634) the father-in-law of the Prophet and one of his most trusted advisors. He was the first of the four 'rightly guided' caliphs of Sunni Islam, after the death of Mohammad. (pp. xi, 26, 27, 30, 31, 33, 34, 35, 36, 38)

Abu Sa'id: see *Mahna's sheikh*.

Adham, Ibrahim: Abu Eshaq Ibrahim ibn Adham (died c.782) was a prince born in Balkh who renounced the world and lived as a wandering dervish. The similarity of his story to that of the Buddha has often been remarked on, and it is of especial interest because Balkh had been a Buddhist area. He is the 'Abu ben Adham' of Leigh Hunt's poem (1838), and the story on which this is based is told in Attar's *Memorials of the Saints*. (p. 146)

Affan: the father of *Osman*. (p. 28)

Alexander the Great: in the Islamic tradition, Alexander (356–323 BCE) is considered primarily as a man who traversed the earth searching for truth, so he is a kind of proto-Sufi. (pp. 65, 195, 237, 251)

Ali: (c.600–661) the Prophet's cousin and son-in-law and, according to the Sunnis, the fourth 'rightly guided' caliph; the Shi'a believe that his rightful position as the Prophet's successor was usurped by the three caliphs who preceded him. (See also the Introduction, pp. xi, xx) (pp. 26, 29–30, 33–5, 36, 38)

Ayaz: Ayaz ibn Aymaq Abu-Najm was the favourite slave of Sultan *Mahmud* of Ghazna. Though Ayaz actually existed (he died in 1057), his life was quickly overlaid with legend. His story became the archetypal tale of the slave raised to the highest honours by his king; his relationship with Mahmud is used as a metaphor of the mystic's relationship with God. The story obviously appealed to Attar, who returns to it frequently. (pp. 65–6, 172–3, 189–90, 210–11)

Aysha: the last of the Prophet's wives (she died in 678). She is negatively regarded by the Shi'a because of her active opposition to Ali becoming caliph. (pp. 35, 37)

Azar: the father of Abraham, who lived by carving idols. (pp. 104, 175)

Azra'el: the angel of death. (pp. 119, 193)

Bayazid: a famous ascetic Sufi of the ninth century (he died in 874), who lived in Bistam (about halfway between Neishapur and Rey; he is sometimes called Bistami). Like *Hallaj* he was given to making apparently blasphemous remarks while in a state of religious ecstasy ('Glory to me! How great is my majesty!'), but he escaped outright condemnation, perhaps by feigning madness. (pp. 87, 139, 158, 163)

Bilal: an Ethiopian freed slave, born in the late sixth century, who became Mohammad's servant and friend, and was the first muezzin (the person who calls the faithful to prayer at the appropriate times of day). (pp. 22, 35)

Dar (Malek Dar): see *Joseph*. (p. 233)

David: in the Qur'an, David's profession is an armourer who makes chainmail; he is recognized by Muslims as a prophet and a king of Israel. (pp. 14, 40, 172, 174, 213)

Dinar: Malek ibn Dinar (died c.748) was the son of a Persian slave. He was taught by Hasan of Basra, who had known many of the Companions of the Prophet. He achieved fame as a calligrapher; perhaps this is what Attar is referring to when he has Malek Dinar say that he receives his bread 'from God's own hands', as he was a copyist of the Qur'an. (p. 111)

Eblis: the devil. (pp. 182, 183)

Esmail: the first-born son of Abraham; in Islamic tradition, it is he whom God orders Abraham to sacrifice, rather than Esmail's half-brother Isaac. (pp. 14, 256)

Feridun: one of the most illustrious of the legendary kings of ancient Persia. (p. 54)

Gabriel: in Islam, Gabriel is the most important of all angels; he was the intermediary who, in a series of revelations, transmitted the Qur'an to Mohammad. (pp. 21, 22, 61, 99, 166, 193, 213, 251)

Gharun: Korah in Numbers 16. (p. 100)

Ghuri: see *Sanjar*. (pp. 146–7)

Hallaj: see the Introduction, p. xiii. (pp. 126–7, 236)

Hanbal, Ahmad: Ahmad ibn Mohammad ibn Hanbal (780–855) was one of the most important Islamic theologians and the founder of one of the four schools of orthodox Islam. He was born in Baghdad. (pp. 148–9)

Hozifeh: (died 625) a friend of both the Prophet and *Omar*; Omar made him the ruler of Ctesiphon, the ancient Persian capital, after the Arab conquest of Iran. (p. 32)

Jacob: the pain of separation from someone dearly loved is a common metaphor in Persian poetry for the soul's longing for God; Jacob's longing for his son Joseph is frequently used as an example of this. (pp. 14, 60, 61, 152, 184)

Jamshid: one of the most illustrious of the legendary kings of ancient Persia. (p. 54)

Joseph: the favourite son of Jacob, he was hidden in a well by his jealous brothers and sold to Malek Dar, who took him to Egypt. Here he became overseer of the state granaries (Attar seems to believe he also became king). The stories of his relationship with *Zuleikha* and his confronting his brothers with their treachery are frequently alluded to in Persian poetry. He was of unsurpassed beauty, and for this reason beautiful heroes (and heroines) are usually compared to him. Joseph is the most frequently mentioned character in *The Conference of the Birds*, closely followed by *Mahmud*; in both cases, Attar is clearly interested in the same themes: physical beauty (Joseph and *Ayaz*), gratitude, authority tempered by understanding and mercy. (pp. 14, 29, 41, 60–61, 68, 69, 115, 145, 151–2, 155, 177–8, 184, 212, 223, 233–4)

Juneid: Abul Qasim ibn Mohammad ibn al-Juneid (died 910) was one
of the most celebrated of Sufis and the chief expounder of the 'sober'
school of Sufism. Of the state of *fana* or annihilation in God he wrote:
'For at that time thou wilt be addressed, thyself addressing; ques-
tioned concerning thy tidings, thyself questioning'; and it is
interesting to compare this with what happens when Attar's birds
reach the Simorgh. (pp. 127, 135)

Kherghani (or Kherghan; Attar gives both forms): Abul Hasan
Kherghani was a Persian Sufi of the late tenth and early eleventh
centuries. He lived near Bistan in north-west Iran. (pp. 140, 142)

Khezr: the immortal guardian of a spring whose waters bestow immor-
tality. His original name, al-Khadir, means 'the green man'; he is
clearly a figure from pre-Islamic legend, and parts of his story recall
the tale of Utnapishtim in *The Epic of Gilgamesh*. (pp. 41, 48, 49)

Khosroe: the name of at least three of the Sassanian kings who ruled
Iran from 229 to 652. Like the name Caesar, it came to mean any
emperor or important king. (p. 54)

Leili and Majnun: the archetypal lovers in Arabic, Persian and Turkish
poetry. The story is originally Arabic. They were the children of
hostile tribes, and their association was forbidden by Leili's father.
Majnun, driven mad by love, lived on the fringes of the desert among
wild animals; both lovers eventually died of grief. There are many
narrative poems based on this story, the most famous being that of
the Persian poet Nezami. Majnun's madness is a frequent symbol in
Islamic mystical poetry of the soul's longing for God. (pp. 184, 188,
231–2)

Loghman of Sarrakhs: one of the 'wise madmen' (*aqala majanin*) who
were companions of Abu Sa'id Abul Kheir (see *Mahna's sheikh*).
(p. 209)

Mahmud: Sultan Mahmud of Ghazna (the ruins of Ghazna are in
modern Afghanistan, on the road from Kandahar to Kabul) reigned
from 998 to 1030. During this period he considerably extended the
area over which he ruled. He invaded and conquered much of north-
west India, and when he died his kingdom stretched from Samarqand
to Kashmir. A poet himself, he filled his court with poets and philos-
ophers; his relationship with *Ayaz* is celebrated in many Persian
poems. Attar obviously thought of him as a benign and tolerant ruler,
but the historical Mahmud was, according to E. G. Browne, 'greedy
of wealth . . . fanatical, cruel to Muslim heretics as well as to Hindus

(of whom he slew an incalculable number), fickle, and uncertain in temper' (*A Literary History of Persia*, vol. 2, London, 1906). See also *Joseph*. (pp. 54–5, 66, 92–3, 149, 159–61, 172–3, 174–6, 185–6, 189–91, 199, 210–11)

Mahna's sheikh (or Sheikh Mahna): Mahna is a small town in Khavaran, a district of Khorasan; 'Mahna's sheikh' was Abu Sa'id Abul Kheir (967–1048), a Persian poet who is traditionally credited with being the first to use the language of secular love poetry to express mystical experiences. (pp. 135, 184–5, 259, 261–2)

Majnun: see *Leili*.

Malek Dinar: see *Dinar*.

Mas'ud: many kings, particularly of Ghazna, were called by this name, and there is no way of knowing which one Attar had in mind in his story of Mas'ud and the fisherboy. At least two manuscripts give the story to *Mahmud*. (pp. 90–91)

Monkar and Nakir: two angels who question the dead on their faith. (p. 158)

Nasrabad: Abul-Ghasem Ibrahim Nasrabadi, a mystic of the tenth century. (p. 218)

Nezam al-Molk: a famous vizier of the Seljuk kings in the eleventh century. He was vehemently against any form of Islam that was not orthodox Sunni, and was murdered by an Esmaili assassin. (p. 260)

Nimrod: the enemy and oppressor of Abraham. He was defeated by an army of gnats sent by God; one entered his brain and by its buzzing sent him mad. (pp. 39, 98, 200)

Nuri: Abu-Hussein Ahmad ibn Mohammad al-Nuri (died 908) was a Sufi of Baghdad, prominent in the circle which gathered around *Juneid*. (p. 229)

Omar: (c.590–644) the second of the four 'rightly guided' caliphs recognized by the Sunnis. He is particularly disliked by Persian Shi'a, partly because the battles that sealed the fate of the last pre-Islamic Persian empire were fought while he was caliph. (pp. xi, 27, 28, 30, 31–3, 34, 38, 252)

Osman: (c.579–656) the third of the 'rightly guided' caliphs recognized by the Sunnis. The most notable achievement of his reign was the compilation of the Qur'an, and the establishment of its authentic text. (pp. xi, 28–9, 38)

Oveis: (died 657) considered to be a Companion of the Prophet although they never met: the two were said to be able to communicate by a form of spiritual telepathy. Oveis later became friendly with Mohammad's successors. (p. 33)

Rabe'eh (pronounced as three syllables, the last rhyming with 'way'): Rabe'eh bint Esmail al-Adawiya, one of the first and most important woman mystics of Islam. She lived in the eighth century. As a child she was sold into slavery, and she spent most of her life in great poverty in Basra. She became famous in her own lifetime for her piety and was visited by other contemporary mystics. She is credited with the introduction of the theme of divine love into Islamic mysticism, and if this is true her influence on the subsequent course of Sufism is incalculable. There is an interesting book in English on her life by Margaret Smith, *Rabi'a the Mystic and her Fellow Saints in Islam* (Cambridge, 1928, 2010). (pp. 36–7, 97, 116, 173, 186)

Rudbar, Bu Ali: Abu Ali Ahmad ibn Mohammad ibn al-Qasem ibn Mansur al-Rudbari, a Sufi of the tenth century. (p. 171)

Saleh: a prophet, mentioned in the Qur'an, sent to an Arab tribe. God also sent the tribe a she-camel which Saleh said they should feed and water. Instead they killed it, and a storm followed by a destructive earthquake punished their lack of belief. (p. 40)

San'an: the story of Sheikh San'an is easily the longest in Attar's poem. Attar sometimes calls him San'an and sometimes Sam'an. Dr Sadeq Gouharin (in his edition of *Manteq al-Tayr* (*Conference of the Birds*), Tehran, 1978) makes the interesting suggestion that the name San'an is taken from a monastery of that name near Damascus. He also suggests that the story is modelled distantly on that of a Sheikh ibn Sagha who travelled to Rome and became a Christian. Attar's story made a great impression on his early audience and was taken as a factual narrative – so much so that Attar himself was said to have been one of the sheikh's disciples who followed him to Rome. (pp. xviii, 68–85)

Sanjar: a Seljuk prince who ruled over Khorasan from 1096 to 1157. He expanded his kingdom until it included all of the Seljuk empire (i.e. virtually all of Islamic Asia) and was formally proclaimed king at Baghdad on 4 September 1119. The later years of his reign were marred by successful rebellions against his rule. To the north-east his possessions were constantly threatened by the kings of Ghur, and it is possible that the rivalry between the obscure 'Sheikh Ghuri' and Sanjar in Attar's story is to some degree a metaphor for this struggle. (pp. 146–7)

Shebli: Abu Bakr Dolaf ibn Jahdar al-Shebli (died 946) was well-born and entered the service of the Baghdad court. Later he joined the group of Sufis associated with *Juneid* and became known for his extravagant behaviour, for which eventually he was confined in an asylum. (pp. 104, 124, 183, 257)

Tarmazi: Abu Abdallah Mohammad ibn Ali ibn al-Hussein al-Hakim al-Tarmazi has been called 'one of the outstanding creative thinkers of Islamic mysticism' (A. J. Arberry (ed.), *Muslim Saints and Mystics*, London, 1966). He taught at Neishapur and indirectly influenced both Ghazali and Ibn Arabi. He lived during the latter part of the ninth and the beginning of the tenth centuries. (p. 139)

Tusi, Bu Ali: Abu Ali al-Fazl ibn Mohammad Faramadi of Tus (a small town near Mashhad in Khorasan) was a Sufi of the elventh century associated with the poet and mystic Abu Sa'id Abul Kheir. (pp. 179, 220)

Uzza: a goddess in pre-Islamic Arabia. (p. 104)

Vasati: Abu Bakr Mohammad ibn Musa al-Vasati was a Sufi of the tenth century. (p. 157)

Yusef of Hamadan: a companion of Abu Ali Faramadi of Tus (see *Tusi*); he lived in the eleventh century and died on the road to Merv, a city in southern Russia, near Samarqand. Hamadan is in western Iran on the site of the ancient Ecbatana. (pp. 184, 201)

Zacharia: in Islamic tradition, Zacharia was falsely accused of adultery with the Virgin Mary. He was condemned to death, but remained silent during his execution. (p. 14)

Zuleikha: the woman known in the Bible as Potiphar's wife. Her illicit love for *Joseph*, who by virtue of his perfect beauty was considered a symbol of the divine, is often used as a metaphor for the soul's need for God. (pp. 177–8)

Zulgharnin: his story is told in Sura 18 of the Qur'an, where he is represented as a lawgiver and the conqueror of Yajuj and Majuj (Gog and Magog). (p. 42)

Zulnun: Abul-Faiz Thauban ibn Ibrahim al-Mesri (*c.*796–859) was an Egyptian mystic who travelled in Syria and Iraq and was for a time imprisoned for heresy at Baghdad; after his release he returned to Egypt, where he died. He is credited by later Islamic mystics with having been one of the first and most important of their number; he also had a reputation as an alchemist. (p. 143)